Charmed & Dangerous

Charmed & Dangerous

Candace Havens

BERKLEY BOOKS, NEW YORK

THE BERKLEY PUBLISHING GROUP
Published by the Penguin Group
Penguin Group (USA) Inc.
375 Hudson Street, New York, New York 10014, USA
Penguin Group (Canada), 90 Eglinton Avenue East, Suite 700, Toronto, Ontario M4P 2Y3, Canada
(a division of Pearson Penguin Canada Inc.)
Penguin Books Ltd., 80 Strand, London WC2R 0RL, England
Penguin Group Ireland, 25 St. Stephen's Green, Dublin 2, Ireland (a division of Penguin Books Ltd.)
Penguin Group (Australia), 250 Camberwell Road, Camberwell, Victoria 3124, Australia
(a division of Pearson Australia Group Pty. Ltd.)
Penguin Books India Pvt. Ltd., 11 Community Centre, Panchsheel Park, New Delhi—110 017, India
Penguin Group (NZ), Cnr. Airborne and Rosedale Roads, Albany, Auckland 1310, New Zealand
(a division of Pearson New Zealand Ltd.)
Penguin Books (South Africa) (Pty.) Ltd., 24 Sturdee Avenue, Rosebank, Johannesburg 2196,
South Africa

Penguin Books Ltd., Registered Offices: 80 Strand, London WC2R 0RL, England

This book is an original publication of The Berkley Publishing Group.

PRINTING HISTORY
Berkley trade paperback edition / September 2005

Library of Congress Cataloging-in-Publication Data

Havens, Candace, 1963–
    Charmed & dangerous / by Candace Havens.
       p. cm.
    ISBN 0-425-20691-2
    1. Americans—England—Fiction. 2. Prime ministers—Fiction. 3. Witches—Fiction. 4. Texas—
Fiction. I. Title: Charmed and dangerous. II. Title.

 PS3608.A878C47 2005
 813'.6—dc22

2005045359

PRINTED IN THE UNITED STATES OF AMERICA

10 9 8 7 6 5 4 3 2 1

For Steve and the boys

Acknowledgments

Thank you to my agent Sha-Shana Crichton for being so brilliant, and to Gail Fortune, Gina Bernal, and the incredible team at Berkley for much the same reason.

I so appreciate the critiques and the friends at DFW Writers' Workshop, RWA, and the North Texas Romance Writers. My beloved West Texas Divas and the Secret Divas, I could not have done this without your encouragement and your wisdom.

Jodi Thomas, thank you for your generosity. To my friend Britta Coleman, this has been a mind-boggling ride, and I'm happy we took it together. Shannon Canard, you came in late in the game, but have become a major player. Thank you, my friends, for reading the multitude of drafts and for listening.

I'm lucky to have such an incredible family. Steve, Jeff, and Parker, you believed in me from the beginning and have held my head above water through it all. Mom, Dad, and Grandma Irby, you taught me to follow my dreams and to pursue them. I know how blessed I am to have you all in my life.

And finally a big thanks to Joss Stone, Sheryl Crow, Mindy Smith, Martina McBride, Faith Hill, Melissa Etheridge, and the Domestic Science Club. Music has become a huge part of my creative process and I couldn't have done it without your tunes.

Prologue

Sunday, 5:30 A.M.
Sweet, Texas

This day has great possibilities. Actually every day does, but this one is special because I woke up next to the man I love. Oh, it took me a while to realize it, but he's the one.

For months he told me we belonged together, but I refused to believe him. What he didn't seem to realize is witches don't have boyfriends. It never works out.

The intimidation factor alone usually stands as the biggest turnoff. A lot of men can't handle a woman with power. The whole reading-minds thing and the ability to turn them into toads sort of makes them insecure.

Even my clients are afraid of me, but they want to use my talents just the same.

Don't get me wrong. I love being a witch. My world's filled to the brim with exciting adventures and people.

But this love thing is all new. My heart's full of an emotion

I've rarely experienced. I've cared for people in the past, but loving is something I hardly ever allowed myself to do.

This man changed all of that. I must love him because there are no other possibilities. It's much like being a witch. It is what I am and what I must be.

Look at him, lying there so peaceful. That jet black hair waving around his face and those bulging biceps. Ooh, baby! He's a human cupcake and I could just eat him up.

Now if only I can get him to come back to life it will be a great day. Because lonely as I get sometimes—I don't fuck dead guys.

One

Dead guys: 0 (But I'm having evil thoughts about a certain twitty Brit)

Miles called. *Ugh.* I was in the middle of one of those terrific dreams where you don't really know who the guy is, but there's like this major connection. We were in a wild bedroom with a huge round bed. Doing the nasty in front of a big fire. So real, my face felt hot and my sheets were wet with sweat when I woke up.

Argh. Leave it to Miles to interrupt something really fantastic.

He's such a snippy little twit. No, "Bronwyn, how are you? So nice to hear your voice. . . ."

Nope, with Miles it's: "Get your ass out of bed. The prime minister wants you here."

"Well, hello, Miles, how are you?" I pulled the twisted sheets off my legs and pushed myself up on the pillows.

He ignored my sarcastic tone. "Be at the airport tomorrow at noon for a flight to Oslo. That's in Norway. He needs you to read the room." Click. He hung up.

Norway? I hate Miles, but I detest cold weather even more. It's the middle of friggin' winter and the PM and his buddies run the world. Couldn't they pick a warmer climate? Somewhere with a beach? I could glamour up a tan, but real ones look so much better.

Cold or not, doesn't matter. I've gotta go. The money's good and it's the easiest way for me to know where the world's headed. If the prime minister knew I got as much out of these meetings as he did, he wouldn't invite me. Lots of other witches out there don't have the ability to read minds, only emotions. But I've used that talent to save his life so many times from assassins that we've lost count. So it all evens out in the end.

Yuck, I've got to get out of this sweaty T-shirt and grab a shower. Oh, darn, and the laundry. I'll have to wash lingerie and dig some of my warmer clothes out of the cedar closet before I go.

A witch's work is never done.

9 P.M.

Casper, the unfriendly cat, is missing again. I don't know what her problem is these days. She won't stay put. Since I moved to the new house in November, she's found a hundred ways to sneak out.

I wonder if she has a boyfriend. It's not like her to take off for days at a time. She's always considered herself my great protector, even though I'm certain she hates me.

Maybe she feels like we're safer here away from the big cities. I love living in a place where I don't have to keep my shields up all the time and no one cares who I am.

People in Sweet, Texas, don't give a hoot who you are. Strangers wave to one another and everyone always wears a smile.

After bouncing around between New York City, L.A., London, and Paris, this West Texas town has been a welcome respite. I love the town square with its funky gargoyled courthouse and short, funky trees.

The whole place has this gothic revival feel that's something out of eighteenth-century Prague. Vampires feel right at home in Sweet, Texas.

But I don't think they put up with any kind of deviant behavior here. There's no sign that says "No Demons Allowed" but you get the feeling that people here like to keep things on an even keel. The sheriff and his deputies are always on patrol, and I haven't heard much about any mischief.

Of course if there's trouble near, it will find me.

The great thing is I'll see it before it gets here because everything is so flat. And unlike the big cities, where demons, warlocks, wizards, and witches feed off of the hustle and bustle, here in Sweet it's all about fresh air and peace.

This town is protected by a strong coven of witches, it's surrounded by powerful white magic, and I don't think anything would get through without the coven detecting it.

I've actually been able to sleep through the nights for weeks now without worrying about some assassin coming after me while I rested. This was definitely a smart move.

11:30 P.M.

I've been out looking for Casper again and fell down in the blustery winds. Some days I hate that damn cat as much as she does me. I hope she freezes.

Gotta pack. Miles wants me in Norway on Thursday so I'm flying my Cessna to Dallas tomorrow and then hopping an international flight.

My brain just flashed to the prime minister. Something big is going down because I didn't even have my mind open to him. Guess I'll find out soon enough. Hope the bad guys show up. I'm really itching for some fun.

Now I'm off to finish packing and I need to grind some medicinal herbs. A witch never knows when she might need help from Earth's bounty. I've let my little black bag get shamefully low on everything from acacia to rosemary.

I also need to do some research on Norway at the library, so I know their magical customs. Kira's the librarian in Sweet and she's become a great friend. She's also one of the best researchers I've ever known.

Wednesday, 11 P.M.
Somewhere over the Atlantic
Spells: 1
Dead guys: 0 (But the guy next to me is a candidate)
I'm so tired, but I can't sleep on planes. The guy next to me is adorable, but he just started sawing logs and I find that extremely unattractive. The sound is a cross between Casper coughing up a hairball and a nuclear explosion.

Time to put him in a deeper sleep. What was that spell I used on Dad? Have to shut this cute fella up. No way I can take six more hours of this.

Earlier tonight I tapped into the PM's mind a bit and discovered he's worried about the meeting. He didn't directly think about the problem, so it was more a feeling I picked up than fact. But he's definitely got some big-time anxiety going on.

Miles sent me files on the rest of the attendees. It's an eclectic group. There are scientists from Norway, a sheik from Dubai, several ambassadors from other Middle Eastern countries as well as Europe, and the American vice president. Supposedly this meeting is to discuss the world's energy crisis, but I have a feeling there's a lot more going on.

Writing all the stuff down helps me sort it all out. After last month when those stupid warlocks tried to use me as a sacrifice to bring back Orne, the King of the Dead, I decided to write everything down. That way if some creep knocks me off, someone will know what happened.

If you're reading this, it probably means I'm dead. Don't worry. Death doesn't scare me. I know what happens afterward.

I also know my purpose: to rid the world of evil. Oh, not in a save the world in a Buffyesque kind of way, but in a destroying bad guys one day at a time way.

When I turned twenty and took the oath to protect, I decided that day I would do whatever it took to rid the world of all this nastiness floating around. For the last five years, I've kept that promise. Unfortunately, I've made some enemies along the way and it's made it difficult to travel anywhere without some magical assassin trying to do me in.

Hopefully, this diary won't be all about maiming and killing. (Although, I really like those stories best.)

I'd eventually like to write down some sexy bits. Geez, it has been a really long time since I've been with a man. I'm not sure I've been through a sex drought this long before.

My job takes me around the world and that makes dating difficult. I don't mind one-night stands but I haven't had one yet that's gone well. Somehow they always find out I'm a witch and it scares them off.

No sex is making me cranky.

Oh, goody, snore boy is stirring. Wonder if he's interested in some mile-high fun.

Two

Thursday, 9 P.M.
Waxing moon
Oslo, Norway
Spells: 3
Dead guys: 1

It's so friggin' cold my tits actually hurt from pointing hard. Actually, Norway's not a bad place. The people are sweet and it's clean. But it's too damn frigid for me.

I hear they have this hotel nearby that's totally made out of ice. People pay three hundred dollars a pop to sleep on a frozen slab of water. Idiots.

If they want to sleep with something cold they should shack up with Miles. That guy's an iceberg. Something's crawling up his pants these days because he's even nastier than usual. And that's pretty damn bad.

After a whopping three hours of sleep the jerk banged on my door. I stumbled across the room in the dark and flipped the lock. Before I could say anything, he pushed the door wide and walked in.

"Miles, fancy seeing you here. Didn't you see the sign on the door? It says 'Do Not Disturb.' " I pointed to the placard on the knob.

"I can read, Bronwyn. The prime minister has a meeting with Sheik Azir. You've got to make yourself presentable in fifteen minutes. Meet me outside suite 903."

"It's five in the morning, Miles."

"Wonderful, you can tell time." Then he strode out of the room like the pansy ass he is.

About sixteen minutes later I met him outside the suite, wearing a black sweater and pants, no makeup, and a ponytail. He didn't say a word about my being a little late, but he did give me the evil eye. I glared back and he pushed me through the double doors.

The PM stood in front of a large expanse of windows, as dapper as ever. Every dark hair in place, and silver Armani suit. Slick, but in a nongreasy way. Dare I say, even kind of sexy? It's hard for me to think of him that way. He's so not my type.

"Hello, Bronwyn," he said, as he continued to gaze out onto the city.

"Good morning, Prime Minister."

He turned around. "You're looking tired." He raised an eyebrow. "Jet lag?"

To which I wanted to say, "It's five in the friggin' morning, you pompous jerk, and not all of us can look like an ad for *GQ* first thing."

"Yes, sir, probably jet lag" is what came out of my mouth.

While he is a bit of a stuffed shirt, truth is, I like the guy. He cares about the people he governs, which is more than I can say about most politicians.

"Bronwyn, I'd like you to read the sheik, but he can't know you're here. Our security fellows will outfit you with a microphone, and you'll be talking to me through this earpiece." He put the clear plastic speaker in his right ear.

You know, the witch business is getting pretty high-tech these days.

I had to find a quick way to get the fuzz out of my brain from lack of sleep so I popped two of my favorite herbal greens with a Coke.

The herbs reacted with the caffeine in the drink. In a few seconds my brain clicked into gear and my body tingled.

The PM's security guys (who are seriously handsome in that stuck-up British kind of way) clipped a microphone to my chest and slapped headphones on my ears. Kind of wished the blond had spent a little more time with his hands on my breasts, but he was all business. We did a sound check and two minutes later the sheik walked in.

God, he was glorious. Exotic. Tall, with long black lashes covering deep brown eyes.

If he didn't have fourteen wives already, I might have applied for the job. Okay, I have no idea if he has a harem or not, but he is a sheik.

From the beginning he gave off a positive vibe, but very strong-willed. He didn't suffer fools and he had a definite agenda. A few minutes into their conversation I caught a glimpse of the sheik's thoughts. *Assassination.* Just the word. But who? Did someone want him dead or was he after the PM?

People think that reading minds is an easy thing, but it isn't. A lot of us think in pictures, not words or conversations, so putting coherent thoughts together is difficult. Not to mention the fact that we all run on different frequencies, which quite often gives me a migraine.

He read pretty high on the emotional scale. His hands were grasped tightly in his lap. The blue aura around him indicated a good soul, which probably meant the assassin might be after him, not vice versa.

A flash of another face, much like his but different. Anger. His cousin hated him. Then suddenly, an explosion.

As he spoke, the images became stronger.

Holy crap. His thoughts were about a cousin who planned to kill him. But if he knew, why didn't he do something about it? Made no sense.

I whispered the facts as I put them together into the PM's ears. To his credit, the man never wavered in the conversation. He gave no indication that he knew of the attempt being planned against the sheik.

The conversation about solar energy wound down and a Swedish temptress flashed into the sheik's mind. The bazooms on that one were enough to make the strongest man drool.

He thought the name *Helga* and the woman had a knife in her hand.

Oops. Poor Sheiky baby. Some men have no luck with women.

She was in on the whole assassination thing and he was playing her game to get info. Clever man, but he's living dangerously by hanging out with that she-devil. She's definitely in cahoots with the cousin.

The sheik and PM shook hands and I wanted to run out and yell, "Don't screw the bimbo." But that's not really protocol.

After he left, I told the PM and Miles everything.

I'd like to think it was coincidence that later in the afternoon a woman named Helga Sorenson was found dead. Evidently she'd been skiing and had a run-in with a tree. Bashed her skull in, poor girl.

Kind of makes you wonder about her karmic debt. Killed

by a tree. Maybe she'd been a lumberjack in a former life. *Scary!*

Friday, 8 A.M.

Crashing headache. Miles has become a regular little alarm clock. At least he let me sleep until six this time. He informed me of the prime minister's schedule of meetings that I had to attend. Nothing starts until nine, so I loaded up on eggs and toast. They served salmon with my breakfast. There's something wrong about fish before noon. Ick.

Talked to Caleb. He's put in a pet door for Casper, who he found mewing at the back door. The potions shelf is also fixed, thanks to his handyman skills. He can be annoying at times, but he's sure helpful.

My brother, Brett, moved to Africa to help the sick and forgotten and left Caleb, his best friend, in charge of me. It didn't matter that I'm perfectly able to care for myself, or that Caleb is a highly sought-after magazine writer with homes in New York and Dallas.

My brother always gets what he wants.

So a couple of times a month Caleb makes the half-hour flight in his Cessna and stops by to help with things around the house, and to make sure I'm not dead on a bathroom floor with my cat eating my face. (Brett's thoughts, not mine.)

I guess it's good that he's taking care of things while I'm here in Oslo, but sometimes he's a bigger pain than my brother.

Tapped into the sheik's head again. I hope he's the one who sent the orders to off the blonde temptress and that it had nothing to do with me. I don't need that kind of karmic debt on my shoulders. I create enough of my own.

Unfortunately, he still isn't out of harm's way. The cousin is here in Oslo, which is bad news all around. I can't use my magic to protect the sheik because he didn't ask. Of course he doesn't know I exist, so that might have something to do with it.

I told Miles and the PM what's going on with the cousin so I have to trust they'll make the right decisions.

If they don't, I will.

11 A.M.
Charms: 1
Terminally bored witches: 1

Blah. Blah. Blah. I've never sat through anything so boring. All this politico doublespeak makes me want to puke.

I slipped a protection charm into the PM's coat jacket. Made it out of a small piece of carved wood soaked in primrose and lavender, and wrapped in a red ribbon. Smells a little girly but it works.

He pulled it out and looked at it for a minute, then winked at me. I think he understands that I do these things for his own good, but he never likes to make a fuss.

Something strange happened this morning. The maid cleaned the room early and I put one of my keep-out wards on the door afterward so no one could come in. Wouldn't want anyone to accidentally stumble into my bag of tricks.

When I came back for lunch someone had tampered with the wards.

I shoved the door open cop-style and took a quick look. Hopefully, none of the other guests saw me jumping around in my three-inch heels and favorite black power suit, pointing my fingers in the shape of a gun. I can be such a dork sometimes.

They didn't touch anything or remove items. Whoever over-rode the ward had to know something about magic. Very weird.

Why would someone be interested in my room? No one except the prime minister, Miles, and the security guys know I'm here.

I— Crap, it's Miles banging on the door again. Geez, I thought I'd at least get lunch.

Midnight
Spells: 3
Dead guys: Almost 2
Holy cow, Batman! What a day.

I opened the door and there he stood looking meaner than ever.

"Come with me, Bronwyn." Miles grabbed my arm and hustled me off to the PM's suite.

There lay the prime minister on top of his bed, as pale as I've ever seen him, which is saying a lot because he's English. Sun worshipers they aren't. Body trembling, he tried to lift his head.

He tried to sit up and I pushed him back on the mattress and went to work. "Prime Minister, what happened to the charm I put in your pocket?"

He whispered through chattering teeth. "Someone spilled a drink on my suit jacket so I took it off. Forgot to put the charm in my pants pocket."

"The prime minister dined with several dignitaries and took ill immediately after the meal," Miles said in his clipped tone.

"Miles, go get my bag out of my room. Then make a list of everyone at that luncheon."

The toady man didn't say a word. He walked out to do what I asked.

I closed my eyes and released the power of the wards on my room. If Miles had tried to go in with them intact, he would have been fried.

"Prime Minister, I want you to take shallow breaths. I believe you've been poisoned."

His frown intensified.

"Do you remember feeling confused the instant you ate something at lunch?"

"No. Wait, yes." His brows drew together. "After the soup. My head hurt and I couldn't concentrate. I thought I might have had an allergic reaction."

I spread my hands a few inches above his body and worked my way down. "No, sir, it's poison. I can feel it."

I had to stop the toxins from reaching his heart or it was all over. With one hand over his heart and the other on his solar plexus I chanted in a low voice.

The shivering stopped and a great calm moved across his body.

Miles walked in with my bag and I set to work mixing. I had no time to test for an antidote so I put together one of my cure-all herbal potions.

I handed Miles the eucalyptus. "Put this on his chest and stomach."

He spread the oil on the PM, while I mixed angelica, bay, and basil to purify the blood and elder, chamomile, and parsley for healing powers. Threw it all in a can of Coke.

"I need heat."

Miles ran to get a lighter from one of the security guards. I gave the potion a quick blast of fire.

Dumped half the mixture down the PM's throat. Put two white quartz stones on his solar plexus and chest. His pale skin glistened in the darkened room.

He took a long shuddering breath and his eyes closed.

Crap. I hadn't been in time.

Just as I turned to Miles the PM gasped for air and his eyes fluttered open.

Thank you, God. The prime minister really is one of the good guys, and it's my job to keep him alive. I don't think I could handle it if he died.

I heard a huge sigh of relief behind me. Miles shook his head. "Good work, Bronwyn."

"Thanks. Keep him still for a few hours and give this a chance to work through his body." I piled the ingredients back in my bag and looked up. "You want me to stay with him?"

"Is he going to be okay?" Miles rubbed his eyes and I wondered if he'd been crying.

"Yes. He needs rest. He fought a tough battle today." I closed the bag and pulled the fluffy, golden comforter up on the PM.

"You go on. I'll keep an eye on him." Miles gave the PM a loving look. Now that's a little too much information for me. If Miles has the hots for the PM, I just don't want to know.

"Give him two teaspoons of this each hour until it's gone." I handed him the can. "This isn't your run-of-the-mill assassination attempt, Miles. Someone used magic to poison the PM. I need to know who was in that room."

"I'll get you the list within the half hour. They're already testing the dishes and food from the event to see if we can find out what was poisoned."

"Tell the investigators to look at the soup first." Something dawned on me. "You'd better check to see if any one else is sick."

His eyes lit with understanding. He made a quick call and discovered the sheik felt fine. Later we discovered Azir hadn't eaten the soup. No one else had been affected.

Interesting.

With the PM out of commission I was left to my own devices for a few hours. Always a dangerous thing, especially when there's a mystery. I had grand ambitions to start my own investigation.

But my stomach had other plans. I didn't want to eat in the hotel. No use in pushing my luck. I walked down to a small coffeehouse that served an eclectic mix of food. I didn't feel brave enough to try Oslo's version of the American burger, so I decided on a cheese sandwich and hot chocolate.

Sitting by the window, I watched the bundled passersby as they waddled around. I've honestly never seen so much Gore-Tex and animal fur. PETA would have a field day here. A light snow fell and it covered the world in white. Didn't see a lot of snow in Houston, where I grew up, so there's always a bit of wonder in it for me.

An hour later I walked back to the hotel and checked on the PM. He rested comfortably.

Miles walked me to the door. "Only the prime minister and the sheik's bowls tested positive for the poison."

I nodded that I understood and walked out.

I had a feeling Sheiky's cousin was up to no good and now he's messed with my charge. I spent the rest of this evening moving the pieces into place.

All bets are off and I'm going to kick that bad boy's ass.

Three

Somewhere over Europe, thinking about country roads

Spells: 2

Charms: 4

Dead guys: 5

I miss John Denver. My grandpa used to listen to him all the time. He died in a plane crash (John, not my grandpa), which is a bit of a bummer since I'm at a cruising altitude of about twenty-eight thousand feet.

I'm about five thousand miles from my country roads but I'm so ready to be home.

People ask me all the time why I choose to live in such a godforsaken place. I don't see it that way. It's hard for the bad guys to hide on the wide-open plains. When I'm in the city they're around every corner, but in Sweet, it's easy to spot a stranger who means to do you harm.

Speaking of bad guys, I'm just happy yesterday is over.

Had a total mind meld with Sheik Azir's cousin. No idea how I picked him up so clear. Maybe because Sheiky baby was so determined to beat the cousin at his own game.

Deciphered that the next move was to take place at a breakfast for several of the politicians. I don't know what these guys have against sitting down to a good meal. Anyway, Mr. Bad Boy Cousin had two hit men set to take out Azir.

No poison. This time a quick two shots to the head would take care of the poor guy. The cousin didn't give me a clear picture of the assassins when I accidentally tapped in, so that part of the plan was a bit hazy.

Told the PM and Miles about the hit and they set their own security guys up as waitstaff. To protect the PM and Sheiky baby I used Malandro's spell. That meant I had to find a way to be in the room.

I borrowed a food server's uniform and glamoured myself into an ash blonde. I started to add twenty pounds to my frame, but the last time I did that I ended up with a huge ass that didn't go away for three weeks. So, I decided being blonde would be enough.

I pretended to fill the coffee urns periodically, and stood at the back of the modern-styled ballroom going from person to person trying to tap into their brains.

Blah, blah, blah. Solar energy. Blah, blah, blah. Oil-rich countries.

Longest damn meal in the history of breakfast.

Then I felt it. A confusion spell spread across the participants. Didn't expect that. A witch or warlock, maybe two, hidden in the room, but I couldn't see who it might be. Up until that time they'd been blocking their powers or I would have picked up on them.

I did catch a glimpse of a man with long dark hair, but blinked and lost him.

The chatter died down and I saw the sheik and PM look at each other. In an instant, two of the waiters pulled guns and without thinking I threw my hands in front of me. The heat radiated from my belly and I shot two balls of fire. Hit 'em both and—*kaboom!*—they combusted. Bits of flesh and limbs blew all over everyone. Blood, guts, and I think an eyeball lay atop pieces of toast, and pieces of skin fell on the eggs.

Then a powerful warlock, who I swear must have had some invisibility thing going, zapped me with black magic. Never saw him. I hit the wall and slid down. As I fell into the "Oh, crap I'm going to pass out" mode, I found the warlock's mind. Idiot. He had no shields.

I blew a slow burn into his brain. *Fry, you evil piece of shit.* My eyes closed and I heard someone scream, "He's on fire!" I sensed another more powerful presence just as I slipped into la-la land.

Next thing I knew I was in the fetal position on the white damask couch in the PM's suite. He and Miles were staring at me like I had two heads.

"It's alive." Miles always has something catty to say.

"That will be enough, Miles." The PM grabbed my hand. "Bronwyn, dear, so good of you to return to us." At least the PM looked happy that I'd survived. Couldn't say the same for the nerd by his side.

"Did you have to blow them up?" Miles said as he tried to help me sit up on the PM's sofa.

At first I wanted to apologize, but then I realized I'd done nothing wrong. "Geez, Miles. We all have our talents. Mine's combustion. Besides, I like explosions."

The PM shook his head. "Bloody mess."

"Did we get them all?" Stretched my arms to see if they still worked.

"Well, something interesting happened. There were two more men in a getaway car. When they started the motor, it exploded. Would you know anything about that?" Miles smirked.

I shrugged and gave them my best "Huh?" look. No way I'd tell them about all the fail-safe spells I'd set up to catch the bad guys.

I tried to stand but couldn't quite make it on my own two yet. Goodness. Whatever that warlock threw at me had a hell of a kick.

"What happened to the cousin?"

"Unfortunately, we didn't apprehend him. He and two of his men escaped," the PM said. "Some magical person must have helped them, because they all just disappeared."

Crap. I may have saved lives, but I didn't extinguish the source. Sloppy work, Bronwyn. The cousin had to have more than one warlock or witch working for him because he'd survived my attack spells.

"You protected the sheik and me today, Bronwyn. I'm quite proud of you." The PM held my hands. "I explained to him about your protection spell and he's in your debt. He tried to wait for you to wake up, but he had to meet with the police. He's promised you anything you want."

"That's kind, sir, but he's still in danger and so are you. I'm sending charms with both of you and I'll work on some long-distance protection spells."

"No one expects you to save the world, Bronwyn."

"You and now the sheik are my charges. I'm not saving the world. Just you."

I tried to stand again and had to sit back down and put my head between my legs. I hate warlocks. That wicked asshole had spread black magic throughout my body. It felt like sludge churning through my blood.

Miles brought me tea and I accepted it hesitantly. After the poisoning fiasco with the PM, no way would I drink anything fixed at the hotel.

"Bottled water, Bronwyn, and I heated it in the kettle myself." He tried to make me understand that he was well aware of my fear.

"You can't be too careful these days, but thank you."

An hour later I made it back to my room.

It took everything I had to get dressed in my jeans and change my hair back to its natural color. Caught a cab to the airport this morning, and now I'm going to sit back and do my darnedest to get some rest. Otherwise I'll have to stay over in Dallas because I can't fly my plane if I'm tired.

Where did I put that belladonna? And I'll need something to put it in. Pushed the flight attendant call button.

He didn't wear a skirt like the pic on the button but he was definitely cute. My little mile-high escapade on the way to Oslo flashed through my brain. But I was much too tired for that kind of fun right now.

"Yes?"

"Could I have one of those bottles of scotch?"

"Miss, it is seven-thirty in the morning!"

"Right. Better make it a bourbon."

Tuesday, 10 A.M.
Waning moon
Sweet, Texas
Clean witches: 1

Jesus. I barely made it home Sunday. I felt like a walking zombie. Caleb met me at the airport in Dallas and flew my Cessna home, because I couldn't get it together.

It's taken two days of purification spells and potions to get that black magic sludge out of my system. Stupid fucking warlock. I hate him.

I thought most of them were all Wicca-loving white majickers these days. But lately, I've seen my share of bad ones. For centuries the male witches got a bad rap, so for years now they've run around doing only good for the world. Evidently my guy didn't get the memo.

Too bad they don't have some kind of Betty Ford detox for witches; there are days when we could use help like that.

Been working out in the conservatory. Caleb's helped turn it into a pretty decent place for my herbs and flowers by installing some solar panels. I swear after that disastrous breakfast meeting I never wanted to hear another word about solar crap, but even in midwinter the panels keep the glassed-in room warm.

Love working in the dirt. Caleb also made me some shelves and a great worktable. Thought he'd been hanging around because of my enormous charm, but now I think he's got a thing for Kira. He keeps asking if I need help with research or if I need him to pick up some books.

What a big goober.

I P.M.

I'd just been thinking about how much I miss Simone and she called from L.A. The demon slayer has come across a tough nut and needs my help.

I sent her a protection spell long distance. Same one I sent the sheik and PM.

Gotta do some research on this demon. She called him a Worgh. He's not in my Book of Shadows so I had Kira email over some ancient shamanic text. Caleb rushed to the library to see if he could help her. Yeah, right.

9 P.M.
Spells: 2
Dead demons: 1
Found it! Worghs need human hearts to stay alive. Just stick their big claws in and rip it right out. Nasty buggers.

When it comes to killing demons the shaman's got it going on. To kill a Worgh, Simone had to find a blessed ceremonial knife, human blood with the hepatitis virus, and good aim. She found an L.A. shaman with all the goods.

Middle-world spirits must turn to human form when they eat. So Simone just waited till the demon got ready to rip out her heart and plunged the knife into his.

The initial wound didn't kill him instantly, but the contaminated blood made him shrivel up like a prune. 'Bout a half hour later he turned to dust.

Love it when that happens. Big ole pile of demon dirt.

Simone promised to come out for a visit. Can't wait to see her.

Also, when I talked to Kira earlier today, she said she wants to introduce me tomorrow night to some new doctor in town. She swears he's the dark, brooding Hugh Grant type.

The only doctor I've seen in town looks more like Gomer Pyle than a Greek god. Oh, well, at least there's food involved.

I'm more interested in seeing if there are real sparks between Kira and Caleb.

I like Kira a lot. She's a former high-powered lawyer turned librarian. She told me once that she had grown tired of representing the scum of the earth. Her hippie parents live here in Sweet, and she came back to be closer to them.

I'm not sure I'd wish bossy Caleb on anyone, especially a friend.

Wednesday, 5 P.M.

Got a call from the hangar. Darryl, who runs the local airport, says a package came in for me. Asked him to drop it by the house. He laughed and told me I better get out there. Whatever.

Butt-in-gear time. Guess I'll go pick up the package before dinner.

6 P.M.

Surprised witches: 1

Drove up to the hangar and Darryl stood behind the counter in the office chuckling like a crazy man.

"So, where's the package?"

"Hangar three."

"Why didn't you bring it in here?"

He started laughing again and pushed me out the door. When he slid the bay open I gasped.

Holy crap.

A jet.

"Whose is that?"

"Yours." Darryl choked on a breath and held his sides.

"Quit shittin' me."

"I'm serious. Some guy named Sheik Azzzzzzy something sent it. There's a note inside."

Sheik? *Oh, my God.* "Where's the pilot?"

"Another jet just like it flew in behind him and picked the pilot up and then took off."

What do you get the witch who has everything? If you're

Sheik Azir you send her a Gulfstream IV-SP. The smoothest jet ever to fly the friendly skies.

The inside was total lux. Creamy leather seats with plush velvet pillows. Dark paneled walls. Gold-plated everything. A bar, small kitchenette, bedroom, and full-sized bath. Awesome.

And he'd filled it with pink roses.

Huh. Friendly guy.

I stood there in awe. Gathered up the pink roses and tried to figure out how I could return one beautiful jet to a sexy sheik in Dubai.

Four

Can't sleep.

The PM finally called me back late last night. The conversation went something like this:

"Prime Minister?"

"Yes."

"Um, sir, Sheik Azir sent me a Gulfstream."

"That is pleasant."

"No, sir, I don't think you understand. It's one of the most expensive private jets available. I can't accept it."

"Well, it would make the sheik very unhappy if you were to refuse his gift."

"I don't want to make him unhappy, sir. But I can't accept a million-dollar jet. It isn't ethical."

Pushed my hand through my hair. The PM is a brilliant man—why couldn't he understand?

"Do you feel his life is worth a million dollars?" His voice became serious.

"You can't put a price on a human life."

"Exactly."

"Exactly what, sir?"

He took a long breath as if readying himself to explain something to an annoying child. "If you were to return the sheik's generous gift, he would see it as an insult. If you send it back, he'll believe you don't consider his life worth the cost of the gift."

"Pardon me, but that's a bunch of . . . hooey."

"What is hooey?"

"I think you know."

The PM cleared his throat. "Why don't you see it as payment for services rendered?"

"Technically, the sheik never hired me."

"Bronwyn, please. This is tiresome. You can't return the gift because it would be a high insult. Accept his generosity."

What the hell could I say to that? The sheik's life is worth a hundred jets. I didn't want to hurt his feelings, but taking a gift like this throws off the whole karmic balance.

The PM continued, "I do remember the sheik's concern that your Cessna couldn't travel overseas. Should your services be needed in an emergency, he didn't want you to have to wait for a commercial flight.

"And as far as the services rendered, I think if you check your packages today you'll see a contract that hires your services for a rather lengthy duration."

I walked through the house to the living room where I found several unopened packages. I've always been bad about mail.

Most of the FedEx drops are potion supplies and I hadn't checked them in days.

Sure enough there was one from Dubai.

Great.

"Bronwyn, are you still there?"

"Yes, Prime Minister."

"I've got to go. Is this matter settled?"

"No, sir, but until I can figure out an alternative, I'll keep the jet."

"Good." He disconnected.

I sat there staring at the contract.

I wouldn't sign it. After careful inspection I discovered he wanted to pay me a hefty fee—about twenty times my regular amount. But he wanted me at his beck and call.

I don't work that way.

Needed some time to think things over and I wanted to talk to the sheik. Maybe I could straighten all this out over the phone.

Left a message with Miles to get me the sheik's phone number. Now I just had to figure out what I'd say to the man.

Oh, and the other reason I can't sleep. Dr. Sam. A gorgeous hunk of beef who turned my insides into goo tonight at our dinner with Kira and Caleb.

Something about him. Gomer Pyle he wasn't. The dinner is all a blur, except that I remember having sexy thoughts about giving the good doc a lap dance.

There's just one problem—I think he's a warlock. He definitely had shields I couldn't penetrate, which indicates someone with a fair amount of magical power.

If that's the case, he's off the I-want-to-have-sex-with-you list. I don't do warlocks, after that guy in college tried to drain all of my powers and leave me for dead. Then there's the whole gang of warlocks who trussed me up like a pig on a spit and hung me up as a sacrifice. I just have no happy thoughts where warlocks are concerned.

It's a shame because I felt this raw, sexual connection with him. Something I've never experienced before with another magical being. And we talked about everything—books, movies— and we had so much in common. I'd worn my I'm-a-slut red top, with the V to the breastbone, and my new Seven jeans. But his eyes never ventured down to my chest, or if they did I didn't see them. He stared into my eyes the whole time we talked.

Even now I can't stop thinking about him. Argh!

3 P.M.
Potions: 30
Spells: 3

I've been working on a new potion to help with memory loss. Margie, who works over at the nursing home in the hospital, is a friend of Kira's. They were coming out of the Piggly Wiggly yesterday morning as I was going in.

Anyway, Margie told me the saddest thing about working with the elderly is they don't remember who they were—or are, for that matter.

"Mr. Gunther is this old man who has wonderful stories," Margie said. "But half the time he can't remember what his name is or what year it is. Doesn't seem fair that you live this great life only to lose all memory of it when you get old."

"Do you have a lot of patients like that?" I asked her.

"Probably seven out of ten at the home are that way. It just makes me feel so helpless when I see them trying so hard to re- member."

If I've got one soft spot it would be for old people. The time I spent with my grandparents before they died gave me some of the best memories of my life.

I didn't tell Margie about the memory spell I've been working on lately, but I did go home and start making a potion, and now it's ready to try out. A spell is just a temporary fix and it seems a shame to give them back their memories only to take them away again. At least a potion will last a little longer.

4 P.M.
Potions: 1
Happy men: 1

I visited Mr. Gunther at the nursing home, and gave him the first dose of the potion. When I arrived he was sitting hunched over in a wheelchair staring out the window. I tried to talk with him, but he didn't respond. He did drink the liquid in a small cup I gave him.

Two hours later I returned to find those piercing blue eyes much clearer.

He was reading a book.

"Hello, Mr. Gunther."

"You're the witch."

Okay, so no beating around the bush here. "Yes, I'm *a* witch. Is that a problem?"

"Nope, just grateful. First time I've been able to read a book and remember what I read in about two years. Most days I sit around reading the same sentence for hours." He patted his wheelchair.

"That's wonderful. And just for the record, I asked for permission before giving you the potion." I smiled and patted his shoulder.

"I know. I signed a release a year ago when my mind first started going, that they could try any experimental medicines or treatments. Any idea on how long it will last?"

I couldn't lie to him. "No, I don't know. I'm sorry. But I'm working on something more permanent."

I pulled out a leather-bound journal. "I think you know what to do with this."

"Yes." He nodded.

"I'm working on a journal too. Gives me a sense of where I've been and how far I've come." Handed it over to him.

"I'll write down every word I can remember." He touched the leather gingerly. "Then if it starts to go, at least I can read about it, one sentence at a time."

I stood to leave and he grabbed my hand.

"You're a good witch."

"Oh, I have my days, Mr. Gunther." Squeezing his hand, I leaned down to plant a kiss on his weathered cheek. "I'll check on you later in the week."

Thought about stopping by to see the oh-so-cute Dr. Samuel McKinney on the way home. But I didn't have the courage. He's absolutely gorgeous and smart. I should at least check him out.

Oops, phone.

Friday, 5 P.M.

Caleb heads back to Dallas tomorrow. He's got several interviews to do for a big cover story he's working on. He tried to talk Kira into taking a weekend trip back home with him, but she told him no.

Good for her.

They've only known each other for a few weeks but those pretty blonde curls and brilliant mind have turned the "I can never be serious about a woman" playboy into a big ole pile of mush.

Oh, and good news. Sort of. Dr. Sam called earlier and wanted to consult with me about some natural healing alternatives for his patients.

Thank God.

I know, I know. I don't do warlocks. But this guy. He's just so—I can't get him out of my head. Maybe if I fuck him it will get him out of my system.

I'd been thinking about ways I could contact him that didn't send the message, "Hey, I'm hot for your body." This was the perfect way to spend some time getting to know the good doctor, and it was all his idea.

We met around one-thirty at Lulu's Café next to the Piggly Wiggly. There's no real Lulu. Ms. Johnnie and her twin sister, Ms. Helen, run the place. Ms. Johnnie bakes all the pies fresh each morning and runs the front counter. Ms. Helen cooks everything else. They're quite a pair.

When you walk in, the delicious smells of just-baked bread and cinnamon assault your senses and you are overcome with the need to gorge. I wore my green cashmere sweater, and a pair of jeans that would allow me to eat whatever I wanted.

Pictures of the women's lives cover the walls. They were quite the lookers back in the day. Several of the photos have them sporting cheerleading outfits complete with pom-poms. And collectively they've been through eight husbands. All of whom are proudly displayed on the walls in various photos along with their children, grandchildren, and dignitaries who have made their way to Lulu's.

On a slow evening, after a few nips of cooking sherry, Ms. Johnnie and Ms. Helen have the place rolling with their tales about the president of the United States getting stuck in the toilet when it was out back, and Helen's fourth husband who she divorced when she found out he was two years older than he'd said he was. Didn't matter that they were in their sixties at the time. She thought she'd married a younger man.

"Just you today, Bronwyn?" Ms. Johnnie, dressed in a lime green pants outfit, handed over a menu.

"No, ma'am. I'm waiting for a friend. Oh, there he is."

Ms. Johnnie turned to see who walked in the door and put

her hand on her heart. "Now *that*, darlin', is a real man. Mmm-mmm. Is that the new doctor?"

"Yes, ma'am."

"Is he your date for lunch?" She fanned her face. "I think I'm feeling a twinge of the vapors." She never took her eyes off of him.

"Um, well, it's not really a date." I tried to set the record straight. "More like a business meeting."

"Damn shame if you ask me."

Sam's black hair gleamed in the sunlight pouring through the windows. How did he manage such a great tan in late February? He must have just come back from a beach holiday.

I'm always jealous of people with tans. With my light brown curls, green eyes, and fair skin it takes a solid month at the beach just for me to turn honey colored.

I introduced Sam to Ms. Johnnie and he charmed her socks off. We ordered the special, which included avocado turkey subs with Helen's melt-in-your-mouth mashed potatoes.

"Thanks for meeting me here." He took my hand in his and my stomach clenched in sexual anticipation. My body heated instantly and I stopped myself from sighing.

Ms. Johnnie brought him some tea and we released our hands.

"I haven't eaten here before." He folded a napkin into his lap. "But I've heard wonderful things about the food."

"I look for any excuse to eat the twins' cooking. I love this place."

"Rumor is, they're something special." He eyed the pictures on the walls.

"And then some. Ply them with a little alcohol and you'll get the entire history of Sweet, Texas, in one sitting."

"I'll remember that." He looked down at his hands. "There's something I've got to ask."

Now what? "Okay, shoot."

"Really it's two questions. Are you a high witch and can you read minds?"

Where the hell had that come from?

He held up his hand in a stop motion. "Wait, I didn't mean it like that. It's just . . . I think you're pretty and I'm sitting here wondering if you already know what's in my head. And I could feel the power emanating off you the other night. I've never met so powerful a witch, and I'm just curious."

I'd been so nervous about our lunch I hadn't even thought about reading his mind. Wish I had. "Yes, I'm a high witch. I have the ability to read minds. No, I didn't read yours."

"I'm sorry. Just curious."

"No worries. When I go out in public I usually put up shields because the noise gets to be too much. But I'm curious why you asked me about it. Most witches don't read minds and I haven't really talked about it with anyone here in town."

"The other night when we had dinner with Kira and Caleb." He took a sip of tea.

"Yes."

"I sensed you were reading their minds."

Actually I had been doing exactly that. All I got were sexy images of the two of them intertwined and I put up the shields. From what I knew, their relationship hadn't gone that far, but they were definitely thinking about it.

"They're my friends and only recently got together. Guess I got a little curious. Now what do you mean by *sensed*?"

Sam shifted in his chair. He started to speak but stopped as Ms. Johnnie delivered our food. After she left, I picked up the conversation. I had to know exactly what he knew.

"So, about the whole sensing thing . . ."

"I'm a warlock. I know, I should have said something when

we met the other night." He put both hands up this time in a stop motion that would have made the Supremes envious. "I don't practice. No one in my family has for the last hundred years or so. We've all become doctors and healers. Like most witches and warlocks, I do have some natural ability besides healing. One of those is reading emotions. I'm an empath."

Okay, here's the deal: I'm prejudiced when it comes to warlocks, whether they practice magic or not. It's been my personal experience that men can't handle their magic. The power's too much for them and they more often than not succumb to the dark side.

My biggest problem with Sam being a nonpracticing warlock is that I didn't sense he held power. Well, I knew there had to be something about him. Usually I can feel a warlock from a mile away. Sam had to have ironclad shields for it not to rub off on me in some way. And it hadn't. Kind of like the guy in Oslo, who zapped me with the black sludge before I could respond.

And in a way, if Sam held those shields in place, he did practice magic. I knew before I ever walked in there what he was, but I had hoped I was wrong.

"Why did your family turn away from the craft?" I tried to act casual but I was angry. And disappointed. If a warlock he be, off the sex list he goes. And it's a very short list these days.

"My great-grandfather practiced in his younger days, but felt he could do more good working as a surgeon. He used his power of healing to make a real difference. My grandfather and father followed in his footsteps, except my dad went into psychiatry. He uses his ability to gauge human emotion by helping people understand their lives."

"And you've never studied or practiced magic?" I watched his face and something shifted in his eyes.

"Oh, yes, I studied. I thought it important to understand my heritage and how to use my powers if needed. But I've never had any real cause to use them except for healing."

Damn. He wasn't telling me the truth. He'd used his powers for something other than healing. I could probe his mind, but knew he would know I was doing it.

"How about your parents?" He shifted again in his seat.

"My father is a neurosurgeon and my mother turned away from the craft when she decided to teach English at NYU a few years ago. They never discouraged me from seeking my own path into magic.

"For the last three hundred years all the women of the O'Hurley family, my mother's clan, have been born witches. It has always been left to the individual whether or not she wants to practice.

"The last high witch in our family was born two hundred years ago, so we were all surprised when my powers came in at seventeen."

He smiled. "I can't even imagine what that must have been like for you. So much power, so young."

I shrugged. "My mom says that a high witch is born knowing what to do and I believe she's right. I blew a few things up by accident at first, but for the most part I've always known how to keep the power in check."

Ms. Johnnie showed up with pie. Chocolate cream for me, and apple for Sam. We dug in. At this point I didn't know what to think.

"I realize this might be a bit much at only our second date." He ran on like an Indy car at the head of the pack. "It's not like I go around telling everyone I'm a warlock. In fact, you're the only one I've told here. But I wanted to be up front with you."

I put on a happy face and smiled, which belied the turmoil I felt inside. "Not a problem. Your secret is safe with me." But in my mind, I decided to do a background check on Sam the Warlock. If he were truly bad, my senses would pick up on it. The only thing I got from him was pure sexual heat. The kind that made me want to jump him right there, even though he was a warlock.

We did eventually talk about the potion I'd put together for Mr. Gunther and perhaps trying it on several other patients. When it came to arthritis and bone degeneration, I had some books about healing herbs I promised to share with him.

"In the ancient Celtic Book of Shadows there are remedies for every ailment." I shrugged. "No real magic involved. It's a matter of mixing the right ingredients, and convincing your patients to make healthy lifestyle changes. I also worked with a witch doctor of the Zimba tribe in Nigeria. He uses some healing techniques I've recorded. I'll get my notes together and drop them off at your office tomorrow."

He smiled and my stomach dipped to my toes. How could I be so attracted to a man I couldn't possibly date? Warlocks are a big no-no in Bronwyn's book of dating material.

"That'd be great." I needed to see if the sheik had called and we'd been at the café for almost an hour and a half. "Look, I've gotta run." I stood up and grabbed my wallet to lay some money on the table. He touched my hand and there were visible sparks. Magic. The warmth spread up my arm into my chest. He had let down his shields.

He felt it too, I could see the blush of it on his cheeks, and he smiled. "I asked you to lunch; I wish you'd let me pay."

"That's not necessary."

"Hey, did I say something to upset you?"

My problem was I didn't want to like him. That whole warlock thing threw me for a loop. I did like him—a lot. Crap. "Not at all. This is more of a business lunch, not a date."

He blanched at that. Evidently he saw it as more than talking shop.

"Okay, see you tomorrow?"

His face brightened. "That'd be great, thanks."

Put the money on the table and waved good-bye to Ms. Johnnie and Ms. Helen, who were leaning on the counter ogling Sam. Couldn't say I blamed them.

Forgot about the time zone difference. Can't call the sheik, but I sent Maridad, his assistant, an email asking for Azir to call me at his convenience.

In the meantime it won't hurt for me to take the jet up for a test flight. Wonder what Kira's doing? She might enjoy a ride and she may have more info on the good doctor since they are such close friends.

I'm so smart.

Saturday, II A.M.
Waning moon
Spells: 2
Potions: 3
Well, Sheiky baby hasn't called but Miles did. Next trip is to Brussels on Wednesday. Never been there but hear it's cold this time of year. Great.

Also had a message when I got back from flying. Dr. Sam said he'd forgotten his office is closed on Saturday and wondered if he could stop by and pick up the books and notes.

I left him a voice mail and told him sure.

Okay, I want to see him again. I admit it. That doesn't mean I'm going to sleep with him. He's a stupid fucking warlock.

During the flight Kira spilled everything she knew about Sam. They'd been friends since college and she adores him.

"If we had the least bit of chemistry we would have dated," she told me, "but we didn't. He and I had English lit together and worked on several projects. When I had boyfriend trouble he'd always come by and take me out for coffee or beer. He's just the best. I've cried on his shoulder many times."

I trust Kira, so I've decided to give Sam a chance to be my friend. Just a friend. After the sparks at Lulu's, I know we have chemistry, but we'll keep it strictly platonic and all will be well.

I can be friends with a warlock.

If he's interested I'll show him how to mix a few remedies for his patients.

My stomach is filled with butterflies and I can't believe I'm so turned upside down by this guy. Get a grip, Bronwyn. Damn, is that his car? Eeeek!

Sunday, 4:30 P.M.
Potions: 2
Cute guys I want to sleep with: 1

Sam brought lunch yesterday and ended up staying through dinner. We talked about everything and made a few potions together. When he left around midnight, he gave me a chaste kiss on the cheek, like we were in high school or something, and my heart did a double take.

We met again at the Methodist church this morning. Nice group of people. The minister and his wife invited Sam and me to the church potluck tonight so we're heading back there. Sort of hoping Sam comes home with me tonight. I've decided I don't care. The more I'm around him, the more I want him. He's so damn kind. Everyone in town loves him.

I want to be a very bad girl and jump him. If doing the nasty with him kills me, well, what a way to go.

10 P.M.

Argh! If I want to be a bad girl, I'm going to have to do it all on my own. At least when he dropped me off this time he kissed me on the lips.

I'm such a bad girl, but I don't care. I want to have a mind-blowing roll in the hay with the man. And I know it would be mind-blowing because every time he touches me I melt. Wiggly knees, the whole bit. Geez.

If he touches me again I'll have to invest in a vibrator. I mean, a girl can only take so much.

Five

Monday, 3 A.M.
Sweet, Texas
Returned jets: Still 0

Sheiky baby doesn't seem to be as worried about time zones as I am. He just called to tell me how grateful he is for my protection.

My sleep-addled brain had trouble producing coherent sentences. I think I said something like, "Sssno problem, Sheiky—I mean, sir."

A long pause on the other end made me sit up in my bed. Had I really said Sheiky?

He cleared his throat. "Yes, well, I wanted to make sure you enjoyed the jet and that it suited you."

"Oh, it's wonderful, but very unnecessary. I simply can't accept it."

I tried so hard to explain that his gift, while generous, was woefully inappropriate, but he didn't get it.

He also couldn't understand why I wouldn't sign his contract. Rude and bristly, that's how I'd describe him. Of course that's all offset because he has a velvety voice that makes a girl's spine tingle. He's going to be in Brussels so I'll try to talk to him again there.

The conversation ended with him giving me the use of a pilot to help fly the plane to Brussels. It's a long flight and he doesn't want me to get too tired. I get the feeling Azir isn't used to the word *no* because when I said it he totally ignored me, wished me a safe journey, and hung up the phone.

Casper, who I hadn't seen since I left for Oslo, lay beside me on the bed. She didn't seem happy about the early wake-up call and stuck her head up under one of the pillows. Smart cat. Think I'll do the same.

2 P.M.

Visited Mr. Gunther again. What a charmer. Those blue eyes twinkled as he told a great story about dancing in the streets of Paris with his wife for their fortieth wedding anniversary. He described every detail, from the twinkling lights on the Seine to the red dress she wore.

"She was as beautiful as the day I met her." He wiped a small tear from his eye. "People say that all the time but with Clara— she had such a big heart and loved everyone and everything around her. Her very presence made life a joy."

"She sounds wonderful." I sat across from him, not knowing what to say.

Lost in memory, he paused for a moment then looked me in the eye. "I know I said it before but thank you for this. Being able to remember my wife is a gift beyond measure. She made me a better person just by knowing her."

I wrinkled my nose to keep the emotion back and took his

hand. "I've got to do some traveling but I'll visit when I get back."

Margie told me that Mr. G's been writing in his journal endlessly. With memories like his, can't say I blame him. I've never experienced the kind of love he talks about when he mentions his wife. Such devotion.

I left another journal with Margie to give him when he fills the first one. There's something about that old guy that just tugs at my heart. I've got to find a way to help him on a more permanent basis.

Man, that 3 A.M. call made me tired. Think I'll grab a nap, so I can stay up late tonight. The girls are coming by for some fun.

Tuesday, 10 A.M.
Hungover witches: 1

I thought it a bit strange that I'd been here a few months and hadn't met any of the local witches. After hanging out with Kira and Margie last night, I realized the magical folks are well integrated into the community.

Turns out the mayor's wife, Peggy, oversees everything to do with the local coven, which explains why the townspeople never seemed to mind having me around. They're used to witches.

She does a fantastic PR job. I've never seen anything like it.

Michael Hughes, the chief of police, is a warlock. His sister, Amber Ann, is a witch, and their mother is Peggy. Oh, and Chief Hughes is a white magic warlock. Could explain why there's not much crime in Sweet. Just about every city council member or person in power in this small town has ties to a witch. I understand now why I felt such a positive pull to the place. With all that white magic energy, how could I resist?

Anyway, I learned about all of this after plying Kira and Margie with margaritas. We'd decided to have a Mexican fiesta in the dead of winter. I hung up bright colored lights all over the living room. Kira brought some massively delicious chicken en-chiladas, and Margie hauled in giant pots of refried beans and Spanish rice. We ate until we were sick, then we dipped into the Rocky Road ice cream. I know. Pathetic.

I made myself the honorary tequila chairman and mixed so many batches of raspberry margaritas that we lost count.

Note to self: Don't mix margaritas with Rocky Road.

Margie had a wealth of info about Dr. Sam. He's pretty hot stuff around the retirement home. The nursing staff fights over who gets to do rounds with him.

"He's not my type, too smart and sophisticated. I like my men big and stupid. But there's something so charming about him," Margie cooed as she pushed her brunette bangs out of her eyes. "Our patients turn to mush in front of him and do any-thing he asks. Old Thomas Wilkins refused to wear his glasses. Thinks they make him look old. He's ninety-three. Runs into walls so much that he's got horrible black-and-blue bruises on his face, arms, and legs. We worry all the time about being charged with negligence because of him.

"Doctor Sam puts the glasses on old Thomas and tells him he looks distinguished. Now he never takes them off. We go in at night and sneak them off his nose so he doesn't break them in his sleep."

Kira turned those brown eyes on me. "So you know he's a good guy. Now what are you going to do about it?"

I made a cross-eyed face at her and moved the conversation to Kira and Caleb. I couldn't share the real reason. He's a warlock. Even though I've sort of gotten over that myself.

Honestly, I have no idea how I feel about Sam. He's smart, funny, adorable, and pretty much everything I'd want in a man, except he's a warlock. I've been kind of upset that he hasn't tried to sleep with me, but at the same time I'm not sure I would go through with it. Except for that one lapse in college, I've never slept with a warlock.

Margie picked up on my change of subject and quizzed Kira. "So do you miss Caleb?"

Kira twirled her hair around her finger. "No. Yes, of course I do." She giggled. "And no, Bronwyn"—she turned on me—"we haven't done the nasty yet, but I'm sure you'll be the first to know."

We all laughed at that and moved the subject to something safer. Ex–boy toys.

It's been so long since I just hung out with the girls. As crappy as I feel this morning it was definitely worth it.

Too drunk to drive home, Kira and Margie passed out on the twin beds in the guest room. Something makes me think Kira might be a sensitive. I've picked up on ghosts in the house, but last night when I showed Kira the guest room she shivered and looked around.

"What's wrong?" I asked her.

"Nothing. Well, I feel like someone is watching me."

At odd moments I've felt a presence in the house, too. Nothing malevolent. About the time I notice it's there, it dissipates. But it did surprise me that Kira felt it. There may be a little witch in her after all.

Darn, just time for tea and then I've got to get to work.

10 P.M.

Had a message from Miles. Have I mentioned what a snippy little twit he can be?

"Bronwyn. Brussels is off. Be in Dubai on Friday. Sending an itinerary via email." Click. Not a good-bye or any kind of real explanation. At least the Middle East is warmer than Brussels. Wonder about the change but imagine I'll find out soon enough.

Wednesday, 7 A.M.
Spells: 0
Confused witches: 1

I have to write all this down because the experience is so intense I don't want to forget a minute of it.

I'd been working in the conservatory, for hours possibly. All of the herbs came up nicely. I was knee-deep in dirt, repotting some of the basil and oregano, which always shoots up too fast, when I felt someone behind me.

I stood and his arms wrapped around me from behind, slipping just under my breasts. I knew instantly from the smell of patchouli that it was Sam. Intoxicating.

Leaning into him, I felt his arms pull me closer. He kissed my ear and nibbled it, gently sending pleasure down my spine.

In the past week we've held hands but nothing as intimate as this.

I turned in his arms, moving my hands around his waist. He opened his mouth to speak and seemed to think better of it. He reached out and pushed my curls away from my eyes.

Our lips met. Always thought it sounded corny when women talked about how kisses made them melt, but now I know exactly what they mean. It's like when that second shot of bourbon hits you and your whole body warms. Only lots, lots better.

Couldn't breathe. His tongue made its way into my mouth and teased mine with its strength. He tasted of peppermint and cinnamon. We explored each other and he suddenly stepped back. The blue in his eyes intensified and the next thing I knew we were in my bed, flesh against flesh.

His body pressed hard into mine and it felt like the most natural thing in the world to be next to this man on the cusp of making love. Never have I wanted anything more.

Moving his hands up and down my body he teased and titillated. Can I just say the good doctor has a great bedside manner and magic fingers? Whispering my name against my ear, he spread my thighs apart and let his fingers do the talking while his kisses intensified. I gasped with pleasure and begged him to come inside.

In one fluid motion he pulled me up and slid me down on top of him. He lifted his hips to meet mine. With that first thrust the magic within us rose to the surface. We made love in a golden haze of magical energy. Senses went into overdrive and I threw my arms back to grab his thighs. He moved his hands to my waist and pumped me harder as I begged.

Our bodies slickened, rising and falling to meet a frenzied pace. I screamed with pleasure as the convulsions tightened and the warmth spread through my body. I grew slack with release and I collapsed on his chest.

"Bronwyn," he moaned. And I trembled.

Slowly he moved himself in and out of my body. I didn't know how much I could take and at the same time I craved more.

Flipping me over to my back, he stood, pulling me to the end of the bed. He brought my hips to his. I wrapped my legs around him and fisted the sheets as he drove himself harder and harder into me.

I heard screaming and realized it was me writhing on the bed begging. I came again swiftly and this time he rode the tide with me. "Bronwyn, yes!" he yelled, his voice coarse with emotion as he fell to the bed beside me, obviously spent.

For a moment our auras shimmered, mixing in a weird shade of purple.

A strange mewling sound came from a distance. I woke to find my bed empty except for Casper, who was none too happy about the noise I'd obviously been making.

He wasn't there. It had been a total Bobby Ewing. Nothing but a dream. I leaned back on the pillows and looked around the room, searching for something that I knew couldn't be there.

I've had vivid dreams in the past but nothing like this. The sheets were drenched in sweat and twisted into a mess.

He had to have been there. I swore I could still smell him. His scent was on my skin.

I need a cold shower then I think I'll take the good doctor some breakfast.

Six

I'm a nervous wreck. Sam will be here any minute and—

I went to meet him at his office this morning, bright and shiny, with cinnamon rolls and hazelnut coffee from Lulu's. I waited in the truck outside, confused about my next move. Should I try the door? Was he even there yet?

Geez, I'm a high witch with more powers than an entire coven combined and I couldn't seem to get up the nerve to walk up to the door. How sad was that? While I pondered, he pulled up in his black SUV. I jumped out and met him in the front of the gothic-style building.

"Wow, to what do I owe this great honor?" He turned the key in the door and flipped on the lights as we stepped inside.

"You're the doctor, figure it out." I laughed, holding up the bag of food.

He offered a confused smile.

"Well, you know better than anyone that growing boys need a healthy breakfast to start their day." I handed him the bag with the rolls and put the coffee on the reception desk.

"True." He opened up the appointment book. "Looks like we have at least a half hour before my first patient. Why don't you come back to my office and we can discuss my nutritional needs." His voice was sexy with innuendo.

"Okay."

He grabbed all the food and I followed him back to his office. I've got a thing for cherrywood and obviously so does he. A huge desk took up a third of the room, and the walls were covered floor to ceiling in bookshelves. One wall had a large window with black-and-white photography displayed on each side of it. For a small-town doc's office, it had a very midtown Manhattan feel.

He put everything down on a small table between two leather chairs facing the desk and grabbed my hands. "So, tell me why you are really here, and why are you so nervous?"

I'm a pro at hiding emotions but hadn't thought to do it around him. I keep forgetting his intuitive nature and the fact he's a warlock. "If I tell you, well, you may have to keep me for observation." My voice was husky with need.

He frowned and touched a hand to my cheek. "Are you feeling ill?"

I laughed more from being nervous than anything. "No, no. It's silly really." I stepped back and sat down in the leather chair. Had to do something with my hands so I pulled out a roll and handed it to him along with one of the cups of coffee. He sat down opposite me and stared intently.

I took a bite but didn't really taste it. Now don't get me wrong, cinnamon buns from Lulu's are heaven. But I was having a tough time sorting through all the emotions rumbling in my brain. I'd just experienced one of the most intense love-making experiences of my life and the man hadn't even known he was there.

I slid my tongue across my lips to get the icing off and he watched intently.

"Bronwyn?" He smiled. "Just tell me whatever it is."

"A dream." There. I'd said it out loud.

"Um, a dream?" He sipped his coffee.

"Yes. A very intense dream—a sensual one."

He choked on that bit of news.

I continued. "Okay, so I know this is totally inappropriate, but I've never experienced anything like it. And I'm not one of those women who is good at holding back and keeping secrets. I like things out in the open with my relationships." I held up a hand. "Not that we have one, but I think we sort of have something."

He raised his hand to talk, but I waved him away.

"Anyway. I had this intense dream, so real. I can't even begin to tell you how it made me feel. And when I woke up, I couldn't believe you weren't there beside me. My problem is, I'm afraid that I may have slipped into your dream accidentally. It happens sometimes when my shields are down and I care about someone. And if that happened and it was your dream too, I'm sorry."

He just sat there staring at me. My nerves were on edge and I jumped up out of the chair and tried to escape. So much for honesty in relationships. Secrets and lies are good things and emotions should be repressed.

I tried to open the door but he shut it again with his hand above my head. He grabbed me from behind and wrapped his arms under my breasts.

"Did the dream begin like this?" he whispered in my ear and trailed kisses down my neck.

My breath caught and he squeezed me tighter as I leaned into him.

We did share the dream.

"Yes, it started just like this." I still faced the door.

"Turn around, Bronwyn."

I did what he asked and he grabbed both arms and pulled them above my head. As his eyes narrowed his lips crushed mine in a passionate kiss. That whole wiggly-knee thing happened again. His body pressed tight against mine was the only thing that kept me from sliding down the door. Our magic mixed and sent waves of heat through my body.

His tongue probed and he tasted of coffee and sugary sweet pastry. I didn't think it possible but it was even better than the dream.

While he still held my arms above my head, he brought one hand down to cup my breast, running his thumb over the hardened nipple. I tilted my head and his kisses left my lips and he nibbled on my ear and neck.

I was ready to drop my pants right there and wrap my legs around him when a knock on the door made us both jump.

"Doctor?"

He pulled me to the side of the door and cracked it. "Yes, Carmen?"

"Oh, you are in. Just checking to make sure everything was all right."

"We're fine, thanks." He chewed on his lip to keep from laughing. "I'm, um, in a consultation right now and I may run over a few minutes. Tell Mr. Blaine I'll be with him shortly." His mouth covered in lipstick and his cheeks pink with emotion, he smiled at the other woman.

"Yes, sir. He's not in yet but I'll let him know."

He shut the door and we both laughed at the absurdity of the situation.

I fanned my face. "Why, Doctor, as the twins at Lulu's like to say, I believe I have the vapors," I told him in my best Scarlett O'Hara imitation.

"You and me both." He led me to the chair and I sat down. I gulped some of the coffee, while he moved his chair in front of mine and grabbed my free hand.

"Obviously," he began, "there is something between us. And I'm not angry that you slipped into my dream. Although, I'll ask that you not make a regular practice of that."

"Not a problem."

He smiled and took a deep breath. "So, can I see you tonight?"

"If you don't, I might just explode." I didn't add that the only thing I wanted to do right now was climb on top of him in that chair and ride him till I couldn't think anymore.

"Why do I have the feeling there's more going on in that head of yours than you're sharing with me?" He stood and brought me to him.

"I have no idea what you're talking about, Doctor." I winked. "But maybe when you come courting tonight I'll share some of my wicked ideas with you."

"Courting? Haven't heard that in a hundred years, but I can hardly wait." He kissed me again, not quite as hard as before, but just as passionately. Then he straightened the curls around my face and buttoned the top of my shirt.

"I have a feeling this is going to be a very long day," he said as he walked me to the door.

"Anticipation is a good thing." I turned and put a hand on his chest. "A very good thing."

When I walked out he laughed and I noticed the bulge in his pants. "You might want to take a moment to, um, compose yourself." I pointed at the evidence.

He shook his head and shut the door. I'm pretty sure Carmen

knew just what kind of consultation the good doc had given me, but she wished me a cheery good-bye just the same.

I spent the day working through the Book of Shadows looking for some special wards to protect the prime minister's and Sheik Azir's homes. I think I found something good. But it involves a few ingredients I'll have to order.

Cleaned the house from top to bottom and did whatever it took to not think about tonight. Will it be as good as the dream? Am I really in a relationship with a guy I met a week ago? I don't care that he's a warlock. I don't care if he ends up killing me. I just want him.

There's his car. Aaaah!

Thursday
New York City
Spells: 1
Dead guys: 1

It's amazing what can happen in twenty-four hours. Well, I'm sort of used to strange events in my life, but I'd put this day right up there with the best of them.

Last night with Sam began a bit awkward but turned out really sweet. Not what I expected at all. He brought white wine, which went well with some of Ms. Helen's chicken potpies I'd picked up that afternoon.

Before he got there I'd made the house look like a seduction zone. Candles everywhere and a fire going. Vanilla permeated the air. I wanted it so delicious he wouldn't be able to resist.

We ate and talked about everything except sex. It's funny. Kept waiting for him to make his move. I may be a modern woman, but once in a while I like the guy to take charge. We discussed our favorite films and I brought up a particular scene in that old movie *Blue Velvet,* which honestly isn't my favorite, but is very hot. He reminded me about scenes from *Wild Things* and *9 1/2 Weeks.* That's when things took a turn for the sexy.

We were naked and doing the nasty on the floor, the kitchen counter, the stairs, and finally in my bed. Whew! And I didn't think it possible, but it was even better than the dream.

By three this morning my body was a vibrating mass of nerve endings, and I'd never felt so satisfied.

He woke up early and fixed me breakfast and then drove me to the hangar so I could get the jet to New York. He waited while I did a flight check and then kissed me good-bye. I'm more confused than ever, where he's concerned. I like him. A lot.

Got into New York just as a winter storm hit and found myself stuck for the rest of the day and night. Called Miles and left him a message that I'd be a day late. He won't be happy about the news but there isn't a darn thing the jerk can do about it.

Called the pilots, and we decided to check in around six tomorrow morning and file a new flight plan. Mom and Dad live here now, but are out of town for a medical conference in Hawaii. Lucky them.

Decided to use my key and crash at their brownstone until the storm clears. The house was chilly but I turned up the heat and went in search of warmer clothes. I'd packed for Saudi and traveling in the desert, which meant light cotton shirts, sandals, jeans, some slacks, and small summer tops. Not one thing to take the chill out of my bones.

I borrowed one of Mom's cashmere sweaters and a kicky pair of Jimmy Choo boots. I noticed she had added at least four more pairs of Manolo Blahniks to her shoe collection. My mom has terrific taste in shoes, and Dad forgives her one vice.

Since they were spending a couple of weeks away, the kitchen was bare. I grabbed Mom's shearling coat and gloves from the hall closet and walked down to the café on the corner. The place was filled with people who didn't seem to mind the wicked weather outside.

After waiting about fifteen minutes I ordered the tomato basil soup, a turkey sandwich, and a cup of orange tea. The tea smelled like a heavenly potpourri and made me think of Christmas. Sat by the window at a small table and people-watched.

The couple in the corner were having an intense conversation and things didn't look good for the man of the house. Sounded like he might have a gambling problem because she kept ranting about his using the rent for a poker game.

I felt sorry for the guy. Poker's so addictive. Every time I play Texas Hold 'Em I get caught up in the game. Thankfully, I've got a lot of dumb luck and I haven't lost too much. Which is good because I'm a really bad player. I could cheat and read minds, but that takes all the fun out of it.

I'd finished my meal when I sensed a warlock walk in. My eyes darted around the room and I spotted him at the same time he did me.

Tried to read his mind but he blocked me. I pushed through his brain and gave him a warning that I'd harm none as long as he behaved.

"You can't tell me what to do, witch!" he screamed from across the room. Everyone in the café turned to see about the commotion. The warlock, dressed in a business suit, raised his arms as if ready to go to war.

"I'm asking you nicely to please put your magic away." My voice stayed calm, but inside my body trembled with fury. Have I mentioned how much I detest warlocks? Well, with the exception of Sam.

"I don't take orders from you," he snarled.

I started a protection incantation to keep the patrons safe. The energy burned in my solar plexus and tingled out to my arms and fingers.

Everything happened in slow motion. He threw something black and nasty at me and I tossed him up against the back wall. Only a little of his magic seeped in, but it was enough to really piss me off.

"Come on, warlock. If you want to fight let's do it. But outside." With my mind I opened the door and tossed him onto the street. Contrary to popular belief, I do try to get people to see reason before I kill them. But sometimes they don't give me much opportunity to save their lives.

This was one of those times.

"I don't want to kill you, but I will. Turn yourself in to the local coven and we'll call this over," I explained.

"You don't get it, witch; I'm here to kill you and I will do it." He stood facing me as if in an old Wild West showdown. Hands on his hips, chin jutted out. If he didn't look like he'd just stepped out of GQ with his blond businessman haircut and Armani suit, I might have taken him more seriously. "You'll die today, witch, and I'll become an even richer man."

I shook my head no. "Not gonna happen, pal. I don't know who's paying you to track me down, but you should have done your research. I can hurt you way more than you can me."

"Not true. My black poison has already invaded your body and your powers grow weak. You cannot defeat me."

Where in the hell did this guy come from? I wanted to blow him up but that causes too much karmic debt. I could just beat his head into the street until his brains oozed out through his ears, but then someone would have to clean it up. And again there's that old what-goes-around-comes-around rule.

While I thought about the one hundred and one ways I could

kill him he summoned another spell to throw at me. Knocked me backward and nearly tripped on my own feet. Jerk. He was strong but absolutely no match.

Now why would someone send some half-assed warlock to fight me? Made no sense.

He raised his hands to throw another spell and I blocked it and threw it right back at him. Oops, he obviously hadn't counted on that. Stupid warlock. The spell took him to his knees. Black sludge fell in tears down his face.

"You know, if you're going to throw that nasty black crap around, you need to learn to protect yourself from it." Idiot. The snow came down harder and a police cruiser pulled up. My wet hair curled around my face and my nose was cold.

I looked around to see everyone in the café pressed against the glass watching. Magical showdowns don't happen often in public. We really do try to keep things behind closed doors.

The warlock still couldn't move, and I explained to the officers what had happened. They called for a special unit that handled crimes of magic, and they let me go. I didn't know if the warlock would die from his own black garbage, but I knew I had to get it out of my system. I couldn't go home to renew, so I'd have to do the next best thing. I pulled out my cell and called Garnout.

"Hello, blessed one. I got sludged by a nasty warlock. Can you help me out?" I coughed. More had seeped in than I thought.

"Bronwyn, my dear, I'm always happy to help you." Garnout's kind voice rang in my ears. "I'm at the same place but upstairs in apartment 24. I'll get everything ready."

"Thanks, Garnout. I'll be there as soon as I can find a cab." Before long I was on my way to be healed by the most powerful wizard I'd ever met.

Seven

Can I just say I'm happy that I've got two pilots sharing the duties of getting this beauty to Dubai? After Garnout's whack 'em sack 'em potion last night I would have never been able to fly this thing on my own.

I don't feel bad, but I'm wiped out and need more rest to replenish my magic. I asked Garnout about the ingredients in the potion but there are some things a great wizard never shares.

"Bronwyn, darling, I can't tell you what's in the potion. You know the wizard's creed. But I'm more than happy to make a couple of extra vials for you to take on your journey." He walked around the apartment picking up bottles of this and that and mixing it with a small mortar and pestle. "You're going to feel nauseous and some pain. I've put a small amount of chamomile and blueberry in to help ease the discomfort."

"I don't care as long as it works." I sat down on the red velvet sofa and looked around the room. Much like his shop, it was neat and tidy but filled to the brim with oddities he'd gathered in his many travels. "The last time I had to desludge myself it took three days."

"Well, even for a high witch three days of purification is good. Most take at least a week. Now drink this." He pulled at his graying beard, his green eyes kind and thoughtful. "In about five minutes you'll think I tried to kill you, but in an hour you'll feel good as new."

Gave him a wary look and swallowed. The stuff tasted like pure ick as it slid down my throat. A bitter ginger flavor remained on my tongue.

"Now lie back on the couch there and be as still as possible. You'll want to vomit, but best to hold it for as long as possible. The toilet is behind the door by the portrait of Beatrice." He pointed across the room to a picture of an elegant woman with strawberry blonde hair, brown doe eyes, and flowing royal blue robes. From the loving way he looked at her, she must have been someone special.

"Garnout, why would they send someone so weak to fight me? The warlock I killed in Oslo was twice as strong as this one. He never had a chance." My stomach roiled and I soon found myself in a fetal position trying to do deep breathing exercises to keep from throwing up.

"Ah, it's working. I don't know about the warlock, but I'll do some checking. Could be someone's put a bounty on your head again, and they'll come crawling out of the woodwork. Remember the last time when that vengeful Sarafan wanted you dead? Every dark witch and warlock in the world descended on this city looking for you.

"You fought those battles and grew stronger with each one.

As you no doubt will this time. I need to run to the shop for a bit, but I'll be back to check on you. I wouldn't leave, but I've got a new employee and he's not quite adjusted to the clientele. Every time a dark lord or demon walks in he tries to kill them. Poor fellow can't seem to distinguish between a tad evil and the really nasty fellows. Not good for business." He gathered his coat.

As he walked to the door, he hesitated. I could tell he didn't want to leave.

"Go, Garnout. I'll be fine. I'm a big girl, and it's just a little sludge." I wrapped my arms tight around my stomach when the rumbling began.

He smiled and left. Good thing he wasn't there five minutes later or I might have tried to kill him. Doubled over in pain, I cursed him—and his "special potion."

Twenty minutes after sipping the potion, I ran for the bathroom. I swear Beatrice watched with a small smile on her face. I know those eyes moved across the room with me.

About an hour later my strength returned. Couldn't say I felt 100 percent back to normal. The queasiness stayed with me for hours.

When he returned to his apartment I tried to repay his kindness but he was insulted. "You've saved my loved ones more than once, young witch, and you owe me nothing."

Guess he's referring to the time I got his nephew out of a tight squeeze in Beijing. The kid had gone to study magic at the Okania School and hung out with the wrong crowd. Before he knew it, he'd been sold into the slave trade. Garnout made sure the human exporters no longer existed while I saved the kid's life from some weirdo who liked to molest and kill young men. That was about six years ago and Garnout had been so grateful he set me up a meeting with the prime minister. The PM liked me and I've been protecting him ever since.

When he, or one of his friends, calls, I go. And I've built a nice little business for myself.

Now I'm living the life of luxury sitting on a sofa in my own private jet, while the pilots plot a course across Europe. Okay, technically it's not my jet, but this isn't such a bad life. Of course, I've still got to find a way to give this baby back to the sheik, but for now I'm just going to wallow on the plush leather couches and maybe even take a nap. After I eat my big juicy steak and drink this champagne the sheik insisted be stocked on board. Yummers.

Saturday, noon
Dubai

Who would have thought all this sand would be so extraordinary? I expected desert, but honestly I've never seen anything like this. Out my window all I see is miles and miles of windswept dunes. It's beautiful in a vast sort of way.

I'm expected at lunch. We got in really late so they were nice enough to let me sleep in this morning. That's unusual considering Miles is a part of the "they."

Guess I should get my butt in gear and find the dining room. It won't be easy. From what I saw last night this palace in the sand has more rooms than most hotels. Wonder what's appropriate to wear to lunch in a place like this?

Sunday, 3 P.M.

Maybe it's jet lag, but I could sleep for a week. The sheik and prime minster kept me in meetings for hours. These guys have no appreciation for the word *weekend*.

They wanted my opinion on security issues.

The problem lies with the sheik's cousin. The jerk has gathered together some of the most powerful and evil warlocks in the world with one purpose in mind: to kill the very people I'm trying to protect. Man, that pisses me off.

"I thought he'd come after me because he wanted control of the family business," Azir said of his cousin. "Now I know it's about revenge."

The prime minister didn't say anything, but I couldn't resist. "What happened?"

Azir leaned back in his chair and crossed his arms against his chest. The crinkling of his brow and frown on his face indicated he wasn't comfortable sharing the story.

"Our mothers were sisters and very close. Years ago when I was at college in England, I received news from home that there had been some trouble.

"I returned here to discover that my uncle had nearly killed my aunt in a jealous rage. He'd been certain that another man glanced at her in town and he blamed her for the attention.

"I'm sure you know that my country doesn't treat women fairly and my uncle had been perfectly within his rights to beat her into a coma according to our laws at the time."

The PM and I sat stunned. Domestic violence is nothing new, but it's hard to stomach when an entire country does nothing about it.

The sheik pushed away from his meal and ushered us into a plush garden sanctuary. Filled with exotic birds, palms, and a running brook, it was an oasis in the middle of his home. We sat at a small table and he continued his story.

"As I look back I'm certain I could have handled it better, but I was young." Azir ran a hand through the waves of his black hair. His eyes had a faraway look as if the memories were just beyond his reach. "My mother suffered great grief by my aunt's bedside, and you must know I adore my mother. 'This cannot be allowed to happen again,' she said. And I agreed.

"I went to my uncle's home and confronted him. Threatened him, really. He pulled a knife to punish me for my insolence. I don't think he intended to kill me, just wound me. There was a fight and he lost. My cousin, who was only fourteen at the time, had been hiding behind the door and saw the whole thing. Later that night his mother, my aunt, died.

"In her honor I opened the Women's Hope Foundation to help those who have been abused begin new lives. I don't know if my aunt would have accepted help, had she had any options. But I didn't want another woman to suffer if she did desire to get out of her present circumstances."

I picked up a flower that had fallen onto the table. "I had no idea you were behind that organization. It's huge in America and there are success stories in the newspapers about women who you helped and then they went on to do great things."

I shook my head. Here I thought this guy was all about business and I discover he's trying to save the world. As obstinate and annoying as he could be, I found myself liking him. It didn't hurt that he's gorgeous.

"I'd like to take you both to visit the safe haven we've built here. But the organization has not made me popular among my countrymen, who have old-fashioned ideas about women's rights. That, along with my research into solar power, has put me on several blacklists. This is why I need your help over the next several weeks."

"Why is that?"

"I have a feeling it's not just my cousin who is trying to kill me. While we try to unravel this mystery, I need your protection."

"Sheik Azir, you've had my protection for a few weeks now, and you will until I round up all the bad guys." Both men stood and I walked in the small garden with them.

Azir pulled on a leaf of a large palm tree. "I understand the prime minister must return to England tomorrow, but I would appreciate your staying for a while longer, Bronwyn. I need you here."

I heard the desperation in his voice. Turning to face him, I almost toppled on a stone. "How long are you talking about?"

"Perhaps a week, maybe two."

I blew out a breath. I'd expected to be here over the weekend but no longer. I had so much to do at home. Simone had emailed that she would be at my house on Tuesday.

"Please know you are a priority and I can protect you from wherever I am in the world. But I can't stay here and ignore my other clients, or the work I do back in the States." I touched his arm to take the heat out of the words and received a flash of energy that curled in my palm.

"I'm asking for two weeks, and you could very well save my life and the lives of several others in the process." If he noticed that our skin touching had created heat he didn't give any indication. From the look in his eyes I knew he held something back.

"Tell me why it's so important. Why now?"

He opened his mouth and closed it again. Ripping to pieces the leaf he held, he told me, "My security detail discovered that someone plans to bomb some of the women's shelters."

I gasped. How could anyone be so cruel?

He continued. "You have to understand that I wouldn't ask you to stay unless it was necessary. If you're here and the people who are planning this are close, perhaps you can 'tap into them,' as you say."

He had a point. The closer I was to the source, the more effective I could be. With so much at stake he was right. I couldn't leave.

The PM spoke from behind me. "Bronwyn, I don't see how you can turn the sheik down. Women around the world depend on that organization. Imagine what could happen if they have nowhere to go."

The horror of the sheik's story about his aunt came back and I saw it played out again a million times over. Simone would understand and hopefully so would Sam. I had to help these women and the sheik.

"Do you have any idea who might be behind the possible attacks?"

"At first I thought it might be my cousin because of what happened. But my people have been watching him and find no evidence of it."

"If your people are watching him, why not eliminate that threat right away? The man did try to kill you." I couldn't believe he'd just let his cousin live after everything that had happened in Norway.

"He's family. It's even more complicated than I can explain."

"I could have killed him in Norway if I had known about the warlocks protecting him. What's the difference?"

The sheik turned away and pushed his hand through his hair again. If he didn't tell me the truth I'd probe his mind.

The PM spoke up. "Azir, if you want Bronwyn to help you must tell her everything."

"I realize that, but—"

"Look, you can tell me or I can read your mind. Either way I'll find out." I stood with my hands on my hips.

The PM raised an eyebrow and I thought the sheik might blow a gasket. His head whipped around and those intense brown eyes bore into me.

"You can't do that without my permission," he whispered angrily.

"I'm not sure who told you that, but it's wrong. Any ethics I have regarding reading minds are my own. There are no rules."

"Well, this is my home and you are a guest and I do have rules. No reading minds!" He punctuated his words by pointing his finger.

I pushed his finger away. Stupid jerk. "See, now here we have a problem. I have issues with authority figures and people telling me what to do. If you'll back off a minute you'll only see I'm trying to help."

The PM moved forward ready to step in, but the look in my eyes must have made him decide not to.

Rubbing his hand across his brow Azir whispered through gritted teeth, "If I say I'd prefer you wouldn't read my mind while you're here would you listen?"

"Yes." I smiled to defuse the situation. "But you need to tell me what's going on."

Just as he was about to speak, Miles walked out into the garden and interrupted. Damn twit.

"Sir," he addressed the PM, "you have a call, and Sheik Azir you're needed in the office on the first floor. From what I understand it's quite urgent."

"Thank you, Miles. I'll follow you in." The PM walked to the door.

Azir started to do the same but turned to me. "We'll talk after dinner tonight. I'll tell you everything and there are some things I need to show you. But understand that you cannot tell anyone beyond these walls." The worry in his eyes said it all.

"Your secrets are safe with me. I've taken an oath to protect you and in my world that covers everything."

He reached out and touched my arm. Not magic but energy so pure it balled into white light and streamed into my body.

"Thank you."

I walked around the garden for a while longer to clear my mind. When stressed, I actually need to be close to plants, because

I do so much earth magic. What was with that ball of energy he passed to me? I'm certain he had no idea he did it.

Azir is one contradiction after another. In a country known for its oil-rich bounty and mistreatment of women, he pushed for the development of solar power and rights for all.

It's a good thing I don't date clients because he's totally doable. Don't even go there, Bronwyn. You can't even handle Sam.

Time for dinner. That sheik will tell me the truth or I'll make him do it. You know I can be a very wily witch.

Eight

Monday, 5 p.m.
Waxing moon
Dubai
Witches with wicked friends: 1

Simone called. She's already in Dallas and Caleb's going to drive her to Sweet. Explained my situation here. After everything I learned last night there's no way I'm leaving.

The sheik is in a truckload of trouble up to his pretty brown eyes. Someone in his family, besides his cousin, wants him dead. He's received several letters with threats against him and the women's shelters. Showed me everything and even my jaded brain had a hard time accepting the facts.

What kind of creep picks on battered women? Bet it's a regular Joe human. I know some wicked warlocks and demons, but the nastiest beings I've ever come across have been of the human variety. No magical powers necessary.

Didn't get much from the letters, except I know it's someone close to the sheik. He received five of them over the last two months. All of them have pleasant sayings like: *You have betrayed your people. You must die. The blood of your family is upon your head.* Sweet tender things that make the heart grow warm. Not.

But Simone also needed my assistance, so I did what I could from ten thousand miles away. That Worgh demon she killed had one pissed-off family. They ganged up on her and messed her up kind of bad. Takes a lot to bring Simone down, and she ended up killing the whole family. But not without some injury to herself. Like most slayers she heals quickly but it'll take a thorough cleansing to get all of the demon poison out of her system.

"I need a fucking break." Her usually upbeat voice sounded flat on the phone. "Haven't had a vacation in four years. Every day, same old crap, and I feel like I'm losing my edge." The poison had worked its way into her bloodstream, and her speech slurred at the end of some of the words.

"You and Caleb have the run of the house. I'll email you exactly what you need to cleanse your system. Right when you get there, go to the fridge. You'll find a blue bottle. The stuff tastes like shit but drink a cup of it. That'll start the process."

"Bron, what's wrong with me? I love my job, but right now I don't care if I ever see another demon."

"You're burned out. But part of that is the poison in your system. Causes a severe depression. Give yourself a couple of weeks. Lay around and read. Play with Casper if you can find her. Watch TV and eat lots of food from Lulu's. That's my prescription for you." I didn't mention that I'd already sent her a healing spell.

"If I forget to say it later, thanks."

"Not a problem, girlfriend. Just play nice with the boys

while you're in Sweet. They're a tender-hearted bunch and there's a coven that will rock your clock if you try any funny stuff."

"I always play nice with the boys; you know better than that."

She made me laugh. "Simone, just try to pick the ones who aren't already attached." She had a problem with the boys, no matter what their marital status, following her around and throwing themselves in front of her. For the most part she ignored them, but when she felt the least bit horny no man was safe from her charms.

"That's no fun. Where's the drama if I only pick on the single ones?" She coughed and I could tell her body was fighting against the infection. The healing spell would take a few days, but she'd be fine.

"What's the demon situation in Sweet?" Simone's throat sounded hoarse.

"As far as I've been able to tell it's fairly demon-free, so no worries there. Oh, and I've asked Dr. Sam to look in on you. For a doctor he's a nice guy and you'll like him."

"You sleeping with him?"

Damn her perceptive little mind. "What in the hell makes you say that?"

"Your voice got higher when you said his name."

"I've only known him a couple weeks." I didn't want to tell her anything. Too new.

"Maybe so, but you're sleeping with him. Don't worry. Hands off the good doc."

Wish I could believe her. We hung up and I called and left Sam a message to look in on Simone. Just hearing him talk on the voice mail made my insides melt. Also let him know that I'm stuck here a couple more weeks.

I keep replaying that last night together and the morning after. Can't remember when I've thought about a man so much. It's so stupid. We made mad, passionate, totally lost-my-mind kind of love, but that doesn't make a relationship. Maybe it bothers me so much because I haven't been able to talk to him since then. We keep missing each other and played several rounds of phone tag.

This boy-girl stuff is the pits.

II P.M.
Spells: I
Used a locator spell on the letters so I could see how close the threat is. Turns out the culprit is tied to someone here at the palace. Problem is, this is a friggin' castle. And the sheik has about thirty people living here and that doesn't include the staff.

There are women who he's protecting, all of whom live in a special wing with guards. Well, there are guards everywhere, but the ones protecting that part of the castle have great big guns.

His family lives in another part of the house. His sister and mother have been traveling, so I haven't met them yet, but his brother is okay. Not the friendliest guy. Get the feeling Alkazir's more old school. He doesn't approve of my wardrobe, that's for sure. My jeans and cotton blouses would be considered down-right proper in Sweet, Texas, but not here. Every time he looks at me he shakes his head and mutters something under his breath. He should be grateful he's the sheik's brother or I might have to hurt him.

Started reading minds of those I come into contact with, but if the person is working with a witch or warlock they may have learned how to put up shields. Doesn't deter me, though, because if someone tries to block a mind probe that's a big clue.

May take a couple of days but I'll figure it out.

Tuesday, noon
Spells: 2
Charms: 20
Hungry witches: 1

I need a big ole fat juicy hamburger. The sheik eats way too healthy. Fish and veggies for every meal. I'm craving beef, a milkshake, and French fries, which is strange because I don't eat fries. Heard a rumor that there was fast food in Dubai. Hopefully I'll be in town tomorrow and can check it out.

Thought I had a lead but no such luck. Did another locator spell and came up with nothing. Haven't sensed any other witches or warlocks on the premises, so the person who's after the sheik may have left before I could get a lock on.

Did get a lead on the cousin and know he's close. I could take care of him from here, but the sheik wants to wait until we find this other person who is after him. Thinks the cousin will lead us to him. We'll see. Still say we should just fry the guy and worry about the new threat later.

I've got a lot of respect for the sheik but the guy's as hardheaded as I am. Spent most of the evening with him yesterday working on protection spells for the shelters. Explained how it all worked and he seemed genuinely interested in the process.

Most of my clients just want me to magic things away and could care less how I do it.

"There is magic and mysticism in my culture, but I have little experience with people who are witches and warlocks," Azir explained in his study last night. "But I studied the history of magic when in school and the subject has always intrigued me." Seated behind his desk, he pointed to shelves of books to his left. "I've read volumes on the subject."

I walked over to check out his selection and was impressed. From Andrea Sikes's *Witch Way* to Slovak's *Witches and*

Warlocks, he had a wall full of books on the occult and mysticism.

"The prime minister tells me that you are a high witch, one of the most powerful in the world."

"Yes, I was born a high witch."

He shook his head. "I've never met anyone like you. I don't understand why you don't sit at home amassing great wealth or live on an island somewhere basking in the sun. With all that power, you needn't work."

"You have great power and you don't sit at home or take vacations." Men, I swear.

"True, but it isn't the same."

I turned to him. "Yes it is. Power, whether it's magical or otherwise, must be used carefully and for the greater good. I took an oath as a protector. There are others of my kind who are hunters. They search out the evil. It always seems to find me no matter where I am, and I felt I could be more use helping to keep people like you and the prime minister alive."

Crossing his arms in front of his chest, he cocked his head to the side. "It fascinates me. The idea of magic."

I understood his interest. It fascinates me too and, knowledgeable as I am about the craft, it still manages to surprise me.

He asked if he could stay and watch as I invoked the Blue Flame Spell. Only had to change a few of the words to protect all of the shelters until I could make charms for each one. Placed the blue candles on a pentagram and lit each one with my fingertips. While doing this I chanted:

> *O flaming pentagram of protection,*
> *hinder harm from all directions.*
> *By dancing flames wild and free*
> *protect these women my mind sees.*
> *As I will, so mote it be.*

We also overnighted temporary charms I made to place above all of the entrances of every shelter. Whenever trouble arrives on the doorstep, the charm rings the small bell attached. It's effective and something everyone can hear except the person bringing the evil. I found it in a text from the old Celtic Book of Shadows. I'll make more charms to cover all the windows to the shelters. We'll set the same system up here but there are so many doors to the place the sheik's going to have to buy stock in a bell company.

I've been one busy witch, but the sheik has been with me all the way.

The man constantly surprises me. He's so far from what I thought when I first saw him at the hotel in Oslo. I've listened in on some of his meetings and he's shrewd in the business department. At the same time he has a huge heart and cares for so many. Not just the small army living in his house but all those women around the world. I get a sense from him that he feels he must save the world. Wanted to tell him that's my job.

He's worried about something we have to do in town tomorrow. Didn't read his mind but can feel his hesitance about it.

Alkazir left this morning and Azir didn't seem happy about the situation. Tapped into Alkazir's mind for just a bit but it was all about business. He has some concerns about a situation in Paris, but everything in his brain had to do with boardrooms and oil derricks.

Another attempt was made on the prime minister's life yesterday, but my protection spell held. It works off of a charm I did that glows whenever danger is near. The PM noticed his pocket glowing red with a warning. The bomb under the car never detonated and his security people found it soon after.

There's a connection between the PM's troubles and Azir's.

We've just got to figure out what it is and we'll have our bad guy.

Azir's mother and sister come in tomorrow and we're taking a trip into town. Better get my bag of tricks together in case we come in contact with the bad guys. From the look on the sheik's face today, I'd say that's a distinct possibility.

That reminds me: need to make a list of supplies. With all the charms and spells I've worked on the last few days I need to replenish. Wonder if I can find mulberry, lavender, and poxy seeds in Dubai. Oh, and a large quantity of bells. This may take some planning.

Midnight
Confused witches: 1

Sam called while I dined with the sheik. Kind of rude to take the call but the sheik told me to go ahead. Sam said Simone would heal but he thought she needed some kind of energy boost in the next few days. I'm emailing him a potion to give her once the poison is out of her system.

His voice sounded strained. Maybe since Simone and Caleb were in the same room that had something to do with it. I said something stupid like, "I'm thinking of you."

He replied, "Hey, that's great."

What the hell is that supposed to mean?

Simone said something and he laughed. We talked about Mr. Gunther and some of the other folks at the nursing home, who are responding well to the memory potion. It's one of those conversations where a lot of words come out but nothing is actually said.

Caleb, Sam, and Simone were getting ready to eat some of Lulu's chicken-fried steak. I'm so jealous. I just want a damn hamburger. Is that too much to ask?

Sam told me to be safe and hung up. Everything seemed so stilted and awkward. I don't get it.

Have I mentioned lately how much I hate this boy-girl crap? And men are jerks and if they didn't have dicks they'd be totally worthless. And—oh, hell, go to bed, Bronwyn.

Nine

Wednesday, 4 P.M.
Dubai
Spells: 3
Dead guys: Almost 2

The trip into the city of Dubai turned out to be an interesting adventure and changed my mind about a few things. The city was very modern and clean, with monolithic skyscrapers.

I'd dressed conservatively for me, wearing lightweight slacks and a long-sleeve blue cotton top. I still garnered some curious stares from some of the people on the street. The occasional cat-call was yelled from a passing car but one look from the sheik, or his bodyguard, and the perpetrator quickly went on his way.

For the first two hours I followed Azir around like a good little witch. Most of that time was spent at Duban Industries, which is owned by the sheik and his family.

The blue-glassed building houses a variety of businesses, from oil and gourmet foods to clothing and golf ball manufacturing. The men here are as obsessed with golf as their American counterparts. There were a lot more women in management positions than I'd expected. I'd heard stories that women had a tough time doing business anywhere in the Middle East. The sheik admitted that Duban was more progressive than most organizations in Dubai.

During his private meeting with government officials about land rights, I decided to take a couple of the guards and visit the bazaar two blocks away. I had to refurbish my supplies immediately or I couldn't finish the work for the sheik.

Through his company he'd already taken care of several ingredients, including the mulberry, the lavender, and some others that we knew I couldn't find here in Dubai. The shipper promised to overnight everything to us for early-morning delivery.

The people in the market were kinder than I expected; of course, they were trying to sell me things. The guards and I hit stall after stall and I couldn't resist picking up some souvenirs. I travel so much that I seldom succumb to the urge for knick-knacks, but I got a brass hashish pipe for Caleb, purely for decoration. And a beautiful woven blanket in a variety of gold and red threads for Kira.

The entire place smelled of incense and exotic spices. At times my senses were in overload from the pungent aroma.

Found candles in every color, which is good. The black and red ones increase the power of the protection spells and the white and blue help with the purification process.

At a display of gold bracelets I sensed a magical presence. Didn't turn to look right away, but knew it had to be a warlock. Tried to tap into his brain and send a warning, but he totally blocked me. It takes a powerful warlock or witch to do that.

I wondered if this might be one of the warlocks working for Azir's cousin. I had to get a good look but didn't want to be obvious.

I bought a few of the gold bracelets and shifted so I could get a good glance. Our eyes met and he dissipated before me. I don't mean ran and hid somewhere. He, like, went, poof! It was only a blur but he was incredibly thin with long black hair. He disappeared before I could get a good visual.

There are only a few witches and warlocks who can dissipate like that and I'm not one of them. The last time I tried I passed out for two days and woke up with Casper sitting on my stomach staring at me with a strange look in her eyes.

The great wizard Garnout told me long ago that if I were to receive the gift it would come to me when the time was right. Patience isn't one of my strong suits, but I don't have a choice.

Have had some luck with astral projection, but that's pretty useless unless you need to spy on someone. And truth is, I can do it awake and a lot more easily by probing minds.

Anyway, I stood there dumbfounded for a minute in the middle of the tiny shops. What kind of warlock had the cousin hooked up with? I knew of maybe five or six who had that kind of talent, but they were all on the good guys' side.

My pocket burned and the small tiger's eye I keep in there glowed through the cloth. The sheik was in immediate danger. The guards and I ran the two blocks back to the office building. Tapping into the sheik's mind I saw nothing but blackness. He was still alive but unconscious.

In his office we didn't find anything that looked like it had been disturbed. A small groan from behind the closed door made us turn and investigate. Azir's executive assistant, Maridad, lay on the floor with a huge gash on her head.

I yelled:

He who disappears I seek
Open ears and eyes for me
Find him now, so mote it be.

A flash of light and I saw the sheik in the stairwell, two floors below. I barked orders to the guards. How the hell had the kidnappers found their way past all the staff and security?

The two guards who had come with me took the stairs and I ran for the elevator to head the bad guys off at the pass.

As I moved I realized that damn skinny warlock at the bazaar had been sent to spy on me. To make certain I was out of the way so they could kidnap Azir. I reached the second floor and ran for the stairwell.

I heard them before I saw them and prepared to do battle. With my feet apart and arms raised I waited. Two huge men around six feet five inches and about six hundred pounds between them rounded the corner carrying the sheik. One at his head, the other at his feet.

"Put him down!" I screamed.

The pair didn't look like they had the IQ of a squirrel between them so I said it again. "Put him down!"

I heard the footsteps of the other guards coming and so did the bad guys. Afraid they'd drop the sheik and cause him further injury, I threw my right hand out to stop any action they might take with a stunning blow. The men were frozen like stone. With my left I levitated the sheik and put him down on the steps beside me.

My energy lagged. Doing two spells at once drains me fast. They started to move so I threw both hands out and pinned the two giants into the wall. The guards came just as my power was about to give out completely. My knees were shaking and I was afraid I might soon end up in a pile on the floor, much like the sheik.

The authorities were called and the two lugs taken into custody. I hear they do nasty things to bad guys in prison here. Good.

The sheik woke up on the way to the hospital. He said his head hurt from the blow but his private physician released him an hour and a half after we got there.

"My assistant, Maridad, and I thought they were guards with one of the officials," Azir told me in the car as we returned to his home. "Before we could move they pulled guns and ordered Maridad into the bathroom. She resisted, but they shoved her in. If I didn't go with the other one they threatened to kill her. Just as we stepped into the stairwell he must have hit me with the gun.

"Once again I owe my life to you, Bronwyn. It's quite disconcerting being saved all the time by such a beautiful woman." He leaned his head back against the plush leather seat and closed his eyes.

"Hey, now stop with the compliments. That crap goes straight to my head." Flipped my hair back Farrah Fawcett style to prove my point. "It's my job to protect you and those goons weren't going to get away with my sheik."

That made him laugh. But his joy didn't last long when I explained that his cousin had been involved in the attempt.

"In less than twenty-four hours I can resolve this problem for you." I shifted in my seat so I could touch his arm. I wanted to make sure he listened. "I don't mind protecting you but it's difficult when I know the threat and can't extinguish it."

"I appreciate your candor, but we need a few more days to find out who else might be involved. Have you discovered anything by reading the minds of those living in the castle?"

"No, but I know that someone within those walls spies for your cousin. How else would he know your every move?"

"I've had enemies for years but it's difficult for me to believe that someone in my home might wish me harm." He sounded truly disappointed by the news and I felt sorry for him.

His mood lightened considerably when we walked through the front door and his mother ran to hug him. Dressed in the traditional chador with jeans underneath, she looked more like an older sister than his mom.

Her straight black hair fell down her back and the same long lashes Azir has framed liquid brown eyes. Easy to see where his good looks came from. Except that she was short, five foot at the most, with a round belly and hips.

Azir on the other hand is more than six foot with a chest, abs, and ass you could bounce quarters off of. Um, not that I've noticed or anything. But give me some change and I could have a whole lot of fun with the sheik.

"My dear son, I worried so much for you."

"Mother, I'm all right. I am." He gathered her in his arms and pulled her to his chest.

Dressed in button-fly low-riding jeans and cowboy boots, topped with a white cotton shirt tied at the waist, the woman I assumed was his sister came down the hall to her brother.

"Why do you let this continue?" she admonished him harshly, her voice filled with disgust. "You know what you must do!" A tear slid down her cheek, softening the hardened edge of her words, and her brother hugged her to his chest.

"Soon, Shera, soon."

"He could have killed you. How many times are you going to let him try?" she cried between sobs.

"He can't kill me, because I have a grand protector." He moved the two women to his side and pointed to me. The look of in-credulity on their faces was priceless.

They stared at me, then back at him. Then looked at me again.

"Hi, I'm Bronwyn." I extended a hand and walked toward the small group.

"This is my mother, Kazamar Alhid Azir, and my sister, Shera Alhid Azir." The sheik smiled. Both women grabbed my hand in a sturdy grip.

"This is Bronwyn, a very powerful witch who has blessed our home with her presence. I trust both of you will do whatever nec-essary to make her feel welcome and comfortable." He raised an eyebrow to accentuate his point.

"Oh, don't be such a bully. If she is your friend we will treat her with kindness, but we would do so no matter what because she has saved your life more than once," his mother chided. "Bronwyn, you are welcome in our home and please let me know if there is anything you need. I trust you will dine with us tonight."

Food. I never did get my burger. I nodded in acceptance.

"Shera and I have brought back two freezers' worth of beef and plan on sirloin strips tonight." She smiled as if she could read my mind.

Hot damn! Meat! "I wouldn't miss it."

I excused myself to set up shop in my suite. Along with a bedroom that would fit two small homes, the sheik had given me another room to work in. I found a computer, and several shelves already stocked with the ingredients I needed to build charms.

But before I do anything else I need to rest. My strength lags and I have a feeling I'm going to need all of my powers over the next few weeks.

Hopefully, I can get a zombielike nap in before dinner.

II P.M.
Witch's assistants: 2

Dinner was nothing short of a hoot. Azir's mother and sister are quite the storytellers.

"We were in London and Mother had to try on a pair of these—"

"Shera, if you tell that story I'll tell them what happened in Rome," Kazamar warned. The young girl appeared to think about it for a moment, then shrugged and went on with the tale.

"We were in this hot trendy clothing shop where they only have these small screens for you to change behind and they're set up in the middle of the store." Shera laughed so hard she almost couldn't go on.

"Mother had picked up a pair of pants and they were too small."

"They were sized incorrectly, I tell you. I wear a size 10 and that's what the tag said," Kazamar, who was clearly a size 14, stated firmly.

"Anyway"—the young girl waved her mother's comments away—"she took forever and then I saw her hopping up and down behind the screen trying to get these pants on. She tripped on the leg and knocked not only her screen down, but also four others surrounding shoppers trying on clothes. Naked people ran screaming all over the store. She just stood a minute. Then put on her own clothes and walked out of the store like nothing had happened."

"Well, there's no reason to make a scene." Kazamar laughed. "It was funny though."

"So what did my sister do in Rome?" Azir joined in the fun.

"Well, it's not so much what she did, but what happened to her. Twice. We were throwing coins into a fountain and pigeons pooped on her head. Not one or two but a whole flock. She was covered in waste and cried all the way back to the hotel." Kaza-mar tried not to smile. Azir laughed harder than I'd ever seen him.

"I wasn't upset about the poop—that's supposed to be a lucky sign. I cried because they ruined my brand-new Carolina Herrera sweater," Shera explained.

The younger woman shook her head. "Then we were on a train, minding our own business, and this man opened the door of our car and flashed us. Wiggling it around so proud. Mother looked up from her paper and told him, 'Really you should put that away. It's absolutely nothing worth showing off in public.' I could have died I laughed so hard."

The stories continued until just a few minutes ago. Before I left the dining hall both women made me promise that they could help make some of the charms tomorrow. It should be an interesting day.

Sat for a few minutes and did a locator spell on the cousin. Don't know if he's doing drugs or just delusional but I had to pull out of his brain. Psychotic pictures of bodies bathed in blood and ripped limbs.

He had better watch out or those pictures in his head will be his death sentence.

Ten

Thursday, 10 A.M.
Dubai
Witches with boy-stealing friends: 1

Simone called. She and Dr. Sam had dinner with Caleb and Kira. Everything sounded so cozy when she described their quaint night out at the Italian restaurant.

I have no right to be jealous. Just slept with the man; it's not like he has given any indication of some kind of future. See, I never do this. I don't have boyfriends for this reason. Men are for sex only. Men are for sex only. Men are for sex only. My new mantra.

"I'm telling you that Dr. Sam is a cutie. I can see why you like him so much," Simone went on and on. "Never been so well taken care of in my life. And he's got a great bedside manner."

Now what in the hell did she mean by that? "So, I guess you're feeling better."

"Yeah, baby. Not quite one hundred percent but I'm getting

there. Oh, good gossip for you. Looks to me like Kira and Caleb are on the way to the heavy duty. They couldn't keep their hands off of one another. I got hot just watching them." Simone has such a way with words.

"Oh wow, you've got another call, hold on." She clicked off and then came back on the line. "Hey, Bron, that's Sam. He says to tell you hi. Gotta go. He's picking me up and we're gonna head down to some rodeo. Can you imagine it? Me at a rodeo? Ride 'em cowboy!"

We hung up and I sat on the bed. Tried to call Kira to get her opinion of the situation but she wasn't at the library or at home. Probably making out with Caleb in a car somewhere.

Won't be long before Sam and Simone are headed that way. Great. Now I have images of Simone with her legs wrapped around Sam. Argh! That's it. No more men. Well, except for sex. Mind-blowing, house-shaking, bone-melting sex. Like I had with Sam that night when we did it on the stairs and the . . . No. Not going there.

Time to get to work on those charms. Better see if the packages have arrived. Now there's someone you can count on. FedEx.

4 P.M.

May not have started out great but it's been one hell of a productive day. Kazamar and Shera turned themselves into a two-woman assembly line. Makes me laugh to think these two wealthy and powerful women sat on the floor making bell charms, but that's just the kind of people they are.

They were intensely interested in the process of what it took to make the charms and why each piece was so important. Touching each ingredient as if it were precious gold, their wide brown eyes hung on every word.

"Centuries ago they used tassels and fringes dipped in lavender oil to protect homes. They thought the swaying of the ornaments would confuse the evil spirits," I explained to them as we set out each of the pieces for the charms. "I still use lavender but have found the adding of a bell more effective in warning against trouble."

The mother and daughter turned to each other and raised eyebrows.

"They've been used through the centuries in different kind of spells and warriors tied bells to their horses' blankets."

"Yes, this something we know from my husband's tribe. They too, sew the bells to the blanket. How does it work in the shelters?" Kazamar rang one of the bells again.

"The ring not only alerts those inside to danger, but activates a general spell I have surrounding each of the shelters, to keep the evil from entering the building. Think of it as an early warning for trouble ahead."

"How can you have such power?" Kazamar sat on the floor in front of the ribbons used to tie the tiny purple flowers to the bell. "I don't understand how you can protect so much all of the time, without draining yourself."

Shera nodded in agreement with her mother.

"It sounds complicated, but isn't. Most of what I use is earth magic, something that already exists. I sort of call it into action. That's why I use so many flowers, plants, and herbs in my potions."

"I noticed you spent at least an hour in the garden last night." Shera positioned herself on a cushion next to her mother. "Do you need to be near the plants?"

The workroom had a perfectly good table with chairs, but they preferred to sit on the floor to work.

"Being in nature does help rejuvenate me and I feel like I'm more a part of the earth when I'm near it. If you ever come to Texas I'll show you my conservatory. It's filled to the brim with plants and herbs from all over the world."

I moved everything from the counter to the floor.

"Anyway, when I use earth magic it actually makes me stronger and the energy grows. I know it sounds a little strange and out there, but it works for me. On the other hand when I have to do blood magic, or in extreme cases dark magic, it drains me fast. Sometimes it takes a few days or weeks to renew my strength."

"The dark and blood magic sound so scary. Aren't you afraid?" Shera looked up at me, curious to know more. "Do you use it often?"

"No, I don't use either very much. When I'm doing big jobs such as this, I like to keep it simple. The lavender and mulberry wrapped with a ribbon tied to a bell is all it takes. Then I invoke a protection spell from my Book of Shadows and we're done.

"Speaking of which, you don't have to help me. I appreciate it, but I feel terrible taking you away from your own work."

Kazamar frowned. "I can think of no better duty than protecting those women. We are happy to be of service and are grateful for your help. This foundation means everything to me."

Remembering the story about Azir's aunt, I realized making these charms had become symbolic for this mother and daughter. I showed them how to make two of the charms and they toiled away. For the first half hour we worked in a comfortable silence but it wasn't long before the conversation flowed.

They asked about my home in Sweet and the other witches that I knew. I questioned them about their family and got the inside scoop on the sheik when he was younger. It came as no surprise to learn that he'd given his mother more than one headache.

"He's never been one to follow what others were doing," Kazamar told me while she tied the lavender to the bells. "In preparatory school his friends all wanted to study math and science. As did he, but he also took classes in creative writing, sociology, and psychology. Every holiday he'd come home and analyze a different family member. He's fascinated by human behavior and why we do the things we do."

"Sounds to me like he should have been a psychologist rather than a businessman." I rose to get more ribbon for Shera.

"He could have been," she told me. "He has a doctorate in psychology and an MBA. He says the two go together when it comes to his job."

Sometimes I hate that the more I learn about the man the more fascinating he becomes. Lost in my own world, Shera caught me off guard with her question. "So, do you have a boyfriend in Texas?"

Had to think about that one.

"Shera, that's too personal. You know better." Kazamar shook her finger as if scolding an errant child.

We worked for a few minutes in silence and Kazamar paused. "So do you?"

I laughed so hard I slid off my red cushion. "Truthfully? I'm interested in someone, but it's too soon to know where that's going. And I think he may be interested in a friend of mine."

"Oh, that is most unfortunate. I'm sorry we brought it up." Kazamar touched my arm in a way of apologizing.

"To have such simple minds, men can be so complicated." Shera shifted on her pillow. "Before I decided to go to graduate school I thought I might marry a friend of Kahab's."

"Kahab?"

"Do you not know? That is my brother's first name. The family goes back and forth but he prefers Azir," Shera explained.

I tucked that bit of info away. "So what happened?"

"My fiancé didn't want me to work or continue with my schooling, which is very important to me. He's somewhat progressive like my brother, but his family is traditional and he bowed to their pressure.

"My family encouraged me to go with my heart and I decided I could not marry a man who would not let me pursue my dreams. It hurt because I loved him with my soul. On sad nights I still do." She pushed her hair back and gathered the black thickness in a band to make a ponytail.

I moved to find more ribbon and returned with another stack. "I saw several women working at Duban. Isn't it acceptable for a woman to have a family and work here?"

"More the exception than the rule, especially in families with any kind of power or wealth." Shera took a deep breath as if trying to rid herself of the sadness. "You know as well as I that there are millions of women around the world who have families and successful careers, but it isn't a suitable lifestyle for his family. It still hurts because I thought he loved me."

"He did love you, dear, but he's a man and he can't help being an idiot," Kazamar stated simply.

In many ways Kazamar reminds me of my own mother. She speaks her mind, protects her children, and runs her home and the women's foundation with the efficiency of a top CEO. Yes, Mom and Kazamar would get along very well.

"So, Shera, what do you study in school and what grad school do you plan to attend?"

"I did my undergraduate studies in physics at MIT, but I'm thinking of studying aerospace engineering at Caltech this summer. I took some time off to help my mother and Kahab with the foundation."

"And to mend your broken heart," added her mother.

"Yes, I suppose I needed time. Perhaps someday I'll find a man who is open-minded and can accept me as I am."

"As far as I'm concerned, unless you have some kind of extreme need to have children, men aren't worth the trouble," I said, trying to lighten Shera's mood.

Kazamar laughed and the sadness lifted from her daughter's eyes. "Bronwyn, you are both beautiful and brilliant, much like my daughter. And your assessment of men is as accurate as any I've ever heard. Now that we are finished with the charms what happens?" She stood and stretched her back.

"I need to gather them all into the center of the room and place candles around the charms." They helped me move the pile and make a circle of light with the red and black candles.

I shook their hands, expecting them to go now that the work had been completed. "Thank you so much for your help. I'm ready to do the spell now." I motioned them toward the door.

"We will stay," Kazamar stated firmly.

Well, okay. I raised my arms in preparation for the spell and noticed Azir in the doorway. His mother turned to face him. "Well, don't just stand there, come in and watch the magic. She's beginning the spell. Your witch is a talented young woman."

"Bronwyn isn't *my witch*, Mother, she is very much her own woman. But I grant you that she is talented." And he winked at me. If I didn't know better, I'd say the sheik tried to flirt with me. He came in to stand between his sister and mother and watch the show.

I don't normally have such an audience for this kind of thing and couldn't for the life of me figure out why I felt so nervous. Breathing slowly, I calmed my emotions so the energy within could build.

In a few seconds I could feel a white light spilling out around me. Waving my hands across the charms, I recited:

Door to door
Window to window
With this flame I protect all within;
Evil shall not pass these borders.
As I will, so mote it be.

A burst of energy flew from my fingertips and circled around the room, then landed on the charms. For a moment they glowed.

I looked up to see Azir's family wide-eyed and openmouthed. Good magic does that to people.

"It didn't rhyme," Shera whispered.

I smiled. "Doesn't have to, just need to get my point across."

"That was incredible. One of the most amazing things I've ever seen, and I've lived a very long time." Kazamar shook her head. "Our Bedouins do magic, but they keep it very secret. I'm most impressed, young woman. How do the charms get to the shelters?"

Azir stepped in. "We're sending them overnight and in less than twenty-four hours each one will be fully protected by her power."

"I don't understand how it works," Shera said, "but I know that it will." She turned to her brother. "Did you see the fire from her fingertips and the white light that flew across the room? It wasn't tricks, it was real magic."

Azir laughed and hugged her. "Yes, little one. She is a very real witch. And we will celebrate her many talents at dinner. Now help her pack these up for shipping and I'll meet you all for dinner in the main dining room."

Argh. Main dining room meant dressy clothes. I'd figured that much out. Unfortunately, I'd only brought enough clothes for the weekend, and had only one pair of nice dress slacks.

Shera and I were about the same size, though she was about three inches taller. Maybe I could borrow something from her.

When I returned to my room I discovered no need for worry. Boxes from Barney's department store were piled on my bed. Two dresses, three pairs of jeans, several tops, nice slacks, a pair of high-heeled Jimmy Choos and some flats, and undergarments.

I prayed that it was Kazamar, Shera, or one of the staff who had picked out the clothes. How embarrassing would it be to have the sheik choosing my Wonder Bras?

Then I read the note:

Dear Bronwyn,
Please accept these gifts as appreciation for staying on with us for the next few weeks. I'm indebted to you for your service.
If any of the items are not to your liking we can return them. I guessed on many of the sizes, so please let me know if something needs to be replaced.
Best regards,
Azir

Great. I picked up the bra to check the size. Perfect fit. I didn't know whether to be flattered or infuriated that he'd guessed my size and that I wear Wonder Bras. In fact everything fit. Some of the bright reds and pink aren't what I would have picked—I'm kind of partial to black—but they looked good.

As much as I appreciated his generosity, I decided it was time to set some boundaries where the sheik was concerned. A jet was one thing, but silk panties with lacy insets were quite another.

Eleven

Thursday, midnight
Dubai
Spells: 3

The sheik never made it to dinner; he stayed locked in his office on a conference call. I'll settle things with him tomorrow.

Tapped into his cousin tonight and the thoughts were more lucid. Made me wonder if he might be schizophrenic. Instead of the blood and limbs from his previous thoughts, I found him worrying about someone called Blackstock. He had no face to go with the name, which made me think he'd never met the person.

Let my mind wander over his and didn't see anything that had to do with the shelters or bombs. Couldn't get a handle on who exactly Blackstock is, but he's important. When the name came up the cousin had a tremendous sense of anticipation. The sheik may be right about someone else trying to kill him. Maybe it's this Blackstock guy.

Huh? Cell phone's ringing.

Friday, 1 A.M.

Sleep isn't going to be easy tonight. Confusion reigns and I don't know what to think.

Didn't get to the phone quick enough but Dr. Sam left me a strange message.

"Bronwyn." Long pause. "Damn, I miss you."

Called him back and he sounded so sexy it made my heart hurt. "I've missed you." His voice filled the line.

After the other day when he couldn't wait to get off the phone to go play with my friends, I was surprised. He spoke like he actually cared. "Tell me what you've been doing the last few days."

Couldn't tell him about my work with the sheik, so I tried to play it safe. "Oh, nothing special."

"Well, if it's not that special, why can't you come home?"

Oops, he got me there. "Well, I guess it's special to the people I'm working with but I can't talk about it. Security reasons."

"Do you see me as some kind of security risk?" He huffed and I imagined him stomping his foot like a small child in a fit of temper.

"Well, no. They asked me not to talk about it so I'm not going to. The phones might be tapped. Could we please just leave it at 'I'm busy,' and move on?" Didn't mean to sound like such a bitch but as a general rule I don't like explaining anything I do.

"Damn, Bronwyn, this isn't at all going the way I meant. Can we please start over? So how's the weather in Dubai?"

I laughed. "It's hot and you can make better small talk than that, Sam. Tell me how Mr. Gunther's doing."

"The man's mind is incredible. He's filled one of the journals you left and is working on the second one. He shows no signs of mental degeneration. Margie tells me that he only stops writing to take his meals and play the occasional game of chess. Old coot beat the pants off me the other night in five moves."

Sam with no pants. Good visual.

"Did you let him win?" I could just imagine the gleam of triumph in Mr. Gunther's piercing blue eyes.

"Wish I could say yes, but no. He beat me fair. I wasn't on my game though. My thoughts kept wandering to a witch on the other side of the world."

That's the Dr. Sam I know, always quick with those underhanded compliments. "Tell me about Kira and Caleb. Are they making everyone ill with their lovey-dovey crap?"

"They're attached at the hip. When we had dinner with them the other night they couldn't stop touching each other."

"We?"

"Oh, they asked Simone to join us for dinner."

Note to self: Bash my very dear friends upside their idiotic heads when next I see them. Did they not clue in to the fact that Simone's in man-hungry mode and goes for anything with two legs and a dick right now?

"Bronwyn? Are you there?"

"I'm here." My jaw tightened at the thought of Simone pawing my man. I know she can't help herself when she gets in these moods, but she'd promised to keep her hands off.

"Anyway, Caleb had to go back to Dallas to work on a new assignment, but Kira's meeting him there this weekend."

Truthfully the news about Kira and Caleb came as no surprise, but I wondered just how much time Dr. Sam and Simone had spent alone together since I'd been gone.

"So you've made friends with Simone?" I could feel my right eye twitch with tension.

"She's quite a woman. At first she's a bit much, but once you get used to her, she's fun. Her sense of humor never fails no matter what the situation."

"Good to hear you're getting along so well." Worked hard to keep the sarcasm from my voice. "What's she up to today?"

"This morning she told me Kira had ordered books on a new martial arts technique and that's how she planned to spend the day. Simone promised to show Kira how to kill a man with just two easy moves, or some nonsense like that."

With Simone it wasn't nonsense. She could kill a guy in one move and she had the strength of five linebackers packed into that lithe five-foot-seven-inch body. What bothered me the most was the fact that Sam knew so many of the intimate day-to-day details about Simone. Could I actually be jealous? Argh!

"Sam—"

"What is it?"

"Before when you said you missed me—"

"I meant it. Every word. But—"

Man, I hate the word *but*.

"—We've only known each other for a couple weeks and it feels like things have turned serious rather fast. Not that I mind," he added hastily.

"I'm sure you have a point in there somewhere." Gritted my teeth and waited for the one-two punch.

"Look, we have some kind of connection. Would you agree?"

"Yes, there's a connection." My mind drifted to the night we made love. Every time we touched, our souls combined into one, so that when we separated, it physically hurt. I'd never experienced sensations like that and to be honest I wanted to run as fast as I could away from them.

"But you're on the other side of the world—saving lives, I know—but I'm here. In Sweet. We lead two very separate lives. I like you, Bronwyn. But—"

Have I mentioned how much I hate that word?

"—I wonder if we shouldn't take a step back and catch our breath. Give us both an opportunity to adjust to this new situation."

What the fuck was he talking about? He sounded like one of those television psychologists spouting psychobabble to the masses.

I wanted to scream and—even worse—cry. I never cry, especially over a man. Didn't he say that he liked me? Missed me? Why in the hell does he need to take a step back? I mean, I'm quite willing to run the other way, but that doesn't explain his actions.

Calling him vile names seemed an inappropriate response, so I did my best to quell my temper. "I understand. Now, if that's all, I'd really like to get some rest. It's late."

"Wait, Bronwyn, I think we need to talk this out. I don't think you understand what I'm saying."

"Sorry, can't hear you. Phone must be going out. Darn battery." Click. I hung up on the bastard.

Why? Why do I do this to myself? It had only been a couple of weeks and I'd let myself get totally into this guy.

I never seem to remember the rule that men were put on this earth to drive us fucking insane.

8 A.M.

Lost boyfriends: 1

Heading back into town with the sheik this morning. He has meetings and wants me to read some of the participants. He's not telling me everything and I may tap into his mind when we get there. I only promised not to do it in his home. Never said a word about the office.

If I let myself, I could feel a twinge of guilt because he was so nice to me last night. After the phone debacle with Sam, I headed to the garden for air.

Hadn't been there long when Azir stepped through the doorway off the east wing. He wore a fitted rib-knit T-shirt and jeans. His feet were bare, and he looked damn sexy.

"Bronwyn, you're up late."

"So are you."

His brown eyes questioned mine and I realized I must have worn my emotions on my face. I slipped my mask into place and saw a hint of a smile on his lips.

"I don't require much rest. Four hours or so gets me through the day." He stepped closer and motioned to a small bench beside the tiny man-made creek that ran through the garden.

"You're a lucky man. I need at least eight and I'm always grateful for more." I yawned.

"So what's keeping you up tonight?"

No way I'd tell Sheik Azir that I had man troubles with Dr. Sam. So I sat like an idiot and shrugged.

"I don't want to pry, but if it's a personal problem, perhaps I could provide some perspective."

"Thank you. That's kind, but I needed some air. That's all." Not in this lifetime would I ever share my personal troubles with a client.

I knew he didn't believe me. Still, he smiled and we sat on the bench just enjoying the sounds of the water bubbling through the creek.

Leaned back on my hands and looked up at the sky, covered with a sheet of twinkling stars.

For several minutes we sat in silence. I moved to leave and the sheik spoke.

"When I turned six my father took me into the desert to commune with the stars. During the day we rested in a small tent and stayed away from the heat as much as possible. But for five nights we stayed up until dawn and he taught me all of the constellations and told me stories of the Bedouin tribe. His people." He turned to look at me.

It was the first time I'd ever heard any mention of his father. The family didn't speak of him. I figured he must have been dead for several years.

"I get my interest in magic from him. He made me believe that anything I dreamed could be possible. We tracked footprints of those who had traveled before us and I learned much in those five days."

"Sounds like you had a wonderful father."

"He is a great man."

"Is?" No time like the present to find out if big daddy's alive or dead.

Azir gave me a strange look.

"I'm sorry. I thought your father died."

"No. He's been away for the last year. Several of the Bedouin tribes in the north have land disputes. He travels around settling arguments. My father is greatly respected among his tribe."

"And he left you to run the family business?"

"He never cared for it." Azir sighed and stood. He reached out a hand to help me up off the bench. "His heart was never in it and when the opportunity arose for him to go, it turned out best for everyone."

Something wistful in his voice made me wonder if life would have been different for the sheik had his father hung around.

"Can I ask something else?"

Those brown eyes honed in on my face. "Yes."

"If your father hadn't left the business, what would you be doing?"

"Teaching."

Okay, talk about the last thing I expected to hear. "What would you teach?"

"There are many wonderful things about my country, but raising individuals with open minds is not one of them. Some blame our faith, but our faith is open to all and much more accepting than most would think." He paced the small path in the garden. His mood intensified as the passion rose in his voice.

"In many ways I'm jealous of you. You live in a place where being different is a good thing. People in America have so many options. And that is what I want for my country."

Yes, we're all so accepting that some jerk's put a bounty on my head. "There's good and bad that goes along with that. Child and spousal abuse and crimes are at an all-time high. And the homeless problem is beyond belief.

"Teaching is a noble profession, Sheik. But look at the difference between crime here and there. You won't find any here, because it's almost nonexistent in your country. And while we do have the freedom to express ourselves, it isn't the rosy picture you imagine." I shrugged.

"Oh, I know of what you speak. It's far from perfect but there are opportunities there for most who seek them. It's not for myself that I want these things. I send my sister to school there with the hope that she will stay and have a life she could never imagine here."

For some reason this guy always had the welfare of others in mind. Where were the flaws? Other than being ruthless in business and a bit bullheaded. I'd been prejudiced when I first saw him and assumed he had a harem at home. Nothing could have been further from the truth.

"What are you thinking, Bronwyn?" His voice sounded husky and I met his eyes. Damn, I know that look. That's the serious I-want-to-get-in-your-pants look. Can't say I don't feel the same way, but the "no screwing clients" rule won't be broken by me.

And if I'm really honest with myself, I'll admit that he doesn't make me feel like Sam does. If that warlock has ruined me for other men, I'll have to kill him.

"I'm thinking that some things are way too good to be true." I stepped away from the heat I could feel from his body. "What time do you want me ready to go into town tomorrow?"

He accepted the change of subject with gentlemanly respect. "My first meeting is at ten. We'll leave at nine."

I checked my watch. Ick. "I'm off to bed."

"Good night, witch." The way he said *witch* sounded more like *darling* or *lover*. Yikes! He touched my shoulder as I walked past.

" 'Night."

Can't even imagine how I could consider the sheik as a lover. Well, that's not true. The guy's gorgeous, brave, and compassionate, and the list goes on. But he's a friggin' sheik. What is it with men lately? Never been into the whole masochist thing, but I'm beginning to wonder.

Twelve

Another long day at the office. At least the sheik didn't get kidnapped this time. Can't say I like the people he does business with in Dubai. Rudest bunch of jerks I've ever met. And I've met a lot of assholes in my line of work.

Some prince from a neighboring country wouldn't shake my hand. Wouldn't touch a single female, especially an *American*. Whatever. He's related to Azir, but I never figured out how. Most of the men Azir introduced me to nodded slightly at my presence, but for the most part ignored the fact that I sat two feet away. Annoying.

Not that I needed any encouragement in the men-are-toads department, but these guys sealed the deal. Most of the conversations centered on land that the prince wanted to buy and evidently Azir had no desire to sell. His office in the sky filled with steam coming off the prince's ears. But the sheik wouldn't budge.

Lots o' angry thoughts coming from the prince and I wondered if perhaps he's our guy. Nothing clear enough to pin the bombs on him but I'll keep tapping in now and then. He's a definite suspect.

The best part of the day happened before we ever left the house. I finally had a chance to visit the women in the "secret wing." I complain about men on a regular basis, but I've got nothing on these chicks.

Before directing me through the doors where the two guards held great big guns, the sheik explained what was about to happen.

"A few of the women have heard about your work to protect the shelters and want to meet you." He talked in hushed tones as we walked through the long corridor so as not to wake any of the women who might be sleeping.

"Each woman has her own set of rooms and they stay here until new identities can be given to them. They come from all over the world. All that I ask is whatever you see or hear today, you keep to yourself. I'm duty bound to protect these women, and it is my wish you understand how far I will go to do so."

The sheik had just thrown a mild threat my way, but I understood his point, so I let it go.

"I've sworn to protect you and your family, and from what I can see these women fall under that umbrella." I grabbed his wrist to stop him before we entered through an elaborate wooden door decorated with tiny pink and green flowers. "What you do for these women is extraordinary; I'd never do anything to put them in danger."

He accepted what I had to say with a nod and knocked on the door. Behind it an African princess lived in what I call the pink room. It had been filled with every shade of pink the mind could imagine. From fuchsia to bubblegum the place was covered. And I haven't seen so many ruffles since my fifth birthday party when my mom decided petticoats were to be worn under all of the little girls' dresses for high tea. It was overwhelming then and almost equally so now.

The sheik stepped back through the door after introducing me to Naraba and left us to our conversation.

"Sheik Azir is a most generous man," she told me as we sat on a plush sofa covered in pink velvet. "I'd spent the last seven years in a prison cell that consisted of stone. No chairs, tables, or beds allowed. No comforts at all."

"May I ask why you were in prison?" I shifted on the sofa and couldn't imagine this graceful, regal woman wrapped in silk sleeping on a cold stone floor for so many years.

"I'd been accused of adultery."

"And they threw you in jail for that? Where I come from they celebrate it in the press when movie stars do it."

"We come from quite different worlds, but you must understand something. I did not commit the act of which I was accused." She clasped her hands tightly as if she could hold the pain to her. "My parents made me marry a friend of my father's when I turned seventeen. He had promised to be a good husband and was quite a bit older than me. He took me to his bed but was dissatisfied with my performance. I knew nothing of the act and was only a frightened girl. After that he ignored me."

There are way too many assholes in the world.

"Two months into my marriage I was raped by another man. My husband, feeling I'd been soiled, wanted to be rid of me. So I was accused of adultery. They threw me in jail and I was given a death sentence."

You know when you have those days and nothing is going right? Well, from now on I've got something to compare those days to because while I tend to think I've been to hell and back, this woman had actually been there.

"How did the sheik find you?"

"He was traveling with a group of human rights activists and talked with me during his visit. A few days later I boarded a plane and I've been here for the last six months. I'm not sure how he did it, but I'll be forever grateful."

I wish I could say that was the worst story I heard this morning but there were more. A Chinese woman from a small village who had been sexually mutilated for giving birth to triplets. Her babies had been killed and she was tortured. Another woman from Russia who had been forced into prostitution at the age of ten to help feed her family. The stories went on and on.

In my line of work I often see the worst humanity has to offer, but nothing like this. My heart hurt for these women. Amazingly, though, none seemed as broken as you might expect. They were strong and each working toward very specific goals.

I left feeling not sorry but proud. These incredible women had survived atrocities most of us couldn't imagine and had managed to move on and create better lives.

But none of them would have been able to do it without Azir. In each case he had stepped forward and pulled these women out of dire situations. In a strange turn of coincidences the villains in each of their stories always wound up dead. I wondered if Azir had something to do with that. On the way into town he wouldn't talk about it.

"There may be a time when I need your help to save a lost soul," he told me in the car. "Then you'll find out how we are able to do what it is we must."

He did promise to consider my offer to make each of the women protection charms to keep them safe in the future. It's so odd to hear these stories from women who think he's the greatest man in the world and two hours later sit in an office with men who think he is the reason their country has gone to hell.

Tried to tap into the prince but couldn't. That means magic is involved. I'll try again later and see what happens.

Saturday, noon
Azir's asked me to travel with him to Oslo. again. Don't really have the clothes for it, but guess I'll pick some things up when I get there. The PM is meeting us but no other dignitaries.

I wish they'd discuss their plans with me. Once we get out of this house and on the jet I'm reading the sheik's mind and he can bite me if he doesn't like it. Stubborn, mule-headed toad.

Sunday, 3 A.M.
Oslo
We just got in and I'm too wired to sleep. We're staying at a private residence, which is nice. Don't have to worry so much about poisoned hotel food. The PM should be here in a few hours. Gotta grab some sleep before Miles arrives and yanks me out of this nice warm bed. I didn't think it possible, but I swear it's even colder than the last time we were here.

Azir's sister loaned me a parka and boots, so at least I got to the house without freezing to death. I'll pick up the rest of what I need later. Have no idea how long we will stay. Guess that's something else to ask about tomorrow.

Snooze time.

Noon
Spells: 2
Charms: 3
This house isn't as big as the sheik's castle but it'll do. It has a whole goth feel going for it, with deep red walls and black

furniture. I always think of Norwegian architecture of being clean lines and light woods, but this is the exact opposite. I don't think there's a piece of furniture in this place less than two hundred years old. But for some reason it suits me. I love the darkness and the oldness. First thing this morning I put protection charms on all of the doors and windows and did a general spell to protect all the inhabitants of the home.

My bedroom is huge with a bay window that looks out onto mountains and a white wonderland. I love the carved mahogany bed with the curtains. Definitely think it's something I'd like to replicate at home. These posts would be great for tying someone up. Not that I'd actually do it, but it's nice to have options.

I had three emails from Dr. Sam. Seems he's upset that I won't take his phone calls. "You're avoiding me," he wrote. "I don't like the way we left things. I care about you so much and I believe there's been a terrible misunderstanding."

Whatever. He's right. I'm avoiding him but I have good reasons. I can't deal with all that and protect these guys at the same time. I've got to focus on the business of keeping my charges alive.

There's a lunch meeting at one to talk about security for both the sheik and the PM. These guys live their lives in meetings. Don't know how they do it. Tapped into the PM when he walked in this morning.

Some corporate mergers in the oil industry have him worried, not to mention the fact that they found another bomb at his home in London. He's mystified about who's trying to kill him.

Noticed for the first time ever that the PM had a woman rolling around in that brain of his. Nothing dirty, just watching her walk into the office and he thought she had a nice smile. That's the really bad part of reading minds. Sometimes you get way more information than you want to know.

Wonder if Miles would be jealous of the PM's love interest. Haven't run into the snippy little twit yet. Thank God for small favors. Darn. Spoke to soon. He's at the door.

11 P.M.

Strange. Strange. Tapped into Azir. He's worried about so many things his mind constantly skips from one trauma to another. He doesn't understand that I could help him if he'd open up and let me.

Decided to confront the sheik head-on but didn't handle it well. We were at lunch and I told Azir and the PM that we had to make a list of suspects. I needed somewhere to start my mental investigation. They both gave me names but at the same time looked guilty of holding back.

"Look, you've hired me to protect you both and I'm doing that." I put the pen I'd been taking notes with down on the table. "But you have to be honest with me or I quit. Right now. I'm going to walk out and get on a plane and go home because I'm tired of the subterfuge."

The PM let out a huff, and Azir's forehead crinkled into a frown.

"Yeah, yeah, I know I'm insubordinate," I said. "Can't help it. I'm made this way. Don't get all huffy on me. Sheik, you know someone close to you, other than your cousin, has tried to kill you. Prime Minister, there was someone specific you were worried about but I know that name never made it to the list. If you don't want to speak in front of each other for fear of destroying business relationships, fine. But I need those names."

Complete silence for about three minutes, then both men rose, pushed in their chairs, and walked out without a word.

"Great." I went upstairs to pack because I'd meant what I

said. If they couldn't be honest with me I had no hope of saving them from the danger they faced.

As I yanked my bag out of the wardrobe someone knocked.

Opened the door to find Azir standing there with his arms crossed against his chest. "I'll talk to you but with the understanding that nothing I tell you leaves this room."

"We've had this conversation before. I'll keep your confidence."

"I cannot say out loud what I think, because if it is true it will crush my family."

"Perhaps I can help by telling you I believe I know who it is you suspect."

He'd gone to stand by the window and his head snapped around. "No."

"No?" I sat down on the bed. Did the man forget I read minds for a living? I knew he believed it to be his brother. All he had to do was say it.

"There's no way you could know anything about who might be behind these latest attacks."

"I'm not here to play games, Sheik. Do you believe Alkazir conspired with your cousin?"

He laughed. "If only it were that simple. It isn't my brother who wishes me dead." The grim set of his face told me that the next words out of his mouth would hurt more than anything he had said in a long time.

"You must understand I do not say this with a light heart."

He ran his hand through his hair and turned toward the window again as he whispered, "It's my father."

Thirteen

Monday, 8 A.M.
Waxing moon
Oslo
Spells: 2
Brain-weary witches: 1

Never in my life have I wanted to say "Back to the Batcave, Robin" more than I do right now. Need time to assimilate all this information. I'm in total overload.

Wish the most shocking news I heard yesterday was that the sheik's dad wanted him dead. No, no. That would be way too normal for Bronwyn these days.

Minutes after the sheik left my room, the prime minister walked in. He talked about nothing for ten minutes and then blurted out, "I'm afraid Miles may be behind some of these attacks!"

Miles? Snippy twit-faced jerk, who always had his panties in a wad? I think not.

"Prime Minister, as much as I detest the man—a fact you are well aware of—he couldn't possibly be behind something like this."

"The evidence speaks otherwise, Bronwyn. Did you know his brother is behind an underground military operation in London?"

"No, sir, but what does his brother's actions have to do with Miles?" I mean come on. The sniveling brat of a man was in love with the PM, didn't he have a clue?

"My security agents have a tape of him talking with his brother at a local pub, less than a mile from my home."

"Well, they are family." I grabbed a pillow off the bed and hugged it. As much as I hated Miles, I knew he couldn't be a killer. But I needed the whole story before I could help.

"That tape was taken twenty-four hours before the car bomb. And quite frankly, I have a difficult time believing it myself. Then only six hours before the bomb was found at the house, Miles met his brother again at a hotel. They had tea and talked, but our agents weren't close enough to pick up on the conversation." His hands twisted in angst. I'd never seen the PM so upset.

"If you're worried about Miles being behind the attacks, why did you bring him to Oslo?"

"Quite frankly, I couldn't bring myself to believe this news. But after talking with you and Azir, I don't know. Would it be possible for you to read Miles so we could know for certain?"

"Yes. Have a seat there." I pointed to a thronelike chair in the corner. "It may take a few minutes, but I think we should settle this as soon as possible. And I'd like to go on the record as saying you couldn't be more wrong, Prime Minister. Of all the lists we could ever make of your enemies, I would never put his name on any of them."

"You have no idea how much I want you to be right." He sat down and crossed his long legs. The idea that his closest associate might want him dead obviously weighed heavy on the statesman.

Took a deep breath and found Miles with my mind. He was in his room returning email. I probed slowly through his brain, weaving in and out of his subconscious. And found nothing. The only thing remotely regarding the PM was Miles handing him papers to sign. When he thought of the prime minister I could feel the warmth. No, if anything my initial impression of Miles's relationship with the PM was correct. He had been in love with the man for years.

Put the pillow back in its place on the furry down-filled comforter. Stretched my legs by walking around the room.

"So is it him?" The PM's voice was tight with worry.

"No." I couldn't invade Miles's privacy by telling the other man that he might be in love with him. Much as I'd like to get my digs into the sniveling toad. "You have the wrong man. That's not to say his brother isn't involved. I'll check that in just a bit. But—"

"Tell me—everything." He stood and touched my shoulder.

Snow fell heavy against the window, obliterating the view outside. Definitely needed some warmer clothes.

"Prime Minister, Miles has absolutely nothing but your best interests at heart. He cares a great deal for you and could never wish you harm. I'd like to know who it was that first threw suspicion on Miles."

"One of the agents on our security detail. She's the one who ordered the surveillance tapes."

Why am I never surprised to learn a woman is behind trouble? "She wouldn't happen to be a redhead with a nice smile, would she?"

His shocked look told me all I needed to know. "PM, your mole is most likely the young woman you believe is so attractive. I'd have your security detail pick her up for questioning if I were you."

"I don't want to know how you came up with that, but I'll make the calls now. And thank you. I cannot tell you what a relief it is to know for certain about Miles."

After he left I did a cleansing spell to rid myself of all this negative energy. Between the PM and Azir's emotional dramas, I felt like I'd been sludged by a warlock.

Azir doesn't have much more evidence than the prime minister. He believes his father is angry with him for liberating these women he's protecting. I can't find the father to tap into, so that one will have to wait. My gut tells me the brother's a better target, but the sheik is doubtful.

Slept well last night and then woke up this morning feeling like something had gone terribly wrong at home. Tried to tap into Simone, Dr. Sam, Kira, and Caleb and came up with nothing. Someone very powerful is blocking me and it pisses me off.

Called on the cell but couldn't get through to anyone. It's the middle of the night in Sweet. Someone should be home.

Crap.

10 P.M.
Spells: 4
Dead guys: 1
Angry witches: 1
Should have checked my horoscope before I got out of bed this morning. Well, it wasn't all bad.

The sheik and PM invited me to dinner at a restaurant nearby. It was one of the chic, dimly lit places where the clientele are dressed to the nines and the clinking of crystal is heard over hushed tones.

Felt a little out of place because I still hadn't had time to shop for any warm clothes. Wore my mom's sweater I stole when I was in New York and a pair of nice slacks. The sheik and PM dressed in dark suits and both looked elegantly handsome. Even Miles looked dapper—for a twerp.

Truth is, ever since my meeting with the PM, Miles has been extraordinarily kind. I wondered if he'd got wind of what had happened. I'm sure he heard about the redhead who had masterminded more than one plot to kill the PM. It's been all over the news today. Wish I could say the PM's troubles were over, but I'm afraid this mess with Azir will keep everyone on their toes for a long time to come.

We sat down at a table in a back corner that gave us privacy and at the same time a great view of the entire restaurant. The waiter handed me a menu and my displeasure at viewing the healthy fare must have shown on my face.

"What is it you always say, Bronwyn, 'No worries'?" The sheik smiled at me.

"I've been known to say that once or twice." The PM and Miles snorted in laughter.

The sheik's smile broadened. "Well, you have no worries tonight. We've arranged for a selection of beef to be presented for your meal tonight."

I couldn't stop the big grin sliding across my face. "Beef?"

"Yes," the PM interjected.

"Oh, I didn't know you guys cared. I'm so flattered." I fluttered my eyelashes and the men rolled their eyes. Of course I had to sit through two courses before they brought out a huge steak. It was worth every bite of salad and soup I'd taken.

Right in the middle of my private beef orgy, I felt a tingle of magic. I looked up to see if someone had entered the restaurant. No one new had come in so I began lightly sweeping the minds of the patrons.

At a table with a man and two women, I came across a block. One of the women turned to look at me as I threw my mind into hers. Nothing. She was a witch and she blocked me, which meant she had power.

She smiled and waved in a nonthreatening way. She motioned toward the ladies' room and I nodded in agreement. Excusing myself from the table, I whispered a protection spell for my charges and the others in the restaurant. I didn't think she meant any harm but one can't be too careful these days.

Wearing a royal blue dress and stiletto heels, the brunette beauty opened her bag in front of the mirror and pulled out a lipstick.

"Are you Bronwyn?" she inquired as I walked through the door.

I looked at her in the mirror. "Yes."

"I am Lesha, a friend of Garnout's. I wish you no harm."

The formal greeting made me laugh. Garnout must have warned her to be up-front because I'm not known for patience when it comes to confronting witches and warlocks.

"Lesha, it is nice to meet you." I stuck out my hand and felt her magic as she gave mine a light squeeze. "How do you know Garnout, and how did you end up here?"

"Garnout was my magical arts instructor at university years ago and I'm here visiting the friends you saw at the table. They don't know I'm a witch, which is why I asked you to come in here.

"But that's not the only reason." She cleared her throat. "There's a price on your head and some very nasty warlocks are determined to collect. Millions of dollars are involved and I know because one of the warlocks is my brother Aruth. He's an idiot who only recently started dabbling in dark magic. He and another man plan to attack you later this evening outside the home you are staying in."

"Lesha, you know what I can do. Why would you warn me against your brother?"

"He is a fool, but I do not wish him dead. I thought per-haps—if it's possible, could you spare his life? I want to get him help and I will if you let him live." A tear fell down her cheek and I heard the anguish in her voice, as well as her heart.

She was a good witch, I had no doubt, but I could not prom-ise what she wanted.

"I only ask if it is possible, and please know there will be no ill will on my end. No matter what happens. He has caused great pain to my family and is considered a traitor to them, but I must try to help him if I can. We are centuries of witches and warlocks who have done nothing but good and he has tarnished our name."

"I'll do what I can, but you have to understand—"

"I know. Honestly, his life does not deserve to be spared, but he is my brother."

My brother, Brett, drives me insane, and even though I hardly ever see him, I know I would be just as protective. It's difficult to let go of our loved ones even when they disappoint us.

She gave me the details of the attack and we returned to our respective tables. After finishing our meal, I prepared the PM, Miles, and Azir for the battle about to take place.

Miles rode with me, and the PM and Azir took another limo. Azir wasn't happy with the plan and said more than once that his security team could take care of the problem. But I fight my own battles. I told him it was some kind of creed. It isn't, but he never needs to know. I don't like nonmagical folks involved in my fights. Someone always gets hurt when that happens.

I saw the tail as we turned the first corner past the restaurant.

"I'll have the driver let me out on the corner, and act as if I need some fresh air," I told Miles. "You have him take the car to the back of the house. I need you, the PM, and Azir behind the walls of my protection spell so I don't have to worry about you while I'm fighting the bad guys."

"I'll make sure we are all inside," he promised and shifted in his seat to look back at the tail. "Bronwyn, before we begin all this, I must tell you thank you for clearing my name. The prime minister told me everything and even that he suspected me, though how he could ever—"

The twit was grateful? Go figure.

"It must be difficult for you, but I can tell you honestly that it was equally so for the prime minister. He refused to believe wholeheartedly that you were behind the attacks." I don't know why I wanted the pansy ass to feel better but I did.

He took my hand in his and squeezed. "Thank you for being a friend."

Well, that pushed the limit; with friends like Miles who needs . . . But I didn't want to ruin our special moment. "No worries. Now here we are. I'm getting out and you do exactly what I asked."

"Okay, but be careful." He raised his hand in a tiny wave.

"Oh, Miles, please. Now be a good twer—boy and do what I said."

The bitter cold whipped through the sweater I wore. I'd left the parka in the limo so that I would have more mobility. I'd only walked a few steps when I heard the roar of the engine as it came toward me. Cowards, they planned to run me down.

I turned and waited as the car came barreling forward. When it was about five feet away I leaped out of its reach and it swerved to keep from hitting a retaining wall. The car screeched to a halt and two men jumped out onto the street.

"Prepare to die, witch!" one of the men yelled as he raised his arms above his head.

"Let me guess: your name wouldn't happen to be Aruth, would it?" He faltered a bit and his arms came back to his sides. Bad guys don't like it when you personalize things.

"Your sister has asked me to spare your life."

Oops, that didn't work. The mention of his sister sent Aruth's arms up again.

"My sister should mind her own business." He threw a ball of fire at me. It flew just to my left and sizzled in the snow. So, the dark one actually had some power.

The other warlock moved to my right and I threw a stun to keep him still. It wouldn't last long, but I needed time to deal with Aruth.

"Look, I promised your sister I'd try not to kill you." Had my hands on my hips ready to go.

"That's too bad because I very much want to destroy you." He threw another fireball. I felt the heat as it passed by. Before it hit the ground I tossed it back to him and it landed at his feet.

The stun wore off the other warlock and he charged me. Why the hell didn't he use his magic? It made no sense. Before I could hit him again with a stun he knocked me down and fell on top of me. The snow caused an instant chill that made my bones feel fragile. Damn, I hate the cold.

He smelled of too many cigarettes and schnapps. Fist shoved into my chest, he meant to crush me. I couldn't catch my breath and I felt a moment of panic when my airway, constricted by his big, beefy hands, closed. I don't know if the cold caused my slow response or the big dinner I'd ingested but as the blackness crept in I gathered my strength.

Brought my knee up to his groin with as much force as I could muster and tried to shove his balls up through his throat.

Angry, the giant fell off of me, clutching his crotch and moaning. I caught his mind in mine. Before I could even think about it, the pungent smell of sizzled flesh permeated the air. His nards were the least of his problems now.

He shouldn't have knocked me into the snow.

He screamed in pain as the fire leaped out of his body and consumed him. Aruth stood still, watching his compatriot burn.

The hatred in his eyes left me no options. I'd have to kill him.

"Please, nooooo!" Lesha screamed from behind me. I had no idea if she yelled for me or for her brother, but it didn't matter.

"Stay away, Lesha. I must kill the witch." Her brother's face contorted into an angry snarl.

"Aruth, I love you. Please don't do this. I'm begging you. She'll spare your life if you'll come with me."

His black eyes burned. "I have tasted the darkness. I cannot come back. I am damned, as are those who go against me."

This time he directed the fireball at his sister. The look of shock on her face was quickly replaced by anger. She tossed it back at him and then spewed a spell.

Bind his arms
And his legs
Take his mind
For me to see;
So mote it be.

Aruth fell forward, paralyzed. Eyes open, he tried to speak but nothing came out. A large van pulled up in the snow and a group of men and women came out and picked him up.

"What's going on?" I wiped the snow from my hair and hands. The stench from the ashes of the burning warlock turned my stomach.

"My family will take him to our home in Brussels."

"You can't convince someone to give up dark magic if he doesn't want to." I walked toward her.

"No, but I can keep him from harming others. Maybe with time, we can teach him to be whole again." She stood shaking in the snow, the shock of her brother trying to kill her still evident on her face.

"You could have killed him in the beginning." She said it as a statement, not as a question.

"Yes, but I was trying not to."

"Thank you. From my heart and my family, we are most grateful."

She climbed into the van with the others. The smell of burned flesh hung in my nostrils and I headed for the front door of the house. Looked up and saw three heads in the window. The sheik, the PM, and Miles waved at me.

I laughed at my little gang and then remembered the trouble I'd sensed from home. Time to make some more phone calls.

Fourteen

Tuesday, 10 A.M.
Somewhere over the Atlantic
On-the-road-again witches: 1
Possibly lost boyfriends: 1

As I pass through time zones I hope my temper calms down. It's a good thing I don't have to pilot the jet because I'd probably be up there playing destruction derby with the airplane. I want to hit something really bad.

After fighting the warlocks I ran into the house to get warm. Changed clothes and then plopped my butt in front of the big fireplace in my room. Tried to breathe and cleanse my system, but the adrenaline coursed through my veins and I couldn't ease my nerves.

My cell phone rang and Simone was on the other end. Her news is the reason I'm heading back home at a time when the sheik and the PM need me the most.

Seems a demon showed up in Sweet and everyone blames

Simone. Not only do they want to kick her out of town, but they also want me to move. The nerve. Just because some nasty Nako demon shows up, that doesn't mean Simone had anything to do with it.

"The sheriff claims they haven't had a demon intrusion in more than five years," Simone yelled over the static in the line. I moved around the room to get better reception.

"That doesn't mean it's your fault one showed up!"

"I know, but this town you moved to has a lot of rules. Like all of the witches are supposed to meet with the coven within one month of moving into town—"

Oops. I'd known that but had been in New York when they met that first month. Then Oslo when they convened again. "Okay, so I'm a bad witch for not registering, or whatever it is they want."

"Well, that's only one of the many things the sheriff ranted about for hours. You're only part of the problem."

"Why don't you just give it to me."

"They're angriest about the fact I killed the demon in front of Lulu's and I wasn't discreet about it. How can you be discreet when killing a Nako?" Her voice rose higher as she continued her story.

"Didn't seem to matter that he was getting ready to eat a little kid who was walking out of the diner with his mom."

"What?"

"Yep. I'd been in town with Dr. Sam picking up groceries and I heard a scream. Turned and saw the eight-foot scaly Nako with his big yellow teeth ready to bite down on the kid.

"Ordered the Nako to put him down nice and calm-like. The demon gnashed his teeth, and Sam and I walked closer."

There's something wrong with me because right in the big middle of this story about a demon eating a little kid, I'm getting pissed off because Simone and Sam are shopping together. Argh! All I really want to know is if they are together.

I could hear the water running as she poured a glass of water from the tap and wondered whose house she was calling from.

"He just stood there in the door with the kid dangling in his big mitts. I didn't have a knife, arrow, gun, or anything else to use. I whispered to Sam to follow my lead and we took off. I rammed the demon with everything I had. The giant jerk only moved a foot or so but it was enough to knock the kid out of his hands. Sam caught the boy and ran him a safe distance away.

"Demon didn't take kindly to me knocking the food out of his hands and he chased me to the center square. We fought hand to claw for what seemed like forever, but Sam said maybe five minutes.

"Then I hear some woman yelling, 'Young lady, young lady . . . to kill a Nako you have to take his heart.' No shit. I didn't say that, though. I was polite and told her that I needed a weapon.

"By now I can't tell if the blood all over me is mine or the demon's. Sam yelled for someone named Ms. Helen to throw him a blade. He tossed it over the demon's shoulder and I plowed it into his chest. Ripped out his tiny piece of a heart. Man, that big gaping hole smelled. Think rotten eggs mixed with bad hamburger. But you gotta admit Sam and I make a great team."

No comment from me on that subject. "Well, from your story, sounds to me like Sweet should make you a hero."

"You'd think. The kid's mom was so thankful and when she and Ms. Helen heard about the sheriff tearing me down they gave him an earful. I never did find out who Ms. Helen was."

"She's one of the women who runs Lulu's," I told her.

"Oh, well, I'm pretty sure she's the one who told me to rip out the heart. And she's a hoot. She had that sheriff by the ear.

Well, not really, but she reminded me of a television mom when she grabs the kid by the ear for doing something bad.

"Unfortunately, she didn't help my case much. He relented and gave me till the end of the week but he really wants me gone. And, um, they're seriously reconsidering your welcome to Sweet. But I swear to you, Bronwyn, I just did what I had to do. Nobody wanted to see that kid get eaten. You would have done the same."

"Don't worry, you're right. I would have. Make sure you treat any wounds the Nako gave you with that potion I left in the fridge. The one in the blue bottle. The demon's blood may be toxic."

"Oh, Sam's already taken care of me." With a hint of admiration in her voice.

Why was I not surprised?

"When can you come home? I really think you need to meet with these people and sort all of this out."

Sweet had been the first place I felt safe in the last five years. I needed to go home and fix this, even though I'd have to leave the sheik sooner than expected. I couldn't risk losing my safe haven.

"Oh, and Dr. Sam's in trouble because someone found out he's a warlock, and he didn't register either. I think he could use your help."

Great. Sam hadn't wanted anyone in town to know, because of the bad rap warlocks get. I wondered if the news would hamper his practice. That is, if the town coven let him stay there.

We hung up and I called for the sheik. He came to my room and I explained that I needed to take care of some business in the States.

"We must travel to Moscow for a few days, so I see no reason why you shouldn't go home." He patted my shoulder. "You are a brave woman and I feared for your life when you fought those warlocks."

"It's my job to fight the bad guys. This time they were after me, not you, which is the only good news I have tonight."

"When I'm finished in Moscow I will return here. Can you meet me in two weeks?"

"Yes, I don't see why not." Provided I didn't have to move everything I owned to a new location.

"I've bought this home and I hoped that you would use it whenever you wish." He stepped closer to me and I could feel his breath.

"You bought it? Why?"

"You told me you liked it and that it felt like home." He put his hand on my shoulder again.

"I can't believe you spent that kind of money just because I said I liked something. This place had to cost a fortune."

"You are worth it. And I could think of no better reason to purchase a home."

Then he kissed me. Not a light peck on the lips, an I-think-you're-a-great-witch kind of kiss. No, this was a deep, invading your mouth, I-think-you're-hot kind of kiss. And I let him do it. It felt good. His lips pressed against mine, his tongue probing and tasting. Everywhere he touched me, I burned, in a good way, and wanted more.

That snapped me out of it. Crap, I kissed a client. Technically, he kissed me but I didn't stop him. Geez! I took a step back and he smiled.

"Sheik Azir, um, you're a client and I can't, um . . ."

"And you are my friend and confidant. If I choose to buy a house because you like it, that's my business. And you should know that I'm not one to follow rules any more than you are. Especially silly ones where a client can't kiss a witch he finds most attractive."

I swear in that moment his chocolate brown eyes peered into my soul. Couldn't explain it in a thousand years, but I really wanted this man.

"That's the one rule I've never broken. I can't date you."

"It wouldn't be dating, Bronwyn. When we touch, our bodies speak to one another. Can you deny it?" He pulled me to the window and we gazed out into the night.

"No." The fire seemed terribly warm. My breath caught, and my brain filled with confusion. The sheik totally wants me. Ahhhh! Bodies speaking. The guy could write erotic greeting cards.

I just wish it wasn't true. The connection between us is so intense. But different from what I felt with Dr. Sam.

Sam. Yes, that was the douse of cold water I needed. I was angry that Sam had fallen for Simone, but I also realized in that moment that I wanted to fight for him. Azir and I had chemistry, but I'd experienced something more with Sam and I wanted it again.

I grabbed Azir's hand and dragged him toward the door. "I've got to pack." He let me shove him out and he smiled, that disarming magnetism oozing out.

"Don't forget to carry the charms I made you at all times. And watch your back. There are bad guys everywhere. Even in Russia."

He pulled the handmade ornaments out of his pocket to show me he carried them. Then he reached down to kiss my cheek. "Take care, witch. I'll see you soon."

He laughed as he walked down the hallway and I slammed the door. Then I sat down on the bed. My cheek felt warm and wonderful from his kiss.

Wizard's dicks, what am I going to do?

Fifteen

Wednesday, 7 P.M.
Waxing moon
Sweet, Texas
Happy witches: 1 (Unfortunately it's not me)

Why do I ever leave this place? Sat in my living room and watched Casper chase an imaginary bird across the yard. Hard to believe it's March and spring's a few weeks away. I've got to get busy with the garden soon.

It's so peaceful right now that it's difficult to imagine the chaos of the last few days, even though I only caught the tail end of it.

Simone became a local hero as of yesterday, when Walter Kiesewetter, the editor of the *Sweet Weekly News*, ran an editorial about her bravery. He lambasted the sheriff and the local coven for stirring up trouble and treating Simone "abysmally." It's my guess Walter doesn't get to use the word *abysmally* much so he made the most of it. It's got to be tough running a town newspaper in a place where newsworthy happenings are few and far between.

Before Simone, the most violent story I'd ever seen in the paper was about a coyote that ate a chicken on one of the local ranches. In that story Walter had taken the side of the coyote.

This demon thing probably made Walter's year.

Finally met with the head honcho of the local coven last night. She came out to the house and brought food and drinks along. It wasn't at all what I expected.

Peggy, the sheriff's mother and leader of the coven, seemed to understand when I explained that I'd been halfway around the world protecting innocents.

"I in no way disrespect what you guys have done·here." I cleared my throat. She made me a little nervous. "The people in Sweet have treated me so well and I think this town is the greatest. I wouldn't want to do anything to jeopardize that. It's just that every time you've met, I've been out of town."

For a good five minutes I rambled on and she didn't say a word.

Peggy sat on the sofa in a long flowing skirt and black sweater. Then she noticed a picture on the side table and picked it up.

She gave a little yelp and then pulled a small tissue out to dab a tear from her eye. It didn't take us long to discover we knew someone in common—my mother.

Small world.

"When we were at Berkeley your mother turned every head on campus, male and female. If she hadn't been such a sweetheart it would have been easy to hate her." As she pushed a graying lock of long brown hair behind her ear she smiled sweetly. She took a deep breath and smiled. "I lost touch with her after she married your father. They moved to Houston for him to do his residency and I ended up here with my beloved Joshua on his ranch. Tell me about your mom. What's she doing now?"

"She and my dad are in Hawaii at some conference but should be headed back to New York in a few days. She took this semester off but she's been lecturing at NYU. I can give you her number. I know she'd love to hear from you." I grabbed a pen and paper from the side table and wrote down the info.

"Yes, oh, that's wonderful. I can't wait to talk to her. And I'm sure she'll be happy to know that her old friend is here looking out for her little girl."

Stifled a laugh about that one. It's been a long, long time since anyone referred to me as a little girl.

"That last year of school she talked about turning away from the craft. What happened?" Peggy put the picture back on the table and stuffed the tissue into her skirt pocket.

"She doesn't practice anymore, but she's guided me in one way or another my whole life. She and my dad let me make my own decision about whether or not I wanted to be a witch. When I chose the path of magic she supported me."

"Well, she's raised a very powerful young witch, and I'm so happy that you landed in Sweet. What a coincidence."

Since I seemed to find myself in her good graces I decided to push ahead with my mission to absolve Simone and Sam of their supposed sins.

"Peggy, I'm glad you understand about my work, and it's wild that you know my mom. But there's the matter of my friends, Simone and Dr. Sam." I took a deep breath to prepare for the onslaught.

"Oh, darling, absolute water under the bridge. We needn't worry about any of it. That young friend of yours is a hero. They even said it in the paper. I don't necessarily approve of her methods but she saved that child's life.

"And we all adore Dr. Sam. Now he needs to do the same as you, and tell us his intentions, but I see no future problems." She stood and walked around, picking up my trinkets from around the world.

"We like to know what's going on with the magical folk in town. Helps us keep the peace. We don't need to know your every move and you don't have to join us or sign anything. It's all very relaxed. You tell us the type of magic you do and what you plan to do with it, and that's about it."

"That sounds fair, but I wondered if you could talk to the sheriff and straighten things out with him. He doesn't seem to share your relaxed attitude."

"Goodness, girl, my son won't give you any more trouble." She waved a hand at me and shook her head. "He does what I tell him to, but he's very protective of this town. We all are. Not to make excuses, but he's only been sheriff for three years and we've never had any trouble like your friend's demon."

Wanted to correct that fact, remind her that Simone had nothing to do with the demon, but didn't want to push my luck.

She looked at the paper with my mother's number. "Oh, I just can't wait to call and find out how she's doing. And tell her how happy I am to have you here in our town."

Damn. She'll be filling my mom in on the details of my life. I love my parents, but there's a reason we live so far apart. Argh.

Thursday, noon

I've been home forty-eight hours and haven't heard a peep out of Sam. Maybe he has his hands full trying to explain himself to the local coven. Although, I thought I cleared all that up with Peggy on Tuesday. One thing's for sure. I'm not going to sit around and wait for him to call.

How dorky is that? But you'd think I would have seen him in town at the grocery, or when Simone and I ate at Lulu's for breakfast this morning. I wonder what he's doing?

7 P.M.

Simone leaves tomorrow morning. Caleb and Kira plan to drive her into Dallas to catch her plane. She decided if she had to fight demons, she'd just as soon do it on her own turf. So it's back to Los Angeles.

Wish I didn't feel so happy that she's headed home. Honestly, I'm mixed up about it all, especially now that I know she and Dr. Sam didn't do the mattress dance.

"Why haven't you called him since you got back?" she asked me while she packed up her stuff in the guest room.

"I've been busy." I sat on her bed and picked at the tiny fringe on the ivory-colored chenille. "And when I was in Dubai things got weird."

"Weird how?" She pulled out her lingerie and some of it scared me. Black lacy things with slits in the crotch. Leather underwear that laced up the back. I like sexy stuff as much as the next girl, but that doesn't seem very comfortable.

"The guy's totally in love with you. All he ever talks about is Bronwyn this and Bronwyn that."

News to me.

"I've never seen a guy so loopy over a woman." She snapped her suitcase closed and tossed her makeup into a large zippered backpack.

Loopy? A week ago the guy said he needed a break, and we didn't even have anything to break from. He was about as far from being loopy about me as a man can get.

When I didn't say anything, she turned to glare at me. "Listen, Bronwyn, I don't know what's going on in that goofy head of yours but don't fuck this up. This guy is head over heels for you. I know because I flirted with him unmercifully."

What a surprise.

"Oh, don't give me that look; I did it for you."

"Me?" Do I really need friends like this?

"I didn't need a man so bad that I would steal one from my best friend, Bron. I decided if he was really the one for you then he'd be able to resist my charms. And I gave it to him full force. If he couldn't resist me, then he wasn't good enough for *you*. And guess what?"

I shrugged.

"He turned me down flat, you idiot. And I didn't make it easy for him. I had to see if he was for real, and he is. So whatever tension is between you it's time to suck it up and fix it."

If only it were that easy. "You know how I am with relationships, Simone. And it's not just about Dr. Sam. I have feelings for—" Geez what was I thinking? I couldn't say those words out loud.

It's ludicrous to even imagine that I might care for Azir. I mean he's a friggin' sheik and lives on the other side of creation. He's got a total God complex and wants to save the world. He's richer than any person has a right to be.

And he's beautiful.

"Bron, if you tell me that you're in love or lust with someone else I'm going to knock the crap out of you." Simone stood with her hands on her hips, giving me the evil stare.

She had it right. I had no business being in love or lust with anyone, especially the sheik. And I do have feelings for Dr. Sam. If he loves me, as Simone seems to think, then I definitely need to at least try to sort things out.

She put her hands on my shoulders.

"Hey, I'm just kidding about the violence, but you do need to set things straight. If you're into something with someone else you have to let Sam down easy. The guy's total for you."

Let out a breath I didn't realize I'd been holding. Had to put the sheik out of my mind. He'd be an impractical choice for a lover. "No, I'm not in love with anyone else. You'd think a high witch would know how to deal with relationships, but that's the one area I'm totally deficient in."

"Don't take it too hard, Bron. It's tough for all of us. Love hurts, but it's usually worth every minute you spend in it."

Simone can be positively brilliant sometimes. Yes, love sucks.

Friday, 9 A.M.

Figures. I call Sam and he's out of town for a long weekend. That's just not allowed. If I get brave enough to call a man, he should be there waiting for me.

Stupid man.

I hope he's not out with another woman. Then he'd be a really stupid man and I might have to kill him.

Not that I have a right to kill him. Maybe I should have returned his calls and email. I just had to do this my way and now it's probably over. Didn't even give him a chance.

Stop. Breathe.

Garden. I need to go get dirty. Oh, great, now I remember the dream in the conservatory with his arms wrapped around me. Nooo! Dirt, hands planting herbs. That's what I'll do. Then I'll till the flower garden. Hard work—the answer to everything.

Noon

Okay, so the gardening thing didn't work. It's going to be a very long weekend if I just sit around wondering what Sam's doing.

Oh, yippee! Phone's ringing. Please let it be someone who can save me from this psychotic behavior.

2 P.M.

The call didn't help. It was the sheik's assistant at Duban Industries. I've got another week here at home before I have to take off for Brussels. I'm meeting the sheik and the PM there for more meetings. At least we aren't going back to frozen Oslo.

I wonder why the sheik didn't call me himself. Probably just busy with something important. I mean, the guy's a billionaire. He doesn't have to make his own phone calls.

But he acted like he had the hots for me in Oslo. Wouldn't he find some excuse to make contact? Am I the only woman in the world who doesn't understand men? And why the hell do I care so much about two men I hardly know?

I need to go back to the old Bronwyn ways. Men are for sex only. Ride them hard and then let 'em go. Can't have sex with the sheik, but if I treat this whole thing with Sam like that, I might just survive. Of course it doesn't help that the man has my heart hostage, and I don't have any idea how to get it back.

Sixteen

*a*fter torturing myself for hours on end and making a mess of the conservatory, I went into town last night. Lulu's had chicken and dumplings and I wolfed down more than my share of comfort food. Add two pieces of pie to that and you'll understand why I felt like I needed a wheelbarrow to roll me back to the truck.

Ran into Margie, who invited me to a party at her house tonight. She told me it's totally casual and just a few friends, great music, and lots of food. After last night's gorgefest I swore I'd never eat again, but I'm already hungry for lunch so that didn't last long.

Still haven't heard from Dr. Sam. I sent him an email and asked that he call when he gets back to town. But now I feel like a stalker chick. I've left messages at his office, home, and cell too. No way I'll tell him about being jealous of his imaginary affair with Simone, but I will apologize for being a jerk while I was gone.

Got a call from the airport and discovered the sheik had the jet returned to my hangar. Bummer. I thought when I left it in Dubai to travel to Oslo that would be the end of it. I'd taken a commercial airline home. But no. The damn jet is right back where we started.

If it weren't almost midnight in Moscow, I'd call and give the sheik a piece of my mind. That's not true. I'm staying away from that guy until I can sort out how I feel about all this.

Now that I'm home, the whole thing with Azir seems like a huge mistake. I just needed some distance.

Sam upset me, because he acted weird while I was gone and I had a momentary lapse.

Still, the sheik's a charismatic fellow and I'm going to make a charm that helps me resist him whenever he's around.

Speaking of which, I better get down to my workroom and put together some charms and potions. I've been seriously slacking and I don't want to get caught shorthanded.

Oh, and I have to go back and check on Mr. Gunther to see how his memory potion is doing. He was resting when I stopped by today and I didn't want to disturb him.

Margie says he continues to write like crazy, so I hope everything is working the way it should.

Sunday, I A.M.

That Margie's a sneaky toot. I think she invited every single guy in town but there were only three women at the party. Margie, her friend Sarah, and me. Didn't matter, though, we had a hell of a time.

There were about five men for every woman. Not bad odds.

She set up a karaoke machine and that provided hours of entertainment. Some of the guys weren't too bad. Bill Thompson, the pharmacist at the drugstore, sang Elvis tunes, and if you closed your eyes it sounded like you were in the presence of the King.

But Cliff, who works out at the Barneses' ranch, needs to think twice before quitting his day job and heading to Hollywood. He warbled through U2's "It's a Beautiful Day" and even the dogs howled.

Surprised myself when Margie and Sarah dragged me up with them to sing "Girls Just Want to Have Fun." We did hand motions and the whole bit. I can't remember being that silly since I was about twelve and my best friend, Mary, decided we had to dress up like supermodels for school. We wore three-inch heels, tight-fitting dresses, and makeup that would make a Sunset Boulevard ho jealous. It was great fun, till we got called into the principal's office. He made us wear school T-shirts over our outfits for the rest of the day.

But at Margie's no one cared. We pranced around like Cyndi Lauper and sang at the top of our lungs. As we were taking our well-deserved bows I noticed Sam standing in the arch of the doorway. The sight of him made my heart dip to my toes. And my lower extremities instantly warmed.

What made me think I could ever just screw this guy and let him go? I wanted to jump into his arms and wrap my legs around him. Hardly appropriate for the moment.

I needed a drink. Moved to the bar and poured myself bourbon and Diet Coke. Crammed a sausage roll in my mouth and waited. Should I go to him? Will he come to me? Shit. Took a deep breath and made myself meet him halfway.

"Hey." Brilliant, Bronwyn. So good with the words.

"That was quite a performance." He touched my arm and his fingertips shot shock waves through my body.

"I don't think we're quite ready for the concert tour, but with a few more rehearsals . . . Um, how are you?" Tried not to slosh my drink, and to look cool at the same time. My hand shook, so it wasn't easy.

"Good. I had to attend a charity event with my mom and dad and just got back to town. Thought you were out of the country for a few more weeks." He led me to the backyard and we sat down on Margie's wooden porch swing. I wondered how long we would be talking around things. At least we were conversing, which was more than I'd expected.

"Yeah, well, after everything that happened last week I thought it might be good to come home and straighten things out. I kind of like it here and I didn't want to move." I looked away from him and stared out onto the lawn.

"You would have been proud of Simone. She was very brave."

There was a small twinge at the mention of her name, but now that I know nothing happened, there's no reason to feel that way. "I am proud of her and she's always brave. She's a little crazy, but she means well."

"On that we both agree." He sighed. "Look, we could talk around this for days but—"

"Can I apologize first?" I turned to look him in the eyes. "I'm sorry about not returning your calls. I could say things got busy and it wouldn't be a lie, but that's no excuse. The truth is, I don't understand what's going on between us. And I'm just confused."

"Honestly, I'm not much better at this." He shook his head. "There's so much I need to tell you and I don't know where to start. All of this happened kind of quick and it was definitely unexpected.

"I moved to this town for many reasons." His brow furrowed. "One of which was to get away from a woman who I had been engaged to for more than a year."

Couldn't keep the shock from my face. And he squeezed my hand as if he feared I might bolt.

"We never talked about past loves and I didn't see any reason to, until now. My relationship with her ended on a bad note. Well, it's a total cliché. Found her in my bed with two guys from her office."

"Kind of a twist on that old cliché, I'd say." I laughed. "Sorry, it's not funny."

"I realized when I told you I wanted to take a step back that you thought I meant never wanting to see you again. Nothing could be further from the truth. I just needed to—"

"I get it, really I do. Sounds like you have big trust issues, and rightly so. Unfortunately, I have the same problem. So it's smart for us to use a slow approach. Now if I'm really honest—and I usually am—you have to know that I don't like to do anything slow."

He smirked.

"Okay, well, that's different." I frowned. "Gutter brain. And for the record, you know I like it fast *and* slow. Actually I like just about any way we can do it."

He laughed. "How about if we date? Like good old-fashioned, I take you to dinner and we kiss on the porch when the night's over kind of dating?" His smile made the butterflies in my stomach take flight.

"No sex?" I couldn't help it. I really like the sex part of the relationship.

"Not right away. Trust me, Bronwyn, it's as difficult for me as it is for you."

"Okay, now you really do sound like Dr. Phil."

"I know you and I were made to be together, but we need to take our time in making that happen. We're both young, busy, and I say we take it at our own pace."

"I agree, but I still don't understand why we can't have sex. I mean, like, are you talking weeks or months of going without?"

"Well, if you keep smiling at me like that it may be minutes." He pulled me closer and hugged me. His spicy scent made my mouth water, and I wanted so much to reach down and touch him.

He whispered. "Let's just play it by ear." He kissed me and then pulled me back into the party. The McClellan boys, who could all be linebackers on a pro football team, were belting out a Bon Jovi tune and swaying to the beat. Sam and I laughed until we couldn't breathe.

He kissed me again at my car and we agreed to meet for church this morning, which is seven hours away and I need my beauty sleep. I like the idea of taking things slow but it's not going to be easy. Just the image of him in that suit, with his starched white shirt and tie, will make me want to jump his bones. Methodists are a forgiving bunch but I think they might draw the line at making out in the church pew.

3 P.M.

The McClellan brothers invited Sam and me out to their ranch for a barbeque tonight. Caleb and Kira are back in town and we made plans to go together. Should be fun.

Sam was sweet in church and held my hand. He had an emergency call at the nursing home so we couldn't do lunch, but we'll hook up tonight. Oh, that reminds me. I need to go by and check on Mr. Gunther tomorrow. Should do it today, but I really want to get in one of those good Sunday afternoon naps.

Monday, 9 A.M.

It felt very couply at the barbeque last night. Kira and Caleb couldn't keep their hands off of one another. I'm not sure if I've ever seen him so happy. She grabs him an iced tea and he gets up to find her butter for her corn on the cob. Hokey, but kind of sweet.

The look in Caleb's eyes when he watches her is nothing short of pure devotion. When they touch, I can feel the magic between them. Never seen Caleb so moony-eyed over a woman.

The McClellans sure know how to serve up a feast. Sam and I were up to our elbows in rib bones. We flirted and ate until neither one of us was sure we could fit behind the wheel to drive home.

I tried to drag him in the house and got him as far as the porch, but he stood strong. Well, sort of. When he kissed me good-bye he shoved me up against the front door and pressed his body hard into mine. There was no mistaking the fact that he wanted me. His mouth didn't leave mine for a good three minutes and he tasted every inch of it. When he pulled away we both gasped for breath.

Put my hands on his chest to keep from sliding to the ground. "Sure you don't want to come in?"

"Oh, you know I do." He grabbed my hands and pulled them around my back, holding them tight. "But we're going to do this the old-fashioned way, remember?"

"Sam, I'm not a very old-fashioned girl and I need you."

"Not half as bad as I want you." His words made my insides feel like a big old pile of mush. Seemed so stupid to deny ourselves such pleasure, but in the dark recesses of my mind I understood. The guy had been engaged and I didn't even know it. We needed time to learn about each other.

I hate it when I'm sensible.

Made him let go of my hands and then I gently pushed him off the porch. "Go away, handsome man, and call me tomorrow." I blew him a kiss and he waved good-bye with a smile.

I'm off to visit Mr. Gunther this morning. Can't wait to see if he's still writing in the journals. I changed a few ingredients in the memory potion that I think may help. We'll see. Margie mentioned Mr. G's been sleeping a lot more and I wondered if it might be a side effect of the potion. Margie said not to worry because old people sleep a lot but I don't know. If I did something that caused him harm, I could never forgive myself.

Seventeen

Monday, noon
Sweet, Texas
Crybabies: 1

*A*rgh! I have to make this work. Mr. Gunther has been sleeping too much. Even Sam said so. The good doctor had finished his rounds at the nursing home when I walked in. He had a frown on his face so I knew something had happened.

"Tell me Mr. Gunther's okay." I yanked on his sleeve like a child. My voice sounded whiny even to me. The nurses looked up from their station and he pulled me off to the reception area.

"Bronwyn, calm down. He's fine, but he's suffering from extreme fatigue." Sam had that doctor mask on. The one where he goes all serious, but at the same time tries to look comforting.

It didn't work for me.

"If I've done something, just tell me. It's the potion, isn't it?" Geez, if something happened to that old man I would never forgive myself. There's something about the guy that just gets me.

"Has nothing to do with you or the potion. At least I don't think so." He flipped a page on his clipboard. "From what I can see it's a side effect of Alzheimer's. Your potion helps with the memory loss but there are other problems that come with the disease. Depression, anxiety, and problems with equilibrium are just a few."

"I didn't know." I blew out a breath. "I thought the memory and disorientation were the big thing."

"They are, and you helped him with those. He's tired, but he's still mentally alert. He's also old, Bronwyn, and his body is giving out."

"It's not just the Alzheimer's, is it?"

"I can't really discuss any more of his case with you."

"Oh, come on. That doctor–patient stuff doesn't apply here. He's perfectly aware I'm trying to help him. And it's me."

"Sorry, but I can't do it." He had that "I'm so concerned look" again, but I didn't buy it for a minute.

"Fine, I'll go talk to him myself. And while I'm at it, I'll ask for permission to work with you on his case."

He shrugged. I swear I could have kicked his ass right then and there. But I had to get to Mr. Gunther.

At the door I took a deep breath. The room had that antiseptic smell of too much medicine. The older man's skin had turned so white his hand almost disappeared into the sheets. If it hadn't been for the purplish bruises dotting his arms from the IVs and age spots, it would have been like trying to find Waldo in one of those insane books.

His eyebrow lifted and one of those steely blue eyes popped open. "Are you going to stand there and stare, or are you coming in?" He pushed the button on the side of his bed and raised it so he could sit up.

"Doc says you're tired today. You been out partying all

night again?" I pulled up a chair. Grabbed his hand and squeezed.

"Well, got all those women to please. A man does what he can." His grip tightened around mine.

"When did all of this happen? Last I heard you were kicking Doc's butt at chess."

"Just been the last two days or so. Woke up and didn't feel like I could get out of bed. Don't suppose you've got something for that in that witch's bag you carry around in your truck, do you?"

That small bright spot of hope in those beautiful blue eyes forced me to lie. I didn't know how to help him, but he didn't have to know that.

"I might. But I need to talk to Dr. Sam before we try anything new. He says you've got to give him permission to work with me." I rolled my eyes and the old man laughed.

"You two have a spat?"

"Nah, nothing that serious. Just a slight butting of the heads."

"Not a darn thing wrong with that, young lady, especially when there's making up afterward."

"Mr. Gunther! I'm not that kind of girl." I batted my eyelashes and he let out a hoot.

"That's not what I heard." He smiled bigger than I'd ever seen, and I let it go. What a charmer.

"Want you to understand something, young lady, and it's important to me."

"Sure."

"I told you before how much I appreciate what you've done, and you need to know what a gift it's been for me."

Opened my mouth to object but he held up a hand. "I know you don't like to take credit, but it's due. Now here's what you've got to understand. I only need a short time more to do what needs to be done."

"What do you mean?" He couldn't give up. I'd just met him a few weeks ago and I wasn't ready to let him go. There are people who come into your life that bring so much to it just by existing. I suddenly realized Mr. G was one of those people for me.

"Look, I'm more than ready to meet the man upstairs." He shook his head at my unvoiced protest. "I've lived a great life, one that would be the envy of most. A woman loved me more than any man has a right, and she gave me two talented and beautiful children.

"We laughed and loved, and if I live a thousand more lifetimes, none will be as wonderful as this one. But I've discovered over the last three weeks, since you brought my memory back, that I want to leave something behind. I want people to know about my wife and kids and, hell, I've just got a lot more to say.

"That's where you come in. Give me some of that magic of yours to keep me going for a little while longer so I can get it down on paper. When I finish up this last journal, then I'll be done and ready to move on. Can you help me?"

Told him I'd do whatever it took and then got the heck out of there so I could sob uncontrollably in the truck. God, this isn't fair. I was so upset I bought a dozen pink frosted cookies, with sprinkles, from the bakery and ate them all on the way home. If I were a bit more twisted I'd make myself throw up, but I think I'll hit the Rocky Road instead. Or the double fudge with chocolate chips sounds good.

Then my ass is in that workroom and I swear I'll figure out something to help Mr. Gunther.

Tuesday, 2 A.M.
Potions: 23

So tired. Got to get to bed and sleep for a few hours. I'm close with the potion but something isn't right. If I boost the energy too much it will affect his memory and that's exactly what he doesn't want. I'll figure it out, but damn it's hard to find a balance.

Talked to Sam for a few minutes and he offered to help, but I work faster alone. He thought I was angry about this afternoon, but I just needed to work. I want to be near Sam, but right now I don't know. I have to do this.

Getting up early tomorrow to start again. I must finish before I head to Brussels this weekend.

Note to self: Call Garnout to see if he has any suggestions on how to better balance the potion. If the two of us can't figure it out, it can't be done. And I refuse to even let that be an option.

11 A.M.
Potions: 26

Garnout returned my message and told me to add pennyroyal and rosemary to the mixture. I've used pennyroyal to treat stomach ailments and cramps, but the wizard believes, mixed with the other ingredients, it will help balance the potion. The rosemary will increase the mental agility.

"Have you found out any more about the hit out on me?" I asked while I had Garnout's attention.

"No, not even a hint of who is behind this one." The sigh in his voice made him sound tired, which is unusual, even though he is over two hundred years old.

"Is there something else going on?"

"No, nothing you need concern yourself with. But do this old wizard a favor and try to keep out of trouble for the next few weeks. I've got my hands full with three new covens moving to the city." I could hear the bell tinkle on the door of his shop.

"That's a whole lot of witches. What's the deal?"

"Capric Corporation has moved its offices to Manhattan and

evidently they like to hire witches and warlocks. They're involved with investment banking.

"But it's not a good thing. Whenever there is that much power that suddenly finds its way into a small area, conflict is sure to arise."

He spoke the truth. Once when I was in Paris a coven of witches moved in and there were fights every day. I likened it to L.A.'s gang problem.

"And unfortunately, some of these witches are known for their dark magic, and that puts a whole new spin on our carefully balanced city."

"I've never heard of Capric. Do you need help? You know I'll come if you ask." I meant what I said.

"I appreciate the thought, but it isn't necessary. I've plenty of magical folk here to assist. You concentrate on your elderly friend and taking care of your diplomats."

We talked a bit more about the potion for Mr. G and we'll see how it works. I've called Sam and we'll test it this afternoon. He wanted to take me to lunch after, but I've promised to meet Peggy and a few other members of the coven at the new tearoom for high tea. Decided I had to at least make an effort. Once I leave, I have no idea when I'll be back and there's a good chance I'll miss their next meeting.

Sam may come over tomorrow night to help me unload some boxes that I stuck up in the attic when I moved in. Caleb came over when Kira left for work this morning and painted the third bedroom for me. The sage green is darker than I had wanted, but I like it. It will go well with Grandma Lily's quilt and spindle bed. Once I get that room finished, I just have the family room in the back, the kitchen, and the downstairs bathrooms to do. Ick.

Guess I better get cleaned up. After messing with the asafetida

I smell like a big-city dump. There's a reason that herb's name contains the word *fetid*. It's off to the shower with me.

3 P.M.

This is rapidly turning into a pretty good day. An hour after we gave him the potion, Mr. Gunther perked up and he was writing in his journal when I left.

If that man were fifty years younger, Sam would have some stiff competition. As it is, I'm goo-goo over him. Swear he's worked some kind of magic on me, but he says he doesn't have a magical bone in his body.

The sheik is worried about something and his thoughts keep popping into my head. My problem is I'm not sure if I'm tapping into him, or vice versa.

I know he needs me, not for protection, but to talk things out. I've tried to call but can't get through. Sent him a mental message to contact me, but he has to be open to it to understand.

I have to stop thinking about Azir. Those big brown eyes and hot body will not pull me in again.

The truth is, I wonder if I'm looking for reasons to be with him, because this thing with Sam is so intense. I hope not. Maybe I'm imagining things. Either way, it's not good.

Sent some protection mojo to Russia. Whatever is going on, maybe it will help. I need to concentrate on things closer to home for now.

Eighteen

Wednesday, 5 P.M.
Waning moon
Sweet, Texas
Happy witches: 12

Met Peggy and her gang for tea at Cinnamon's Tee House yesterday. Can't say the rest of the coven is as crazy about me as she is.

I remember in high school when there were kids at lunch no one would sit next to, but I looked for those people and always sat with them. Most of the time they were a lot more interesting than the people who sat at the jocks' or cheerleaders' tables.

I now know how those loner kids must have felt because at the tea no one would sit next to me. And I looked so darn cute.

Peggy had placed me at the opposite end of the table from her and as the other witches filed in, they chose to sit at least one space away. Each woman would come in and nod with a tight smile. Then they'd go sit as far away as possible.

That is until Ms. Helen walked in. She plopped herself down, and I poured her a cup of orange spice tea.

"You look adorable in that dress, Bronwyn. I'm pretty sure I had one just like it back in the sixties." Helen smiled and grabbed one of the tiny cucumber sandwiches off of the platter.

I'd worn a red and white polka-dot shift with a white sweater. Added three-inch red pumps and a pearl necklace. Very Jackie O. Not my normal garb, but I'd had tea enough with my mother's friends to know what was expected. Most of the other women were dressed the same.

"It might *be* your dress. I found it at a secondhand shop in Dallas." I laughed and handed her the sugar.

"Well, it sure looks better on you than it ever did on me." She took a sip and squeezed my hand. "How's that young man of yours doing?"

When she said it I'm ashamed to say the sheik's face popped into my head before Sam's. Bad Bronwyn. Bad. Thought I'd been over that little matter. Move on, girl! Move on! The sheik's a big fat no-no. Well, he's not fat. In fact, those abs are enough to make a grown woman cry with joy.

I looked up to see Ms. Helen staring at me with a strange look in her eyes.

"Oh, um, Sam's good. I saw him at the nursing home just now and everything's great."

I wondered if she could read minds. She cocked her head to the right as if to evaluate me in some way. Before I could think about it, Mavis Calright walked in.

Next to the words *prim* and *proper* in the dictionary is a picture of Mavis. Her hair is never out of place, she always wears gloves, and her dresses are couture. I've seen her tooling around town in a silver Mercedes.

She didn't seem happy at all that the only seat left open in the room was the one to the right of me.

She stood for a moment looking perplexed. Peggy, who had been burning the ear of Leslie Clark, a beautiful blonde witch with curls down her back, gave Mavis a wicked stare and motioned her to the chair next to me.

Mavis shook her head tightly and refused to sit down.

Peggy pushed back her chair and walked toward the other woman. "Please, Mavis, sit down." The words were said through terse lips and gritted teeth.

She shook her head again. "You know I can't."

"Yes, you will. Or you can leave." Peggy's sharp tone made the woman wince.

Mavis's hands twittered around as if she were ready to take flight. "She's a high witch and anyone who sits to her right might be seen as one who wishes to challenge her power."

Mavis's voice was little more than a whisper but it had been enough to cause a hush around the room.

What in the hell was she talking about? I'd never heard such nonsense. It must have been some coven thing.

"Mavis, you"—she looked around the room—"and the rest of you, need to read your books more carefully. It's only seen as a challenge if the witch is a part of our happy little group, which she isn't. And even if she were, there are several other things that have to happen before a challenge can be made."

The relief made Mavis's shoulders visibly drop. She turned her back on Peggy and reached out a hand to shake mine.

"My apologies, I'm sorry." Her willowy fingers felt surprisingly firm against my own.

"It's no problem really. Can I get you some tea?" I reached for the pot when she nodded yes, and poured her a cup.

"We've heard so many stories about you and your powers, and we're all terribly frightened of you." Her eyes widened in surprise. "Oh, no, I just said that out loud, didn't I?"

I laughed and she put her head in her hands.

Ms. Helen reached across the table and patted the woman's wrist. "There, there, Mavis. It's okay. Bronwyn has a great sense of humor."

The older woman turned to me. "You've got to forgive her. She's had foot-in-mouth disease since the day she discovered her powers. She looks about as close to perfection as a woman can get, but she never says the right thing. Isn't that so, dear?"

Mavis rolled her eyes and blew out a breath. "I'm afraid that's true. Please forgive me. I'll say the wrong thing at every turn through the entire lunch. By the end of the meal, you'll want to knock me out with one of the teapots."

"Oh, I've dined with worse, believe me." I meant it. Through my years protecting various diplomats, I'd had to eat with some offensive and often ugly people. And I don't mean scary looking. Just wicked on the inside. But Mavis wasn't that way.

After that, she relaxed, as did most of the other women at the table. In all, eleven witches were there, and I talked with most of them.

A few of them continued to eye me with a wary look, but that's something I'm used to when dealing with other magical folk. Tried to make it clear that I in no way wanted to harm anyone, but it didn't help. Oh, well, never cared much about being the popular girl.

It was fun to sit and listen to some of the other women talk about their daily lives. The conversations centered on family, work, and children. Like any gathering of women, but it seemed strange since these women were all part of a powerful coven.

I believe that's the secret to the success behind Sweet. People with power, and those in powerful positions in the town, want everything to be as normal as possible.

Some of the women invited me to their homes, and I may take them up on it. I've never been part of a community like this and it's important to me.

Have just enough time to change into my ugly clothes before Sam and his protectors get here. Guess he thought he couldn't handle a night alone with me, so he begged Caleb and Kira to come over too.

"We'll get done a lot faster with help," he promised.

"Yeah, right," I told him. But I knew the game.

They're bringing Chinese for dinner. Hope they don't forget the dim sum.

Nineteen

Thursday, 7 A.M.
Sweet, Texas
Witch's friends who are boys: Too many

Oh, what a tangled web . . . Not gonna go there. It's not my fault the fates conspire against me in the love department. Okay, maybe it's a little bit my fault, but please. Even I couldn't have foretold what happened last night.

Sam, Caleb, and Kira arrived, in overalls, loaded down with Chinese food, pink frosted cookies from the bakery (almost threw up when I saw them), and two six-packs of Mexican beer.

We set up in the breakfast room where I'd put Grandma Erma's breakfast table and chairs. It's a cozy nook with a bay window that looks out over the conservatory. It's one of my favorite places in the house and I painted it red, to match the dining room, which is off to the left.

"I thought Kira and I could work on your downstairs bathrooms." Caleb smiled at the librarian and grabbed her hand.

"She loves to use power tools, and can put up the new hardware after we paint. Then I can move on to the next one."

"We figured with the four of us working for a couple of hours tonight we could get tons done," Kira chimed in. "And what I learn from your house, I can turn around and do to my own place."

"In case I forget to say it later, you guys are the best." I raised my bottle of beer, as did the others. "Here's to the best friends a girl could have." We clinked bottles. "I'll be forever grateful, and anytime you need anything I'll be happy to help."

Kira and Caleb glanced at each other with suspicious smiles.

"What are you two up to now?" I raised an eyebrow and gave them my best "You better tell Mother what you are doing" look.

"Well . . ." Kira blushed.

"We're talking about getting a place together here in Sweet." Caleb finished her sentence.

Honestly, I thought it was kind of quick. They'd only known each other a couple months. But they were happy, so who was I to judge.

Smiled and hugged them both. "That's really great." I tried to sound like I meant it.

"That *is* a surprise. Did you find a place yet?" Sam had a secretive look that made me wonder what he really thought. When he glanced at me I realized he thought the same thing I did: it was too soon.

"No, we're just in the talking stages. We thought about my place, but it's so small." Kira twisted a blonde curl around her finger. "We're curious about the house down the road from you, Bron. Would that bother you?"

"Don't be silly. There's a good ten acres on this place so it's not like you'd be right next door, and even if you were, that would be great. Can't imagine better neighbors."

"From the outside it looks like a great house, but we haven't been able to figure out who lives there. Harry, the real estate guy in town, says it isn't occupied but it's not listed either. He's doing some research to find out who it belongs to."

I'd noticed no one lived there but hadn't thought much about it.

"What about the magazine in Dallas?" Sam interjected.

Caleb had freelanced for the last ten years and lived in New York most of that time. Last May he moved to Dallas to work on a business magazine that had gained national recognition. It was Caleb's investigative reporting on corporate fraud that gave the magazine all the media attention.

"Talked to my editor and he doesn't care where I live, as long as I turn my assignments in on time. I've got a friend who wants to lease my apartment and says I can use the spare room whenever I'm in town."

"Well, it sounds like you've got it all figured out. I want you both to be happy." I gathered up the dishes and Caleb put his hand on mine.

"I know it may seem too soon, but we want to be together. This is right for us." Caleb cocked his head and lifted an eyebrow.

I turned to look at Kira, who wore a hopeful face with tears brimming. They need my reassurance. I'm still not sure why, but I wouldn't be the one to rain down on their love with my usual pessimism.

"You guys, I really am happy for you. And I'm here if you need me." I smiled, my most genuine smile.

We tossed the remainder of the food in the fridge and Sam and

I headed to the attic. I moved the boxes to the edge of the opening and he carried them down the ladder and into the bedroom.

When it came time to move furniture down, Caleb helped get the dresser and side tables into the new space. I opened up boxes and pulled out the art I wanted to use in the room.

Several of the pieces had been painted by my family. Grandma Erma's water-colored mums blended seamlessly with Aunt Patricia's acrylic paintings of whimsical fairies dancing in a forest filled with golden light.

"How do you do that?" Sam opened another box with the cutter and looked at me with amazement.

"What?" I had no idea what he was talking about.

"I've watched you hang photos and paintings and not once did you measure anything. And the crazy thing is, it all works."

I laughed. "I've never been much on measuring except when it comes to potions. My mom can do the same thing. We look at something and just know when it's right."

"You know those photographs in my office?"

"The black-and-white ones?"

"Yes. It took me almost a month to decide exactly where they went. Then I consulted a book on the proper placement for photos and measured for hours to get the exact spot. My house has bare walls because I bought too much art and have no idea where to put it all."

He put his thumbs in the straps of his overalls and looked like a good ole boy ready to plow the farm. The sophisticated Dr. Sam in overalls. Sweet really did rub off on people.

"Maybe I could help you with that."

"Sure, just let me know when you want to come over."

I realized in all the times we'd been together, never once had he invited me to his house. Discovered that I was more than a little curious to see how he lived. I'd seen his office, which looked like something off of Madison Avenue. Would he have the same taste at home?

"You know, you look pretty damn adorable in those overalls." I pointed to his dusty denims.

He looked down and laughed.

"Caleb loaned them to me. I had on jeans and a sweater and he told me that wasn't appropriate for the kind of work we'd be doing. He grabbed these for me out of his truck and made me put them on. Actually, they're kind of comfortable."

"Well, Farmer Sam, I think this room is just about done. How do you feel about doing some painting?"

"I'm yours for the evening; use me as you please."

"Oh, you know better than to say something like that to me. It conjures up some very sexy, albeit wicked thoughts."

He grinned. "Can't say I haven't thought about christening your new bed in here. But you know . . ."

"Yes, yes. We're taking things slow. Any idea when we can get back to the sex part of our relationship?"

"Soon." His eyes turned a deeper blue and the look he gave me made my insides melt like butter on a hot cinnamon roll.

"Okay, long as you know patience isn't one of my best virtues." I smiled and left him to ponder that as I walked into the hallway.

Noticed it was suspiciously quiet downstairs. Found Kira and Caleb in the kitchen looking more than a little guilty.

"Are you two making out in my kitchen?" Crossed my arms and waited in the doorway.

"No," Kira said with her mouth full. "We're eating all of the cookies. These things are heaven with icing."

I would have agreed, had I not eaten an entire box so recently. Shook my head and walked to the fridge to get another beer.

"You guys eat all those you want, just make sure you leave a couple for Sam."

He came up behind me and wrapped his arms around my waist. I could feel a certain part of him had grown excited, and it made me laugh. All through the evening he'd found excuses to touch me.

"Did I hear you mention my name?" He squeezed me tight.

I turned in his arms and planted a kiss on his lips. Just for good measure I pressed my pelvis bone into his hardness to show him that I knew exactly how he felt. Then I pulled away to find the paint for the kitchen.

"If you want a cookie, you better hurry up. Kira and Caleb have just about eaten the whole dozen."

"Hey, you guys, no fair." Sam pushed his way between them. "Those are my favorite." He sounded like a little boy who hadn't been picked to be on the winning team.

"You children play nice and give Sam his cookie. He's going to need all this strength tonight." He turned and looked at me with a raised eyebrow. "Well, this kitchen isn't going to paint itself."

That made him chuckle.

Caleb and Kira pushed themselves off the kitchen counter and grabbed two paint trays. "We'll help. We've got to do some touch-up's in the bathrooms and we have to wait for the paint to dry first."

Three hours later my kitchen had taken on a Mediterranean look. Dark golden walls with hues of brown and red made it very old world. A few more coats of glaze and it would be perfect. I needed to strip and refinish the cabinets and put up a stainless steel backsplash and it would be done.

At midnight we threw some sheets on the furniture in the living room to protect it from the paint and flopped down for a rest.

"I can't thank you guys enough for everything tonight.

You've done more for me in a few hours than I've been able to do in the four months I've lived here."

"No problem." Kira raised her teacup in a cheer. "Here's to Bron's happy new home."

The others raised their cups in agreement.

"Thanks again and you're welcome to crash here if you need to." I gave Sam a look that told him exactly what I wanted.

"Oh, that's sweet," Kira said. "But I've got to open up the library early tomorrow. I'm in desperate need of a shower and my own pillow."

"And my appointments start at seven-thirty tomorrow morning." Sam tried to keep his voice light, but I knew he had no plans to stay.

Caleb and Kira gave us both a confused look but didn't say a word. My guess is they figured Dr. Sam would sleep over and I'd take him to the office tomorrow. No such luck. Argh!

They all carried their cups to the sink, and then I walked them out to the truck. Two cars came up the driveway as we headed out.

"You expecting company?" Caleb asked.

"No."

Two black Suburbans parked on each side of Caleb's truck. The tinted glass kept me from seeing who was inside. The door opened, and Sheik Azir got out.

What in the hell?

"Bronwyn, so good to see you." He took my hand in his and squeezed it.

"Sheik Azir, this is more than a surprise. What are you doing here?" I realized I'd been staring at the man and that he still held my hand. Glanced at Sam, who didn't seem happy at all.

"We had mechanical difficulties with the plane and decided to land here to see if we could switch out jets."

I shrugged. "Sure, no problem. As far as I'm concerned they're both yours and you can use them whenever you like."

"Bronwyn, you know that jet is yours free and clear. I gave it to you and I'm not taking it back. I only meant to ask a favor." He frowned and touched my arm.

Sam, Caleb, and Kira had leaned against the truck and were taking in the conversation. The sheik suddenly realized they were there.

"Oh, my apologies. You have guests. How rude of me. I'm Azir. It's nice to meet you." He put out his hand.

They each shook it in turn.

Kira cocked her head to the side, taking in Azir's caramel skin and chocolate eyes, laced with a fringe of long lashes. "So *you're* the reason Bron's been gone so much."

At this revelation, Sam crossed his arms against his chest and his jaw tightened. Yep, that was one unhappy camper.

"I'm afraid I've kept her busy the last few weeks with some difficult projects. She's become quite important to me." He turned and smiled at me. But there was something sneaky in his eyes.

When Sam took a step forward Caleb grabbed his arm. "Well, come on, good buddy, we better get on our way. You've got those patients in the morning."

Sam didn't say a word, but if a look could kill, the sheik would be as flat as a pancake run over by an eighteen-wheeler.

Before Sam got in the truck he walked over to me and planted a hard kiss on my lips. "I'll see you tomorrow. Nice to meet you, Sheik," he said as he stomped back to the vehicle.

"Would he be the reason you were so sad in the garden that night?" The sheik eyed me suspiciously.

"If you'll hold on a minute, I'll grab my keys and take you to the jet."

"Avoiding the question, Bronwyn? I've always thought of you as a woman who tackles things head-on."

"No, I just don't discuss my private life with my clients." I put my hands on my hips.

"So many rules where clients are concerned. But I thought we established in Oslo that we were more than business acquaintances." He pointed a finger toward my house. "And if you remember, you offered your home to me anytime I wanted to visit."

"You want to stay here? Tonight? I . . . um, we just painted, and it smells really bad. Wouldn't you be happier at a hotel somewhere?" No. Way. He couldn't be in such close proximity. I hadn't made that charm yet to help me resist him.

"In Sweet?"

He had a point.

"We have some very nice bed-and-breakfasts in the area. Beautiful old mansions where I'm sure you"—I motioned to his people—"and your entourage would be quite happy."

He made a motion toward the car and a man came out with a bag. "Are you afraid of me?" He shook his head. "I've been on the plane for the last eighteen hours and I'm exhausted. And I must admit I'm also very curious about this world you have separate from your work."

"Well, it's really hard to do that when my work shows up on my front lawn. Are they staying, too?" I pointed to the cars.

"Only my executive assistant, Maridad. You met her at Duban Industries. I didn't think it proper for me to stay in a single woman's home without some kind of chaperone. Maridad fits the bill quite nicely."

"Whatever, sure. Hope she doesn't mind the smell of paint." I opened the door and he motioned for the woman to leave the truck and come inside. She suppressed a laugh and I knew she had something she wanted to say to me, but she didn't dare.

I put them in the other two guest rooms and climbed into my bed. What the hell is the sheik thinking? Stupid man. And why am I so damn happy to see him? I hate this. Really I do.

Twenty

Thursday, 11 A.M.
Sweet, Texas
Houseguests: 2
Frustrated witches: 1

It's my fault. I know it. When I sat with those witches sharing tea the other day I thought of the sheik and I accidentally brought him here through telepathy. Now I can't get rid of him.

When I went downstairs to fix breakfast I found Maridad in the kitchen hovering over the coffeepot waiting for it to fill. Someone was addicted to caffeine. I can relate, but my poison is Diet Coke.

The place smelled of paint, with the warm aroma of rich toasted beans mixed in. With the sun streaming in, the golden walls made the room even more beautiful than I had imagined. I had to thank my crew from last night again for their hard work.

"Good morning," I said to Maridad as I pulled out the eggs from the fridge. "Would you like some breakfast?"

"Coffee and toast are all I need, thank you." Even at eight in the morning she had that formal clipped tone. Not rude, but efficient. I wondered if she ever let her guard down. "But I'm certain Sheik Azir would enjoy a full breakfast. He's out in your conservatory looking over the plants."

Grabbed a Diet Coke from the fridge and poured Azir a cup of coffee. Sighed as I watched him through the French doors. Such a gorgeous man.

I had a feeling he'd been lying to me last night and a call to the hangar this morning confirmed my suspicions. There wasn't a damn thing wrong with his jet.

"Sheik, please don't touch that." I stepped through the doors.

He had been reaching up for a vine and pulled his hand back.

"That's nightshade, also known as belladonna. Too much of it can kill you, just by touching the flowers." I handed him the oversized cup and he sipped cautiously.

Even in the conservatory the air was cool, and the smell of damp earth mixed with the perfume from the flowers overloaded the senses. I love it.

"Do you have many deadly plants in your garden?" His right eyebrow raised, and he flashed stunning white teeth in a smile that would turn most girls to mush.

I'm one of them.

"They are only dangerous when not handled or used properly." I pointed to a beautiful ruby red rose. "This gorgeous dame can be mixed with honey for love potions and is quite harmless. The vine growing above it—there with the almost black buds—those flowers can also be crushed and mixed with honey, but bring about convulsions and internal hemorrhaging seconds after being ingested."

"Remind me to never make you an enemy." He more snorted than laughed and shook his head. "Don't you worry about a child or an idiot adult wandering in here and hurting themselves?"

I shrugged. "Don't have many visitors, and usually those who do make it through the door know better. As for children, that's why the poisonous ones are up high. Only the idiot adults need worry."

He ignored that last comment and walked toward the herbs. "Are all of these used in your potions and spells?"

"Most of them, yes."

"I smell sage. What do you use that for?" He bent over sniffing, but I noticed he kept his free hand in his pocket.

"Sage purifies everything from the air when it's burned, and your body when used in lotions and soaps. Centuries ago it was thought to bring wisdom and clarity. It does have a knack for getting rid of negative energy. And it's great on chicken."

"I've never seen this. What is it?"

"That's meadow rue; it's used to break hexes, as a flea repellent, and against predatory animals like werewolves."

His head popped around on that one. "There's no such thing."

"Just because you haven't seen something doesn't mean it's not real." I turned on the mist over the rose garden. Watering in the morning keeps the plants from molding.

"Have you ever seen a werewolf?"

I shrugged. "No, but I've heard lots of stories. And I've met people who swear they are real."

"I'm not sure what to believe anymore." He faced me and the serious tone told me he had a lot more than plants on his mind. The handsome smile was gone.

"What is it?"

"I'm ashamed." He crossed his arms and turned away from me.

"Of what?"

"Of my need to be close to you." He faced me again, brown eyes staring intensely.

"Oh." What the heck could I say to that? "Look, I thought I made it clear that we can't be any more than friends."

"Just because you want it so, doesn't make it happen." He blew out a breath. "But that isn't why I needed to talk to you. Is there some way you can keep people from hearing what I have to say?"

"We're in the middle of nowhere, at least five miles from town." I closed my eyes and used my mind to search the house. "And Maridad is working on her laptop in the living room so no one will hear you."

"It's not enough. There must be a spell or something you can do to block out everyone." He frowned and crossed his arms against his chest. "Including witches, warlocks, wizards, or anyone else in the magic world I don't know about."

"Why would you . . ." Understanding dawned. "Oh! No problem."

I waved my hand in a circle around us and asked for protection from prying ears and eyes. The sounds of the birds and wind outside ceased and we were engulfed in silence.

A white mist surrounded us that would keep all ears and minds at bay. He pulled out a wooden stool from under the gardening worktable and sat down.

I did the same. "Okay, it's you and me. Tell me why you're worried about warlocks and wizards listening in."

"Someone seems to know my every move, and it has to be more than a leak in my family or at Duban Industries." He shifted on the seat, shoulders hunched.

I'd never seen him like this.

"When I said I didn't know what to believe, I mean about

everything." He placed his hands on his knees and the sadness in his eyes yanked at my heart.

"You can tell me anything, Azir. I'll help you."

He tapped his foot in a nervous action. "Bronwyn, you are the one person I trust right now. The only one. And it makes me feel guilty for lying to you about the jet. I only did it so that I could see you. I think clearer when you are around."

"For future reference, you didn't need to lie about the jet. If we're going to be friends and business associates, I'd appreciate nothing but the truth in the future. Lecture's over. Why are you so upset? Is it your father?"

This strong, proud man suddenly looked like a lost boy. "My father is dead." He rubbed his hand over his face as if trying to erase the anguish the words caused. The action tugged my heart and made it difficult for me to swallow. Such grief.

"I'm sorry. Wait—didn't he try to kill you? I don't understand." I reached across and gathered his hands in my own.

"That's the worst of it. Someone tried to make it look like my father was involved. The attacks began two months ago, but I found out that my father has been dead for months."

"But you told me that you keep in contact with him."

"The woman my father had been living with found me earlier in the week. She's been hiding in Dubai for months with a child who is my half brother."

"So some woman calls and says that he's dead and she has his kid. Come on, Azir. You see the worst of humanity on a regular basis. You know how it works. She just wants money from you."

He held up a hand. "No, no. It isn't like that. She didn't ask for anything. In fact, she risked her life and the child's to contact me. She did it out of love for my father."

"Maybe you should just start from the beginning." I shifted my seat closer to him.

"I told you that my father had been working with several tribes trying to find a fair and peaceful resolution to some boundary issues. Everything had gone well and he'd even managed to get some of the tribes to work together on different projects.

"One night rebels invaded the camp where he stayed and they took my father hostage. He escaped a few days later but he'd been shot. By the time he made it back to the camp he only had a few more hours to live."

He met my eyes. The misery in him tore at my soul.

"He told the woman everything and made her promise to give me a message. She said that he warned me to trust no one, including those I hold dearest. Even my mother and sister were under suspicion because someone in my family wanted me dead."

And there it was. The final blow. He had known for weeks that someone in his family had been involved but none of us suspected his mother or sister. I still didn't.

"It doesn't mean they're directly involved, Azir. Only that they may be unknowing pawns in someone else's game." I thought about the tears in his sister's eyes when she greeted him that night, and his mother holding him so tight as if she never wanted to let him go. Those women loved him. I was certain.

I jumped off the stool and turned to face the door of the conservatory. I let my mind race across the miles and found Shera asleep in her bed. I flitted through her thoughts and saw nothing except she still longed for the man she loved.

Skipping to Kazamar, I probed more. I delved through the recesses in her mind. I unfolded memories and searched for any clue that she might betray her son. Again nothing.

"They're not involved, at least not willingly so," I told him.

"You read their minds that fast?"

"Yes, my connection to them helps me find them quickly. And, Azir, I found nothing."

"That leaves my brother."

I sighed and closed my eyes. I combed the earth for him and could not locate his brother. I tried again and nothing. Opened my eyes and turned to face the sheik.

"Bad news or really bad news first?"

"Bad news?"

Optimist. Even in his darkest time he had hope. I admired that.

"Okay, the bad news is your brother may be dead."

Azir took in a sharp breath. At his stricken look I decided to get it all over with at once.

"The really bad news is, if he's alive he's under the care of some powerful magic. I can't tap into him at all—his presence has been erased from the earth."

Azir shoved his hands through his hair. His watery eyes broke my heart. I knew I sounded callous, but I was afraid his brother posed a grave danger to the sheik.

"It would explain a lot. Like why I got nothing but business deals from him when I prowled his mind before. Most people at least have thoughts about relationships or what they had for dinner. All I got from him was work-related details. Nothing else. Someone protected those other memories from me."

"That doesn't make my brother guilty of trying to kill me."

"No, but would you prefer to believe that it's Shera or Kazamar? I'm sorry. I don't mean to be cruel, but it's time we did something about this and ended the threat once and for all. Do you have any meetings scheduled with your brother in the next few weeks?"

"He'll be in Brussels this weekend while we are there. Are you certain it is him?" He let out a slow breath.

"No, and I won't be until we can talk to him. Do you know

of any reason why he would work with your cousin, why they would both want you dead?"

"You know about what happened with my cousin and uncle, but my brother took my side in the ordeal. He stood by me through everything and grieved as hard as I did for the death of our aunt."

None of this made sense. I'd seen the brothers together and knew they had a loving relationship. "It's possible he's not aware of his actions and that he's being manipulated by magic. They may be using him to get to you, much like they did your father. And I'm sorry, by the way—about your dad. Have you told the rest of the family?"

"I can't. Not until we find out who is doing this. It's important for them to believe that I think my father is still alive."

"Why?"

"Because I've been getting notes and sometimes emails from my father the last few months."

"Oh, so unless his ghost has been busy— Wait, emails from the desert?"

"Yes, there is such a thing as wireless communication, Bronwyn. Not as effective as your ability to whip in and read a mind, but it serves the rest of us well. We know how to trace the emails and letters, but those things take time."

I might have a way of speeding up the process but didn't want to give him false hope. "When will you leave for Brussels?"

"I thought perhaps we could go together at your scheduled time tomorrow."

That meant another day and night here at the house. Great.

"Sure. Um, I've got some plans this afternoon but I could show you around town. It should take all of about six minutes."

He laughed.

"Only you could make me smile at a time like this." He reached out to pull me into a hug.

Wanted to remind him of the "no hugging the clients" rule that I made up when we were in Oslo, but it didn't seem the right time. The man needed comfort. Caring arms to soothe a sad soul.

But it was just a hug. While we did have chemistry, I couldn't stop thinking of Sam. I wanted to be in Sam's arms.

I stepped away and cleared the spell. The mist dissipated, leaving nothing but bright sunshine filtering in through the glass. I took one last sniff of the earthy scent of my garden, and we went into the kitchen for breakfast.

Getting ready to meet Sam for lunch. I'm sure he's going to be way excited that I've got the sheik and Maridad along for the ride. Oh, well.

Twenty-one

Thursday, 7 P.M.
Sweet, Texas
Boyfriends who get along: 2 (Okay, technically, they are friends who are
boys. Only one of them is a boyfriend, and I'm not even sure about that.)

I don't know what kind of karmic wickedness I'm trying to
work out but I wish it would hurry up and happen.

With the sheik and Maridad in tow, I checked the jets at the
hangar and made sure we were good to go for tomorrow. Then
we headed over to Lulu's for lunch with Sam. I had a chance to
call him and let him know that we had extra guests for the meal.
He had been surprisingly accepting and said he might be a tad
late, but would definitely be there.

At the diner Ms. Helen and Ms. Johnnie threw a fit over the
sheik. Seems Ms. Johnnie had herself an Arab lover back in the
day, who bought her a Bentley. Every once in a while he sends
her a new car, even though they haven't seen each other in more
than thirty years.

The sheik marveled at the collection of photos sporting Ms. Helen and Ms. Johnnie, spread over the walls of the cozy café.

"You've lived an interesting life." Azir pointed to the photo of Ms. Johnnie with a college basketball team from Austin. She must have been about twenty at the time, and every man in the picture had his eyes on her.

"Oh, my, yes. Those boys were absolutely delicious." Ms. Johnnie winked. "See that one, third left from the bottom? He was husband number one. Such a wonderful boy. I really loved him, too, for about a year."

Then she walked off to check on some other patrons.

The sheik looked at me, and I only shrugged. "I have no idea, but I guarantee you if she ever shares the story it'll be an interesting one."

We sat down at the big table in the back just as Sam, dressed in dark denims with a deep burgundy shirt, walked in. He smiled, no hint of the previous night's jealousy in his face.

My gorgeous Sam. I sighed, and Azir looked at me strangely.

Sam shook hands with Maridad and the sheik, and then leaned in and kissed me on the cheek.

Damn, he smelled good. Sandalwood with a hint of orange spice and patchouli.

"Oh, how's Mr. Gunther?" I asked Sam as he sat down at the table. "I thought we might stop by and see him this afternoon if he's up to it."

"He's doing much better. Whatever you did seemed to work." Sam grabbed one of the plastic menus from the center of the table and put his napkin in his lap. "And I know he'd enjoy a visit before you leave town again."

Ms. Johnnie came and took our drink orders. It was quiet for a few minutes while we perused the plastic-covered menus.

Sam grabbed the sugar and put two of the packets in his iced tea as he spoke. "I don't know what you like, but everything here is good."

Azir and Maridad watched him and then they did the same thing. Never dawned on me that they might not have had iced tea before.

"Is the chicken-fried steak a chicken steak? I've never heard of such a thing." Maridad's puzzled look made me smile.

Sam turned to her. "Well, it's not really chicken. It's a beef cutlet that is battered and fried to perfection. This is one of the best places to try it if you're willing."

When Ms. Johnnie came back we ordered a round of chicken-fried steaks, mashed potatoes, and Texas toast. I'd worry about the food coma later.

Again the conversation lulled. Without the distraction of menus to hide behind, the tension around the table became palpable. With these two handsome men in the same space it was difficult for me to think.

"We'll definitely go by and see Mr. G today." Okay, so I repeated myself, but I was desperate to get the convo going and I'm not exactly the queen of small talk.

"You'll be surprised by how much better he looks. He's made quite a turnaround."

"Who is Mr. Gunther?" The sheik stirred his tea slowly. Took a sip and then smiled. It's hard not to like Lulu's tea.

"He's a patient at the nursing home. Bronwyn's been helping with his case. He suffers from Alzheimer's and she found a way to help with his memory." Sam grabbed a piece of corn bread from the red basket Ms. Johnnie had put in the middle of the table.

Again the other two diners followed his actions and

slathered butter onto their bread. I bit my lip to keep from laughing.

"Um, yes—he's a great guy, full of wonderful stories." I coughed into my napkin to get myself under control. Watching Sam and the sheik play Simon Says gave me a fit of giggles. "I devised a potion that gives him mental clarity. Had to go back to the drawing board earlier in the week, though."

"Back to the drawing board?" Maridad asked before she took a small bite of her corn bread. Her eyes widened and she looked at the bread and stuffed the whole thing in her mouth. Ms. Johnnie's baked goods do that to people. She absolutely inspires pigdom.

"I had to rework the potion so that we could boost his energy. Part of the disease—it's okay if I talk about this, Sam?" I'd remembered his doctor-patient thing and didn't want to cross any lines.

"Sure, you're not a doctor and Mr. Gunther's given his permission anyway."

"OK, so fatigue is also a part of the disease and I had to find a way to boost his energy without crashing his immune system or causing more memory troubles. It wasn't easy but it sounds like we're on the right track."

"Fascinating. So do you normally use magic in your practice?" The sheik turned to Sam. He said it in a way that made the other man smile. Not condescending or reproachful but more in awe. I wondered how he knew Sam was a warlock.

Knowing Azir, he'd probably had the doctor investigated.

"Not to the extent of what Bronwyn does. I'm a natural healer, so yes, I guess magic comes into it."

I'd never heard Sam talk to anyone else about his abilities. He seemed so comfortable with the sheik. I hadn't known what to think about the two men dining together.

Well, that's not true. I thought for sure there'd be some jeal-ousy, but they were genuinely interested in one another. The sheik asked about Sam's practice and Sam questioned the other man about his work with Duban Industries.

"The company name sounds familiar, and not just because I know my father uses your golf balls." Sam flagged Ms. Helen over when she came out of the kitchen and asked if she had any fried okra today. She ran back and then brought a huge basket with ranch dressing.

I wasn't sure what Maridad and Azir would think of the heart-clogging meal, but what the heck. They seemed to enjoy the experience of trying something new.

Sam thumped himself on the head. "I know. Did you work with my father on the new wing of Children's Hospital in Chicago?"

"I was involved, and hired the architect."

Turned out Azir and Sam's father were old friends and Sam knew about the sheik's humanitarian efforts. After that it was a virtual lovefest between the two men. It ended, after slices of chocolate pie, with the sheik offering to take Sam on his next mission to save the world.

Whatever.

Later in the afternoon we checked in on Mr. Gunther and I took him another journal. I know it's wrong but I keep thinking that if he feels like he has to fill another one, maybe he won't give up on life too soon.

I've got to pack for the trip to Brussels and then we're going over to Kira's for dinner with everyone. She's decided to put on a last-minute Mexican fiesta for Maridad and the sheik.

I'm bringing the margarita mix and sparkly lights to decorate the living area. It should be an interesting evening.

Friday, noon
Waning moon
New York City
Confused witches: 1
Spells: 1 (I did it for mental clarity)

I flew us into New York and we are refueling. The other pilots, who (under Azir's insistence) are flying us to Brussels, are doing a final flight check.

The sheik is all business today but he cut loose more than I've ever seen him last night. He and Maridad don't drink, it being against their religion, but they did enjoy the virgin margaritas I mixed. I did the same since I had to pilot the plane this morning.

Kira fixed every kind of enchilada known to man. There were cheese, sour cream, chicken, beef, and spinach along with a giant pot of refried beans and bowl of Spanish rice. I'd never seen so much food in one place.

After the artery-damaging lunch we had, I was surprised to see Azir load his plate with one of everything. Cocked my head and raised an eyebrow as I stared at the contents he'd piled on. Could this be the same guy who served fish and vegetables for days on end?

"I hear Americans eat their emotions, so I've decided to join the crowd." He smiled.

"Well, at the rate you're going you're headed for a nervous breakdown." I'd meant it as a joke, but when his face turned into a frown I mentally clonked myself in the head. If anyone had the right to lose it big time, it was this guy.

"I think I'll join you." I laughed, trying to take the edge off my words.

Kira's dining room wasn't large enough for all of us, but

she'd spread large pillows throughout the living area. I loved her style. It was like hippie meets old world with a lot of bold colors thrown in. The sofa and pillows were tapestry with touches of deep maroon velvet. But in the doorway separating the dining room from the other part of the house hung beads, which had been formed into a picture of the Mona Lisa. Anywhere else it would be absurd, but in Kira's home, it worked.

I watched from the archway as the sheik was drawn into conversation with my friends. They made a real effort to make him feel welcome. He looked more relaxed and happy than I'd seen him in weeks, sitting there on the floor of Kira's living room.

"Is he in danger?" Sam stood beside me. I'd been so absorbed in what was before me that I hadn't noticed.

"I can't talk about it"—I turned to him—"but yes."

"And it's your job to protect him?"

"You know it is."

"He's a good man, but it hurts me to see you with him." Sam stared at me.

"Really? You seem so comfortable around each other. . . ." Tried to act nonchalant, but he saw through it.

"Oh, don't for a minute think I'm not jealous, Bronwyn. I'm absolutely seething with it. That man can offer you the world. And while I could make you comfortable, the most I have to give you is me."

I didn't think it possible but my heart caught in my throat. "Sam," I whispered.

"Do you love him?"

What a question. And it wasn't easy to answer.

"I care for him." I shook my head. "I know what you think, but I have a rule about getting involved with clients. I just don't do it."

"I wish I could believe that. You can fool yourself if you like, but the rest of us can see when you look at him that you've gone way past caring. And I'd bet my life savings that he's in love with you."

"No, Sam, you'd be wrong. He might be in lust with me, but it isn't love."

"Open your eyes, Bron. Really open them. You're the one who is wrong. That man is in love with you. Trust me, I see it in the mirror every day."

Sam didn't sound angry; sad more than anything. He took the plate from my hand and drew me into the corner nook of the dining room where Kira had set out all the food.

"I love you." He cupped my face in his hands. "No matter what happens in the next few weeks, I want you to know that we belong together. You are my heart."

He kissed me long and hard as if he knew I had no response. That isn't true. I loved him, too. I just couldn't say it yet.

I also had feelings for the sheik, but not what I felt for Sam. Unfortunately, in that moment I couldn't verbalize the way he made me feel.

He showed me words weren't needed.

· He leaned against the wall and pulled me with him. Wrapping our arms around one another, we stood in silence just hugging. I could see the shimmer of a purple aura as our magic mixed. In many ways he completed me, and I didn't even know how exactly.

I nibbled at his lips and then deepened the kiss, sliding my tongue into his mouth as I pushed my pelvis into him. I wanted to show him what I couldn't tell him. And I prayed he understood.

Someone cleared a throat behind me and I turned to see Maridad. "I'm sorry, I—the enchiladas are quite tasty and I wanted to try the ones with the cheese." She rambled on nervously. "I didn't mean to disturb you."

"It's okay. They're the ones with the sour cream sauce." I kissed Sam on the cheek and squeezed him tight one last time. Then I turned to help her.

Sam walked into the other room.

"I apologize, I didn't realize you were in here." She put her hand on my shoulder.

I smiled. "Don't worry about it."

"Your doctor loves you very much. You can see it in his eyes." Funny, Sam had said the same thing to me, only he'd been referring to the sheik.

"He's a good man."

"You are unsure of your heart?" Maridad's questions hit the point rather quickly. She never minced words.

"I guess you could say that. I care for him more than I thought possible, but . . ."

"Again, I say I'm sorry. I didn't mean to intrude into your private business. I worry about Sheik Azir. He too seems to care for you, and I wouldn't like to see him get hurt."

"Nor would I. And I think you're right about the caring thing. If I'm more honest than I should be, I'll tell you it goes both ways. Hence my troubles with the good doctor."

"My mother, who seems to understand the relationships between men and women better than anyone I've ever known, says that when the heart is certain it makes the choice and it doesn't matter what our minds tell us." Maridad smiled as she added refried beans to her plate.

"That sounds exactly like something my mom would say. How about you? Is there someone you love back in Dubai?"

"Yes, very much. But he has no idea." She looked through the beads at Azir.

I wondered what she meant by that. Was she in love with Azir? She didn't act like a scorned woman, and she had treated me with nothing but respect. I didn't get the chance to ask because she joined the crowd in the living room before I could question her.

The sheik and Maridad?

No one wanted to leave the party, but with the early flight, we had to go a little after midnight. I obviously break the rules when it comes to getting involved with clients, but I take the rules of flying seriously and I needed my beauty sleep.

As I sit here watching the sheik dictate a business proposal to Maridad, it's hard to imagine the man in the blue pin-striped suit and starched collar as the same guy in jeans and T-shirt with ranchero sauce on his chin last night.

He looked up at me a few minutes ago and my stomach fluttered with the wings of a million butterflies. Then he winked at me and smiled.

Geez. I wish he wouldn't do things like that. It makes me all confused.

And if Maridad is in love with the sheik then all bets are off. I can't even think about it.

There are so many other things I need to be worried about, like keeping the PM and Azir alive over the next few weeks. Both men are in serious danger, something I sensed yesterday, and it all centers in Brussels.

Twenty-two

Monday, 1 P.M.
Brussels
Ghost hunters: 1

Azir is seriously into castles. This time we are on the side of a mountain looking down over Brussels in a home that was built in the fifteenth century. We're talking drawbridge with a moat. Insane. But very, very cool.

I don't know who owns this spread, but there are about twenty politicos hanging full-time and there's still plenty of room.

My room is almost a duplicate of the one I had in Oslo. Dark velvet draperies and a huge bed so tall I need a step stool to get into it. There are strange tapestries of not so pleasant battle scenes on every wall. Gives the feeling that the owner has a boner for war.

The history of the place smacks you in the face at every turn.

But it's weird. I'm having déjà vu so much I have trouble figuring out what reality I'm supposed to be in. When I walked through the huge wooden doors of the castle I knew exactly where the kitchen, dining rooms, and everything else was located. Never have I experienced such a connection with a place.

Everything is so strange that I called Garnout for wizardly advice and he's checking into my past-life history.

"Sometimes when you intuitively know a place, it's an indication that you've visited either through astral projection or in a past life," Garnout told me. I could tell he was busy helping customers. The cash register dinged and once in a while he'd pull the phone away and in a hushed voice say, "Please come back and see us again."

"If you're busy we can do this later." I touched one of the tapestries and closed my eyes. The battle had taken place only a few miles from here. The smell of horses and blood . . . so strong . . . and a feeling of extreme dread. The bile rose and my stomach tightened in pain.

"Bronwyn?" His voice pulled me from the void.

"Sorry, Garnout."

"Yes, well, good to have you back. Now if you can stay with me a few minutes and let me get some details I'll see what I can do. Oh, and you must be careful while you're there."

"What's going on? I'm slipping back and forth into something that feels like memories. Nothing like this has ever happened to me before." I moved to the window to look out on the cliffs of white snow. Brussels was warmer than Oslo, but still cold.

I remembered peering out this window before and begging for springtime. Argh! Too weird.

He cleared his throat, which told me he knew I had drifted off again. "My guess is the place is tied to a past life or to one of your ancestors. These things do get passed down, but only a few of us have the capacity to tune into them.

"If I'm right, you may experience memories as if they are

reality. You'll also have a stronger sense of the dead. Most of those old European castles are teeming with ghosts."

I could hear him flipping pages in a book.

"Do you feel displaced—right place but wrong time perhaps?"

"That's exactly what it feels like. And you're right about the spirits. There are many throughout the castle. The weird part is there's no negative charge that usually comes with a ghost. This is more like leftover auras walking around. I know it's impossible, but . . ."

"No, not impossible at all. Again, my dear, I stress that you must be very careful. Before leaving your room, do a clarifying spell that keeps you in the present. Sounds as if we are dealing with a combination of magic—"

He placed his hand over the phone, but I heard him.

"Oh, really. Young man, please put that down. That sphere is filled with blood magic and you'll die a terrible death if it should happen to break. Thank you. I believe"—I could hear the rustle of Garnout's robes as he raised his arm to do a spell—"you've accidentally found yourself in the wrong place. Please allow me to assist you to the door. You'll remember nothing of this place or its contents. Be gone." I heard the door shut and the bell tinkle.

I laughed. Some numbskull had obviously wandered into the shop by mistake. Any idiot knows you don't touch a Garion sphere unless you're trying to kill a Kalmàk demon.

"My apologies."

"No problem." I glanced at my watch. "Thanks for the help, but I've got to go. I need to get things ready for our visitors. If you find something, give me a call."

"Be aware that someone may be using magic to cause you harm there." His voice was more serious than usual. "You've been up against some powerful magic and someone like that could have researched your past lives as I'm about to do. Information like that, in the wrong hands, can be extremely dangerous. You must protect yourself."

I don't talk about it much, but I envy Garnout's ability to travel through time, into the spirit world, and pretty much wherever he wants to go. It's one of the big perks of being a wizard.

We rang off and I did a quick clarifying spell to protect me from other magic and to keep my head clear of the past.

Had a lot of things to get ready. Gave the sheik and PM brand-new charms and used Malandro's protection spell.

But there's one big problem: someone else used magic here, recently, within the walls of the castle.

As we drove through Brussels, I had felt the magic emanating from several sources. Nothing negative, but every now and then I sensed a glimmer of something powerful. Tugged at me. About the time I sensed it, the source dissipated.

The closer we moved toward the castle the more intense the magic felt. Perhaps the witch or warlock is here. I'm so tired; wish I could grab a nap, but no time. Have to—

4 P.M.
Pissed-off witches: 1

Someone's screwing with me in a big way. I passed out for almost three hours. Woke up stretched across the bed with my clothes on, holding a man's jacket in my hands. Some kind of tuxedo jacket but from way back. Smells like Grandma Erma's closet. A cross of mothballs and lilac cologne.

I'd still be asleep if nerdy Miles hadn't barged in.

"Bronwyn, I've banged on the door for two minutes. What the hell?"

"Miles?"

"Don't you know we have guests coming? I thought you needed hours to do all of that magic crap." He walked into the room like he owned it and tilted that head with a disgusted smirk on his face.

"I must have fallen asleep. Get over it, Miles. I'm running on empty as it is. Haven't had more than about twelve hours' sleep over three days." That must be it—my body just gave out. Thanks to the sheik's visit to Sweet and my troubles with Sam, I hadn't had much rest. Most nights were spent wondering why I'd found myself in this situation with two men.

"We could all do with more rest, but this is an important party tonight and everything must be perfect." He flitted around the room. "If the prime minister's plan goes awry, all hell will break loose."

I pulled up to my knees on the tall bed and towered over him. "What plan?"

His eyes rounded and lips tightened. The squirrel had said too much.

"What fucking plan, Miles?" I gave him my evil witch stare and he rolled his eyes. Asshole. That usually works on nerds like him.

"If the prime minister wanted you to be privy to the information, he would have told you." When he stepped away from the bed, I knew he was afraid I'd physically harm him. At least he'd been a little scared.

"Let's put it this way, panda bait, either you tell or I go to the PM and spill that you let me in on the game."

He didn't like that ultimatum at all and pushed his curly brown hair away from his forehead. His face scrunched into an ugly grimace. The PM wouldn't appreciate Miles sharing state secrets, but that wasn't my problem.

"I'll only tell you that he and the sheik have invited three power brokers who have much to lose if Azir declines their offer." He picked an invisible hair from his sleeve and headed to the door.

"You try to pass through that door before you tell me everything and I'll turn you into a fluffy poodle with sassy pink bows in your hair." He'd probably like the damn bows, but he stopped in his tracks.

A brass paperweight from the end table zoomed across the room and landed an inch from Miles's foot.

"Now, there's no need for violence, Bronwyn." He paled.

"I didn't do it."

His wide brown eyes toured my face to see if he could believe me. "Then who did?"

"Don't know, but it looks like I've got a friendly ghost hanging out with me, and he or she wants you to spill your guts."

After that, Miles couldn't tell me fast enough. Seems the PM and Azir had set these power brokers up because they believed one of them was working with the cousin. The PM's security staff found a paper trail from the redhead in his office that led to the three men. It was possible they were all involved.

Probed the house for a witch or warlock and found three on the premises. Yes, this could be an interesting evening and I might be able to speed along this plan of Azir and the PM's with a little magic and catch myself a bad guy.

Almost midnight
Bad guys: Too many

Not sure how much I helped the sheik and PM tonight. I had my own power struggles with the magical community. During cocktails I positioned myself near my charges. The event took place in the library, a large room filled from floor to ceiling with books. The ornate wood and brass accents gave the room a warm and cozy feeling, but that didn't last long.

Before I had a chance to take a sip of my fizzy water, two warlocks approached.

The taller of the two had beady black eyes that were nowhere close to friendly, and his charcoal black hair with a silver streak had been smoothed back into a ponytail. He introduced himself. "I am Wallace; I wish you no harm."

Wally the Warlock. Oh, please.

When I shook his hand I felt the power emanating from him. He didn't try to push his magic onto me, but his strength was palpable. He reminded me of someone I'd met before, but he didn't act like he knew me. Strange.

I turned to the other man.

Rotund would be a nice way of describing this basketball with a head and legs. A small amount of power, but enough to do damage. "I am Sphere; I wish you no harm."

"Happy to meet you both. I am Bronwyn. Are both of you here protecting someone?" The pair of them looked like Laurel and Hardy.

"Don't believe either one of them—they lie as easily as they breathe," a familiar female voice said behind them.

"Lesha, what are you doing here? And how is your brother?" I reached out and she clasped my hand. Her long dress fitted sensually to her perfect form.

"He's still in a coma but my family looks after him." She stared at the floor for a second and then met my eyes. "I'm still grateful you didn't kill him when you could have in Oslo. And I'm here for the same reason as you, to protect a charge." She let go of my hand.

"These two disreputable characters are here for protection but you shouldn't turn your back on them." She motioned toward the two men.

"I for one resent your implications that we are here for any other purpose than the safety of our charges," Sphere whispered indignantly to Lesha.

Back and forth they went with the insults until we were called in to dinner. I noticed Wally didn't say much, but his eyes darted around the room every time Power Broker One—John Stamon, the owner of Stamon Enterprises—moved.

He also kept an eye on the prime minister and Azir. I didn't like Wally. Something smarmy about him, but I didn't see him as much of a threat.

Sphere's charge, Power Broker Two—Sheik Kamar—seemed a likely suspect for our bad guy of the week. More than once I caught him in the middle of a heated discussion with Azir.

Lesha's client, international financier Paul Nash, treated her more like a date. He led her into the dining room and arranged for her to sit next to him.

I was so busy keeping up with the magical folk that I had little time to get involved with my own charges' plans. Whatever maneuvering they did seemed to work. When the evening was over and we headed upstairs, they both smiled and whispered to each other like schoolboys.

I'm a bit cranky over the fact that neither of them has bothered to share a word with me about what they tried to accomplish. If it hadn't been for Miles, who was conspicuously absent tonight, I wouldn't even know what they were up to.

I've made my own list of suspects, and I have a feeling Wally may be my dissipating warlock in Dubai. His hair is a slightly different color of black but he could have used a glamour spell to change it. And I think he's holding back on his powers.

Sphere's a blowhard. I'm not sure what his game is, but he's up to no good. One thing I did discover is that the two warlocks aren't working together. They fought constantly at dinner, throwing out innuendos and cutting remarks. There's a competition between them, but I'm not sure what it is.

Lesha on the other hand kept to herself and didn't join in the fray. Once in a while she'd catch my eye and smile. I don't trust her exactly, but she's low on my list of suspects. She did try to save my life in Oslo.

That creepy feeling that someone watches me constantly is something I can't get used to. I'm sure it's a spirit, but who knows? Checked my voice mail to see if Garnout had any news, but he didn't leave a message.

Did hear from Sam, who said he missed me and that Mr. Gunther felt better. That's the best news I've had all day.

No one claimed the old tuxedo jacket when I took it downstairs. This is so weird. I put it on the back of the chair while I'm writing. The smell is familiar, but I can't place it.

Aack! Chill on my spine. The presence is here again and damn—

Twenty-three

Tuesday, 4 A.M.
Brussels
Perturbed witches: 1

Woke up with a start and heard the wards protecting my room buzzing. Realized someone was standing outside the door. Ran across the room, threw it open. Nothing.

Peered down the hall but didn't see anything. Someone had been there, I know it. Thought it might have been Wally, who I'm certain possesses the power to dissipate. The wards I had on the door were strong and no matter who might have been on the other side, no one would have made it through without experiencing a great deal of pain.

But the ringing of the wards isn't what woke me. The presence in this room is what startled me into consciousness. In fact I'm sure it yelled, "Wake up, witch!" A strong, deep, bellowing voice.

Argh! I'm all wrinkled again because I passed out in my clothes. I've got to stop doing that.

I must make contact with this spirit, but I'm too tired right now. Need more sleep. And if the prime minister and Azir don't need me, I'm turning into Detective Bronwyn. Enough with all this warlock subterfuge, I'm doing some sleuthing.

The tapestry in my room reads in Latin, "Know thy enemy."

I damn sure will.

9 A.M.

Sick twerps: 1

Miles the nerd came by. He had a flu bug and that's why he missed dinner last night. The color of a swamp frog, he still didn't look terribly healthy.

"It came on rather suddenly, right after I left your room yesterday." The pale green of his skin gleamed ghastly with perspiration in the morning light. "I wondered if you might have some herbs or a potion to help with the nausea."

"You should have come by last night. I'm sure I could have helped you through the worst of it." I moved around the room gathering ingredients off of the massive mahogany desk where I worked.

"I would have tried but it hit me hard. I vomited for about an hour and then passed out. The next thing I knew it was four in the morning. I made it to your door but when I tried to knock something zapped me. I ran back to my room across the hall and passed out again."

So it had been Miles outside the door. He must have run like a jackrabbit and I probably just missed him. I didn't realize his room was so close.

It made sense. I couldn't imagine why a warlock or witch would try to get past a ward. They would have felt the protection spell long before they came upon it.

Miles had been holding on to the back of the chair but moved around and collapsed into it. Didn't want to scare him, but I feared he might be the victim of some dark magic.

"Miles, do you still have the charm I made you a few months ago?" I put the final ingredients, including chamomile and licorice, in a small glass and gave it a stir.

"I thought so, but when I looked for it this morning I couldn't find it anywhere. In fact, I don't think I've seen it since that night you fought the two warlocks in the street in Oslo."

Gave him the potion and did a deep cleansing spell. Before he left he felt well enough to tell me that I had a meeting in twenty minutes with my charges.

Thanks for the notice, jerkwad.

Guess I'll have to put off my plans to check out Lesha, Sphere, and Wally for now.

Oh, well.

3 P.M.

That didn't last long. The prime minister and Azir wanted to make sure I'm ready for their meeting this evening. We're going into town for some bigwig get-together.

Need to check my wardrobe to make sure I have something business dressy to wear. Hope I remembered my jacket with the velvet trim.

The strangest thing happened when I came back to my room. I heard singing. A soft Irish lilt. Sounded like one of those songs my grandma used to sing when my brother and I stayed with her during the summers at the beach house on Block Island.

We'd spend hours searching for shells, staring into tide pools with magnifying glasses, and making sand castles. Every night my grandmother would fix a huge meal and let us help. Then we'd eat out on the back porch and listen to the black water hit the sand. The waves sang us to sleep each night. It's one of the few times in my life when I can remember being at peace.

I couldn't find the source of the singing here at the castle. I have a definite feeling it was meant for me. The sound gave me a strong sense of inner calm and made me feel comforted, even though I didn't know I needed that kind of thing.

Curious, I cleared the room with sage and tried to meditate. Sent my mind out to the dead walking the castle and discovered a multitude of souls clustering around.

It's more difficult to read the dead than the living. Mostly because they remember only what they want to. Flashes of light and then pictures moved through my head at an alarming rate. Then they all seemed to fade and focus on one scene.

Tiny wisps of memories trailed along, bringing pictures of a young servant lacing up her beautiful lady's gown and brushing the elegant woman's hair into an upsweep of shining blonde curls. I could smell lavender and roses.

A man, with a formal tuxedo coat, the one I'd had in my hand, bowed gallantly. He reached for the elegant woman and guided her to the ballroom. I may have been projecting, but he looked so much like Sam it was eerie.

They danced, twirling in circles. The glow from candles lighting the room blurred into a golden haze.

Then the man stood over her grave, the grief weighing heavy lines on his face. She had been a witch, but her potions couldn't save her from the disease that wracked her body. His despair tore through my body.

He placed the jacket over the mound of dirt and walked away. His sobs echoed through the forest.

Another flash of light and he was laying the jacket on my shoulders as I slept. Someone came to my door and he turned an angry face to it. Protecting me. He wanted me to know he was there.

He needs my help. Something holds him here and he can't move on the way he should.

Dark magic, the same kind that's been causing me to feel confused and so tired. That's what's kept him here, along with many of the other souls.

I never did find the source of the beautiful Irish soprano.

But before I can get to the bottom of that, I have some testy warlocks to hunt down. Darn, phone's ringing.

5 P.M.
Sam called.

"How's everything going?" He tried so hard to sound casual that I knew something was up.

"Good, but this place is weird." I stared out at the snowy mountains and shivered. "I keep having déjà vu. There's a lot of ghosts in the castle and I think some of them are watching me."

"It's not like you to be afraid of some spirits." I realized he didn't sound upset, so much as distracted.

"I'm not afraid. They're trying to tell me something, and I'm not getting it. I'm good at making people dead, but not so much at conversing with the spirit world."

"Is there someone you can call to help?" I heard him slam a file drawer.

Something wasn't right.

"Yes, I've asked a friend of mine in New York for some info. Sam, what's wrong? And don't say nothing. I know when your voice gets like that, something's up."

He sighed. "It's not really anything that concerns you, just my own little drama to play out."

If it didn't concern me, I had no business prying. But I'm not one to give up easily. "Maybe if you talk to me about it—"

"It's not a big deal, just sort of hit me out of the blue." I heard the papers rustle on his desk.

I sat on the bed and waited in silence.

"Bronwyn? Are you there?"

"Yes. Just tell me what's going on."

"It's not like ghosts are watching me or anything as dramatic as that."

"Okay, now you're making fun of me."

"No, no. I'm sorry. Look, it's my ex-fiancée. I told you about her. Well, she just called and wanted to make sure that I'll attend her wedding next month."

"Oh." What the hell was I supposed to say? What kind of woman would invite an ex, one she cheated on, to her wedding?

Did Sam still love her? That would be even worse.

He cleared his throat. "I can hear your brain clicking. Don't go there, Bron. I don't have feelings for her. Well, not like that anyway. But going to her wedding? Why would she even imagine that's something I would want to do? Murder her, yes. Decapitate, perhaps. But attending her nuptials is last on my list."

I'd never seen this darker side of Sam. It was kind of sexy. "Maybe she thinks you guys are friends." Weak, but I didn't know why either. Bad form if you ask me.

"I think the friendship part of our relationship ended when I found her in bed with my supposed best buddies."

"Is that who she is marrying? One of your former best friends?"

"No, neither of us have seen those guys since that night. Well, as far as I know. The man she's marrying works at the hospital where my father is building the new wing. He's a neurosurgeon.

She's terribly happy and wants to share it with everyone she cares about."

"Sounds more to me like she wants to shove it in your face, which hardly seems fair since she's the one who betrayed you. Far as I'm concerned, you have every right to be upset. I'd just forget the whole thing." The room grew cold again and I jumped up to stick the poker in the fire.

Glanced around to see if any specters might be hanging out. Sensed a presence close, but didn't see a thing.

"Well, that would be the easy thing to do. Unfortunately, my parents are involved. They think I should do a bygones kind of thing."

"Yuck."

"That's the smartest thing I've heard today. Yuck. Why do relationships have to be so difficult?"

Something told me we weren't talking about his ex anymore. I wanted to mention that I was a proponent of the sex-only kind of couplings, but I knew he didn't want to hear that.

Stretched my arms above my head with the phone crooked in my shoulder. The movement helped release some of the tension in my muscles. "Um, I don't know. If I did I'd write a book and be the next Dr. Phil. I could go on national television and tell everyone how to get along with their chosen mates."

He laughed, but it wasn't a happy sound.

Checked my watch and grimaced. I had to get down to another meeting with the prime minister and sheik.

"Sam, I've got to run. Can we talk about this later?"

"Sure, sorry."

"Don't be sorry, I'm just late for a meeting."

"With the sheik?"

Uh-oh, here we go. "Um, he'll be there but it's primarily with the PM."

He blew out a breath. "I'm trying, Bron. It's hard when someone you love is halfway around the world with another man."

He so loves me. And yes, I kind of like the jealousy thing.

"Well, take care of yourself and I hope you find out who's haunting you."

"You do the same, and hopefully I'll have an answer soon. These spirits aren't bad, but they need help. I'm just not sure I'm the right person for the job."

We rang off and I changed into my suit with the velvet trim for the meeting.

Couldn't believe Sam had almost married that bitch. He deserved so much better. Maybe I should throw some bad mojo her way. Nothing awful, just a big zit for her wedding day. Right on top of that perfect nose. Well, I've never seen her, but I'm sure she's pretty if she was engaged to Sam. Or a third eye in the middle of her forehead.

But was I any kinder? Didn't I pit him against the sheik in some way? The man loved me and I couldn't even say the words back to him.

I remembered that kiss in the corner of the dining room that last night in Sweet, and wondered what would happen if I really gave in to my feelings for him. I liked that he'd made my legs tremble, and that his hands held me so tight I couldn't breathe.

Would it be so bad to spend my life with a man who made me feel that way?

Checked my face in the mirror and saw the flush from the memory glazing my cheeks. Oh, well, no need for blush today.

Twenty-four

Tuesday, 11 P.M.
Brussels
Worried witches: 1

This castle is so frigid, but these days I never know if it's ghosts or the drafty stone walls.

Still haven't heard from Garnout. He doesn't answer at the store or at home. Now I'm worried about him. I tried to locate him with my mind, but didn't connect. That doesn't necessarily mean anything. He's a wizard and often blocks all incoming probes without really thinking about it. But I'd sure feel better if I could find him.

The meetings with the PM and Azir were more eventful than I could have ever imagined. We had to go into town to this old but elegant hotel where the summit took place.

About fifty men and women had gathered in a large ballroom filled with tables and telephones. Golden chandeliers with beautiful crystals hung from the ceilings. The one in the middle was so huge that it lit a majority of the room.

The walls were trimmed in gold. Anywhere in America it might seem over the top, but here in Brussels it gave an old European vibe that was comforting in a way.

Translators sat in the back of the room and those participants who didn't speak French and English, the two languages used during the conference, wore headphones.

Azir and the PM asked me to sit in and read the group of dignitaries. Feelings were mixed over the topics at hand.

I noticed the room shifted to a more positive note when Azir approached the need for more worldwide funding for the human rights activists. This group appreciated the work he'd done over the last couple of years.

The PM nodded to me.

"He has them on his side," I whispered.

He smiled. "That's good. He's going to need as much help as he can get later this evening. Watch the room turn when the subject of the energy crisis comes into play."

A few hours later the prime minister's prediction came true. A diplomat from Sweden talked about the depletion of fossil fuels, and a general feeling of ill will permeated the room.

These people believed that the oil-rich countries were responsible for the current shortage and were draining the smaller countries financially.

As far out as Azir's ideas concerning solar power might seem at first, I knew this particular group would be amenable to his research. That is, if they could open their minds.

I mentioned it to him on the way back to the castle on the mountain.

"They want a new way of solving energy crises," I told him and the prime minister. "I'm sure they'd at least listen to your ideas."

"The prime minister and I have discussed this, and we may take a stronger approach to the subject in tomorrow's meetings." Azir smiled and touched my knee. "Your understanding how the room felt gave us the incentive we need to push forward."

From the look in his eyes, I wondered if that was the only reason. On the trip to the hotel, Azir had found every opportunity he could to touch me. I wondered if he somehow knew I'd been talking to Sam.

The big problem was that I liked it when he put his hands on me.

"By introducing this idea to these men and women and gaining their support, we feel we can strengthen our momentum as we discuss it with other countries," the PM added, oblivious to Azir's blatant flirting. He also didn't notice the energy that whipped around the inside of the limo like lightning.

After ignoring me for days, Azir had done a total change in attitude. He wanted me, and he didn't hide it at all.

I couldn't help staring into his eyes and I tapped into his mind.

I know you can hear me, Bronwyn. And yes, I want you.

Okay, well, no bones about that. The blush rose on my cheeks. He laughed, and the PM looked at him like he was insane.

"What's so funny, Azir?" The PM glanced around the limo trying to see the joke.

"Not so much funny as exciting." Azir gave me one more sensuous glance and turned to the PM. "We have a great opportunity to take advantage of a situation that could propel us into a whole new adventure."

Talk about listening between the lines. So he wanted to take advantage.

I'm not at all sure how I feel about that. I don't like the idea, but I have to talk with him. In a sane and totally calm manner. He has to know that a relationship with me, no matter how damn sexy he might be, isn't in the cards. I care about Sam and every moment I am away from him makes me ache.

Closed my eyes and leaned back against the cool leather of the seat. I closed my mind against Azir's and tried to think of a way to let one of the most powerful men in the world know I was in love with another man.

Ahhhhhh!

Wednesday, 1 A.M.
Creeped-out witches: 1
In my line of business I see a lot of whacked things, but tonight is a new one for the top of the crazy list.

I'd been in bed for about an hour when someone knocked on the door and then yelped. After last night, I'd supercharged the wards on the door to act like an electric fence.

Opened it and found the sheik on the other side shaking his burned hand. He had a strange glazed look, not the I-want-your-body stare from the limo, but the I've-checked-out-and-don't-know-where-I-am look.

"Sheik Azir?" I touched his arm and he cocked his head.

"Yes?"

"Um, Sheik, would you like to come in?"

He walked on stiff legs, almost as if he'd forgotten how to use them, and then stumbled into the chair next to my bed.

"Is everything all right? Have you been drugged?" I touched his chin and lifted it to check his eyes. Maybe he'd walked here in his sleep, but he definitely wasn't coherent.

"Bronwyn?"

"Yes, I'm here."

"It's a pleasure to meet you." What the hell was he talking about?

"Azir, you've known me for months now."

"Silly girl, I'm not this beautiful specimen of a man. I'm Darby O'Hurley, and I've come for a visit."

Now it was my turn. "Who?"

Then it dawned on me: the sheik's overly pronounced, haughty tone had been replaced by a soft Irish lilt.

"Your ancestor, Darby O'Hurley." The sheik crossed his legs in a feminine motion. A deep contrast to the usual powerful moves of the sultan of sexy. It made me laugh.

"Surely you've heard of me?" If it was a game, he'd gone all out.

Darby? Oh, my God! Could this be for real? A two-hundred-year-old ghost had taken over the sheik's body.

"Are you the Darby who left Dublin in search of adventure and never returned? The powerful witch, who had no match in the world of magic?" I scratched my head. No way.

"Yes, yes, that would be me. The witch who failed her mother and her country, and could never return to the shame she had caused."

I'd heard the stories a million times from my mother and grandmother, but no one ever mentioned failing a country or anything about shame. The stories about Darby had been about a witch so powerful that she had few foes, and she had used that power to save Ireland from countless warlocks. She was the first in the family to be born a high witch.

"I don't understand. I know the stories but never heard anything about you being a traitor to your country."

"No, a traitor I wasn't—but I betrayed my homeland just the same. For I broke my promise to my countrymen to protect them from evil." The sheik's eyes were downcast.

"I chose love and in the end disappointed a nation I truly honored. Ah, but I have no time to dwell on the past. I can only borrow your lover here for a few more minutes."

I wondered what she meant about choosing love over her power. My mother had done the same. There was no shame in it.

Then it occurred to me that she thought the sheik and I were a couple. "Oh, he's not my lover."

Those brown eyes looked up and the right eyebrow rose. "You are mistaken, young lady. His heart beats only for you, and I couldn't have taken him over had it not been filled with love for you."

The sheik loved me? No friggin' way.

"You may not know of his love, but it is strong within him. Can you not tell by the way he looks at you?"

"Lust maybe, but it has nothing to do with love."

"You are wrong. But as I said before, I have no time to dwell. I've a message for you. The darkness is close, and he is set on destroying you."

"What darkness? He?"

Darby looked confused.

"There are two warlocks at the castle. Could it be one of them?" I couldn't decipher what she was trying to say.

"Only one wishes you harm. I've tried to protect you from his spells of enchantment. Your magic is quite strong but you can't see him for what he really is." She took a deep breath.

"Can you tell me if it's Sphere or Wallace?" I sat down on the bed.

"I know not these names of which you speak. Sir William Blackstock is the evil you should fear. I fought him two centuries ago, and he has become more powerful since that time.

"But you, dear, you must prepare. He's stronger than anyone you've ever faced. I know not where he dwells—he hides himself well—but he's close. Ohhh . . ." Her voice sounded strained.

"What's wrong?"

"I must go, but know, dear witch, I am with you." Her hand

rose to rest on my cheek. It felt odd to see the sheik make such an intimate and feminine gesture. "And tell my beloved Lance to come to me as soon as possible."

"Who is Lance?"

"The jacket . . ." Her voice faded. "Blackstock's final blow was to make certain we could not be together in eternity. Send him on his way, young Bronwyn, so that I can be with my true one."

The sheik's chin hit his chest so fast I worried he might get whiplash.

"Sheik Azir?"

His head lifted and he ran a shaky hand through his hair. Eyes opening slowly, he asked, "Where am I?"

"You're in my room."

"I don't remember." He focused on me and shook his head as if to clear the cobwebs away.

"What do you remember?" I didn't want to tell him that he'd been possessed by a ghost. That freaks people out sometimes and it can take them years to get over it. I watched as he tried to think about the events that had transpired.

"I was working on a paper at my desk and felt tired. I put my head down for a moment . . . now I'm here."

"My guess is a sleepwalking incident." Well, it was sort of true. He hadn't been conscious when he made his way to my room.

"You may be right, but I've never done this before."

"It happens when people are under a lot of stress. You've only been here for a few minutes."

"Did I say anything?" The worry frowns across his forehead told me he wanted to make sure he hadn't revealed anything intimate in his altered state.

"No, you seemed confused and had to sit down." The frown disappeared and his shoulders sagged with relief.

"My apologizes for disturbing you at such a late hour." He

rose and steadied himself with the chair. "I'll lock myself in this time, so it won't happen again."

"No worries. But the lock isn't a bad idea; it could keep the bad guys at bay long enough for the wards to work."

He wanted to say more to me, but he was too embarrassed by the situation. Opening the door, he turned to me.

"You're certain I didn't say anything?"

Well, technically Darby had done all the talking so it wasn't a lie when I told him, "No."

He walked down the hallway to his room. I sat back on the bed and blew out a breath.

The sheik really was in love with me.

Huh.

Twenty-five

It had been so quiet around here at the castle I thought the other witch and warlocks had left. No such luck.

When we traveled to town for the second round of meetings, I noticed Sphere and Wally standing at the back of the ballroom. They both acknowledged my presence with a nod and turned their attention to their charges.

Which one was after my charges? I had a difficult time believing Sphere could harm anything larger than a Chihuahua. He had power, but I didn't believe he knew how to use it. I focused my powers on Wally's mind. He blocked me and gave me an irritated look.

Lesha didn't come in with her client. He sat alone on the third row. Curious.

That's when I realized Sphere and Wally might be up to no

good. They hadn't bothered to attend Tuesday's meeting, but now all of a sudden they were at attention, ready for battle.

Hmmm.

Took a deep breath in order to sense the room and detected another magical entity. A handsome warlock with curly blond hair gave a slight wave and smiled. Tipped his mind, and he answered back, "I offer no harm."

Seemed friendly enough, but after last night I didn't trust anyone. Darby's warning about a deceitful warlock stuck in my brain. I would have walked across the room to meet him and get a better idea of what he was up to, but the sheik was about to give his speech.

My stomach turned flip-flops when I looked at him, so handsome in his three-piece suit. His tanned skin dark against the white starched collar of his shirt.

I sent him a quick good-luck spell and clarity of being that I hoped would help his message be understood. His eloquent speech and relaxed but professional manner won over the crowd.

They stood and clapped when he was done and that's when it happened. A large boom, like thunder clashing, and the huge chandelier fell. I used both hands to stop it midair and it hovered over the heads of more than half the dignitaries.

Everyone froze, uncertain of where to move. Total deer-in-the-headlights syndrome.

"Move!" I screamed and the room erupted in chaos. You've never seen so many pin-striped suits sprint for a door. Wally and Sphere, the rats, joined them.

The other warlock stayed and moved close to me. "Tell me how I can help."

"I can't let go and I can't lower it on my own. I'm fighting against someone else's magic." I could feel the sweat on my brow, but couldn't wipe it away.

"If you'll allow me in your circle, I can perhaps float it to the ground with your help." His voice was calm.

"Anything's better than it crashing down on top of us. See if you can push it to the left so we can lay it down."

He raised his arms and mumbled an incantation. I don't know exactly what he said but it worked. The huge crystal piece moved down and gently fell across the tables.

A few of the crystals broke, but nothing like what could have happened.

It hadn't been easy because someone's magic had been pushing the thing so hard it would have shattered to a million pieces, killing everyone underneath it. Including me.

"Bronwyn, are you okay?" Azir shouted from the stage. He and the PM ran across the room to grab my arms. The magic I'd just fought was more powerful than anything I'd ever come across. I tried to act like I hadn't been sucker punched but my body was about to give out.

Ignoring them both, but grateful for the assistance, I raised my head to the blond warlock. "Who are you?"

"Cole Jameson. I'm a friend of Garnout's. He sent me to help and said he's busy researching your problem and that it's deeper than you might think. He should have an answer for you soon."

The PM and sheik frowned. But I wasn't about to explain about what had happened to me at the castle. I didn't have energy.

"I'm grateful for your help and Garnout's." A cleansing breath gave me renewed strength and I pulled my arms away from my charges. "I'm okay, guys, but that was some powerful black magic."

"Did you sense it just before it happened?" Cole gazed around the room as if looking for something. "I thought perhaps it was one of those other two, but when they ran I knew it came

from someone else. That thing"—he pointed to the chandelier—
"could have killed most of the people in this room."

"Bronwyn wouldn't have let that happen, even if it put her
own life in danger." I heard the undertones in the sheik's voice.
He'd been more than a little worried.

"I'm tired of this chickenshit warlock or witch who is afraid
to face me." Put my hands on my hips and surveyed the room.
"He or she may be powerful enough to shake the earth, but obviously has problems going one-on-one with a five-foot-two
witch."

Cole laughed. "Can't say that I blame him. You're the most
powerful witch I've ever come across, and I've met quite a few in
my line of work."

"Which is . . . ?"

He glanced at the two men beside me. "We'll chat about that
later. I think it might be a good idea to get all of you out of here
and to a more secure location."

He talked like a cop. He might be a part of the spook
brigade. They round up renegade witches and warlocks and do
God knows what with them. I've seen more than my share of
magical folk hauled off, but never knew what actually happened
to them. As long as I didn't have to go along for the ride, never
had reason to care.

"Won't you join us for dinner? It's certainly the least we can
do," the PM asked as we walked into the lobby of the hotel. Most
of the diplomats had left immediately, but a few hung around, cu-
riosity getting the best of them. They thanked me for stopping
the thing and I just smiled. Didn't really know what to say.

"I'd be grateful for a good meal. I've been traveling for the
last twelve hours to get here." Cole shook hands with the PM
and the sheik. "But I need to make arrangements for accommo-
dations in town. Would it be okay if I meet you later?"

"Why don't you come back with us to the castle?" the prime minister interjected. "We're thankful for what you did in there and we are more than happy to accommodate you."

Cole looked at me and I shrugged my shoulders. If Garnout sent him, then he had to be a good guy. I'd have to keep an eye on him, though. Too much had happened the past few days to let anyone go unchecked.

"That settles it." The PM turned to Miles, whose normally pale skin was even whiter than usual. I hadn't even noticed he was there, but evidently the incident had shaken him. "Make arrangements for Mr. Jameson."

As we climbed into the car, Miles popped open his cell phone and called the house to get a room ready for Cole. I needed to be alone and to sleep in order to renew my energy. The idea of having one more suspicious warlock in the castle wasn't appealing, but at this point I didn't have much of a choice.

One thing I know for certain: Wally and Sphere had known something would go down. But why would they run and not protect their charges? Those toads better answer my questions by the end of the evening.

II P.M.

So Cole's a cop. A cute one. Argh, Bronwyn, get a grip. You're turning into Simone. Not everything in pants is something at an amusement park for you to ride.

Technically Cole's called an agent and he's part of the international spook brigade. He had planned to come soon to Brussels anyway to check on Lesha's brother and make sure he was under control. He'd been in Australia working on a case when Garnout called him, and he rushed to get here.

Glad Garnout can take the time to phone him but not me. Then it dawned on me. I hadn't even looked at my email in days.

Plugged in the computer and found a message from Sam, two from Simone, and one from Garnout.

> *Dear Bronwyn,*
> *I'll be incommunicado for a few days while I look into your little mystery. Traveling, you know. Sending someone to check on you.*
> *Best,*
> *Garnout*

Traveling, you know. Meant he was going through time, which is why he couldn't answer his page. It all made sense, but I still didn't understand why he felt it necessary to send Cole.

Sam's email had asked for a few potion recipes we'd talked about, but there wasn't a darn thing about him missing me.

He had gone by the house and found Casper on the roof. After several tries he'd finally coaxed the cat down with some of Lulu's chicken. As soon as she smelled the fried goodness she shimmied down the front porch post and curled against his legs.

My cat has good taste when it comes to food and men. But she can be stupid when it comes to heights. She's afraid of them, but can't seem to help chasing after birds in trees or up to the roof. Usually I levitate her down from wherever.

By the time we had made it back to the castle, Tweedle Dee and Tweedle Dum, otherwise known as Wally and Sphere, had vacated the premises along with their charges. The rest of the summit had been canceled and everyone had left as soon as they could charter a flight.

It's a shame. I'd really looked forward to turning those cowardly warlocks into two fat hens. I also wanted to know if they had any inkling of who was behind the near tragedy.

The arrangements had been made for us all to depart in the

next twenty-four hours. I expected the sheik to ask me to go back to the Middle East with him.

"I won't be going home for a while and plan to travel back to America next week," he told me at the informal dinner we had in the small dining room. By small I mean my house could have fit into it and there still would have been extra room. The table sat thirty, but our little group, consisting of Miles, the PM, Azir, Cole, and myself, took root at one end.

"Oh, do you have business there?" I took a sip of wine. A bit smoky and bitter for me, but I needed the nerve-soothing power of the drink.

He looked at me pointedly and said, "Yes." His husky tone told me it was nothing but monkey business and it involved me. Great, just great. Here I am trying to save his ass from the evil in the world and he wants to play hide the tamale.

"Aren't you worried about the need for protection?" I tried to be casual about it, but just a week ago he'd shown up at my house fearful of the world.

"The prime minister and I will travel together and we have your protection spells and charms with us at all times."

"That's wonderful and lovely but have you forgotten about what happened earlier today? That magic—warlock, witch, or whatever—is nothing like I'd ever seen before."

"Yes, well." The PM fidgeted in his chair like a choirboy during too long at a sermon. "The thing is— Before you came down—" He cleared his throat. "Mr. Jameson told us about the danger you are in. This Mr. Garnout you talked about says that there's a hit out on you."

I turned to look at Cole. That asshole had no business telling my clients a damn thing about my personal affairs.

He obviously knew what I thought and held up a hand. Probably from the daggers I'd thrown with my eyes.

"Bronwyn, I know I crossed the line but the investigative team looking into the incident at the hotel today thinks the whole thing was aimed at you. The person behind the magic wanted to kill you and didn't care who else was in the way. Do you have any idea what would have happened if any of those people had died? It would have been an international incident in proportions we haven't seen since the last war."

"What makes them think it was aimed at me?"

"The residue from the magic is an exact match of what we found on the warlocks who attacked you in New York and Oslo. They were pawns and someone had tried to use them against you but it didn't work. That black sludge Garnout helped clear out of your system is the same magic that we found around the chandelier."

Cole pointed to the men across the table. "The prime minister and Sheik Azir were nowhere near when that incident took place in New York, so . . ."

I folded my arms across my chest. The small twinge of a headache moved from the base of my neck and threatened to become a full-blown migraine in a few minutes.

"So you think I'm endangering my charges by being around them?" If my jaw tightened any more they'd have to get a crowbar to open it. I still hadn't been able to rest after the fiasco at the hotel and my energy waned. Now this jerk was blaming me for everything. Enough.

"If you gentlemen will excuse me, I need to pack." I pushed away from the table and headed for my room. I wanted to be angry, but everything he said had been true. They both could have died—and a whole lot of other people—because some asshole wanted me dead.

An overwhelming tiredness surrounded me and it was all I

could do to climb the stone steps to my third-floor room. I barely made it to the bed before I passed out.

Strange dreams rolled in my head. The sheik ran around wearing the jacket I'd found, and then Sam stole it from him. I was on a broom riding around their heads yelling, "Run for the hills, boys, the demons are coming, the demons are coming."

Wouldn't a therapist like to get ahold of that one?

Twenty-six

Wednesday, II P.M. (continued)
Brussels
Witches who want to go home: I

I woke a couple hours later to the sheik calling to me from outside my door.

"Bronwyn? Hello, Bronwyn?"

He couldn't touch the door thanks to the wards. My head still felt fuzzy, but I shuffled over and let him in.

"Are you okay?" He touched my arm and the familiar heat rushed through my body.

"No. I feel like crap."

He guided me to the bed and sat beside me with his arms around me. "It's not your fault."

It took me a minute to decipher his words. He thought I meant about him and the PM.

I really felt like dog doo, rolled over by a lawn tractor.

His concern brought all the uncertainty back into focus.

"The hell it's not. Both of you could have been killed," I whispered, not wanting to believe it. "I couldn't have forgiven myself if something had happened to you. Either of you."

He lifted my chin and stared into my eyes. At first I thought he might kiss me, but then he spoke. "Do you have any idea how worried I was? Bronwyn, the prime minister and I were never in any real danger, but you were directly underneath the thing. It would have crushed you."

I laughed. "I'm tougher than I look."

"Don't make jokes. Please, not this time. I want you to be safe and I'm afraid it's my troubles that have created this ill will toward you."

"What makes you say that?" His scent was a combination of piney aftershave and a musky soap. Intoxicating to my addled brain.

"The attack in New York happened after you helped me in Norway, and you were on your way to meet me at my home, remember?"

"Yes, but what you have to understand is that there's always someone who wants me dead. It's just a part of the job. That's why I moved to Sweet so I could see the bad guys coming. They're always out there." I shrugged and circled my head around to pop my neck. Talking to him had helped to ease the tension.

I took a deep breath. "To be honest, neither one of us is to blame. It's the bad guys, whoever is after you, and me, that we should be targeting our anger toward."

He massaged my shoulders through my blouse and pulled me closer to him. "After I watched you today I realized something important." He leaned down and kissed me, his lips soft and gentle. Nipping my lip, he gently opened my mouth with his tongue and investigated every inch of it.

I lost myself in the moment. My body came alive as his hands slid down my arms and grabbed my waist. The sheik might have had control of my mouth, but Sam had invaded my thoughts. I couldn't sit here and kiss another man, knowing I was in love with someone else. Even I'm not that low.

I stood and put some distance between us.

"I know you don't date clients, Bronwyn, but I would not let another day pass without kissing you." He stood also and held up a hand to keep me from speaking.

"Don't ruin it by saying something flip. Please." He backed away toward the door. "I'm going to leave you to rest now."

"I liked it."

"What?"

"The kiss. I just wanted to say that I liked it. But we can't ever do it again."

He considered what I said, and with a puzzled look asked, "Is it because of Sam?"

"Yes. I like his kisses too, and I think I'm in love with him." It was more honest than I'd been with myself in months. Saying it out loud made it so real, and right.

Azir frowned. "Perhaps some time in Sweet will help clear your thoughts. Cole tells us that you have more power on your home territory, so you'll be safer there."

Cole had been right about the power. I needed to recharge and the best place to do that was at home.

I walked to the door and hugged the sheik. "You're a good man. Keep your charms with you at all times."

"I will." He waved and left.

I walked back to the desk where my laptop whirred. Darby had finally found a way to get me a message without possessing someone's body. My screen saver on the computer read, *Danger from the dark one.*

Geez, clear as mud that one is with the messages. Did she mean the sheik? Sam? Another warlock? Argh!

All I wanted to do was talk to Sam. I moved to the bed and dialed him on the cell.

"Are you okay?" He must have caller ID because he knew it was me.

"Yes." I sighed.

"You don't sound okay. You've been in another battle?"

"Of sorts. I don't want to talk about that. I just needed to hear your voice."

"If you tell me what's bothering you, maybe I can help." His deep voice soothed my nerves like no other. I wished he could hold me, then all would be well in the world.

I ended up telling him everything about the hit on me, the chandelier, what had happened with the PM and the sheik, and the news about Cole.

"My God, Bron, no wonder you feel so bad. Tell me what I can do to make it better."

"Come here right now and make love to me. Help me forget all of this crap and let me lose myself in you."

I heard a big sigh on the other end. "Baby, if you want I'll drive to Dallas and take the first plane to Brussels I can get. I can be there by tomorrow afternoon."

I laughed. "You would do that for me?"

"Of course. Just say the word."

"Well, it isn't necessary. I'll be home tomorrow and then you can help me to forget."

"Tomorrow? Excellent. I'll get everything ready for you. Sounds like you need some serious R&R, and I'm just the guy to help you out.

"Let's see. We'll need an exercise plan. That will involve sex. Um, a nutritious diet of chocolate syrup and whipped cream;

that will also include sex. I am worried you won't be getting much sleep though, at least in the first several hours."

I giggled. "Thank you, Sam."

"I'm going to take very good care of you."

"I can't wait. I'll see you tomorrow."

I'm so damn lucky. So, very, very lucky.

Thursday, 2:30 A.M.

Slept for a couple more hours and then went foraging for food. I hadn't eaten much at dinner and my stomach grumbled so loud I couldn't ignore it.

After a few wrong turns and about ten minutes of searching, I found my way to the kitchen. The large room was completely surrounded in a gray stone that made it about twenty degrees cooler than the rest of the castle. A blessing I'm sure when the six ovens I saw in there are turned on.

I opened the large fridge door and pulled out some of the beef tenderloin and other things left over from dinner. I put everything on the large wooden table in the corner. A beautiful view from the bay windows, even this time of night with the stars highlighting the tree shadows in the snow.

Before he came around the corner I sensed Cole. I saw him reflected in the glass before me, and turned around. Mouth full, I gave him a small salute.

"That looks good." He walked to where the desserts sat on top of the counter. I'd done my best to avoid that section of the kitchen but there was an array of delectable sweets, from hand-made chocolates to a raspberry torte.

He grabbed two chocolate-filled croissants and a glass of milk, and joined me at the table.

"So, are you angry with me?" He pulled apart the pastry and

bit in. "Garnout said you might not appreciate my help, but insisted I come anyway."

I wasn't in the mood to talk, but even I have trouble being rude for no reason. "Don't mind the help, but I didn't care for you sharing private information with my clients."

"In all honesty, I didn't realize you hadn't told them about the hits on you. I tried to cover but it didn't work. The prime minister and his friend the sheik are much too observant."

Something about this guy sent my warlock radar into high gear. Adorableness aside, he seemed too casual about everything. He hadn't batted an eyelash when the chandelier crashed, and nothing fazed him.

"So why are you really here?"

"I'm hungry."

The man was nothing short of infuriating. "You didn't come here just because Garnout asked you to. You're a major player in the international spook squad. Traveling two thousand miles out of your way because some wizard asked you to isn't going to work for me."

His hooded blue eyes stared a full minute as if he were considering how much he wanted to share.

"Trouble follows you intimately, Bronwyn, and I thought, as did my superiors, that perhaps I could observe you for a few days, and track the warlock behind all of this."

"I'm curious how you know so much about the situation. Except for the PM, Azir, and their security teams, the only other person who knows anything is Garnout. As angry as I am with him right now for butting in, he isn't usually so open with my personal business."

"This has nothing to do with anything personal." His voice took on an edge. "We're on the same side here. The only thing your friend Garnout shared was that you were up against a powerful warlock. The rest of the information we picked up from accounts in Oslo, Dubai, New York, and, of course, here in Brussels.

"You've left a trail of dead warlocks behind you, and it's our job to take notice."

"There's not a one of them who didn't deserve everything they received." If Cole and the spook squad were on my side they had a strange way of showing it.

"Trust me, you're a hero as far as most of us are concerned. In the last three years you've rid the world of more evil than all the witches in the world combined."

"I find that hard to believe. And you don't seem to share the hero worship. Not that I'm complaining." The room became even colder and I wondered which ghost might be listening in this time.

"I've a great respect for what you do. I may not always agree with the way you go about it"—he held up a hand before I could chime in—"but you get the job done.

"You asked why I came to Brussels. I wanted to see you work and to talk with Lesha's brother. There's a good chance he knows the warlock behind all of this. But his mind is gone. It may never heal enough for him to think in complete sentences."

"His sister is the one who did that to him. I had nothing to do with it." I threw up my hands in my best "I'm not guilty" motion.

Cole laughed, a nice sound, his head shaking back and forth. "For such a tough witch, you sure are defensive."

"No offense, big guy, but I don't like the idea that I'm being watched. I have a job to do, and I do it. I don't want to have to worry about the squad picking me up because I've killed a few too many bad guys."

"I don't know what else to say to convince you, but it isn't you we're after. You felt that magic—whoever is after you and your charges means to kill. We want to make sure that doesn't happen."

He looked around the kitchen and shivered. "Does it feel colder in here to you?"

Several ghosts had come into the room. The temperature had dropped at least ten degrees in the already cold room.

"Um, no. I've got to get some sleep. Early flight and all. If I were you I'd take a look at the two warlocks in the back of the room today. They were ready for something to happen, so they must have had some idea of what was to take place."

"We're on it. Good night." He held out his hand to shake. "I'm happy I finally had a chance to meet you."

I shook it, but didn't bother to lie and say I felt the same way.

The coldness followed me to my room. My great protector has returned. I have failed Darby, my lovely Irish ancestor. We will be leaving in less than four hours, and I haven't been able to reunite her with her lover.

I picked up the jacket on the back of the chair and let my fingers trail along the soft collar.

So much love between this man and woman. Maybe someday I can come back and help them. But for now I can't wait to get home.

I'm determined to figure out what is going on with Sam. Our relationship has taken a turn, and I feel like I'm missing out on something fantastic every moment I'm away from him.

And Azir. That's one thing Cole may be right about. He and the prime minister may be safer without me around.

Twenty-seven

Friday, 10 A.M.
Sweet, Texas
Relaxed witches: 1

Feels so good to be home. Springtime in West Texas is a heck of a lot warmer than Brussels this time of year.

The weirdest thing happened when I walked in the door. Casper actually greeted me and acted like she was happy I'd made it back. She never does that.

She hasn't left my side since I got here. Cats are so hard to understand.

Sam had been called in on an emergency at the hospital but he rang this morning to check on me.

"You doing okay?"

"A little tired, but good."

"What time did you get in?"

"About two this morning."

"I'm so sorry I missed you, baby; one of my patients took a turn for the worse and I had to be here."

I was disappointed but I understood.

"Is there any chance you can meet for lunch at Lulu's? Ever since you emailed the story about the fried chicken, I've been dying for some."

"Sounds good to me."

We decided to meet at noon, which gives me just enough time to feed Casper, shower, and find something stunning to wear. I want to knock his socks off, which is strange since I already know he loves me. I just want to be certain he makes good on that promise for some great R&R.

Midnight

I don't know why I feel so uneasy. Today was as close to perfect as a day can get. Sam and I had a wonderful lunch. Afterward we went to see Mr. Gunther, who wrote like gangbusters the whole time we were there.

I'd picked up another journal for him in town and gave it to him. He smiled, those blue eyes penetrating but friendly. "Thank you."

"You know you're welcome. Have you been feeling better since the last potion?"

He frowned then and put down his pen. "Yes, but I don't want to take any more."

"Why is that?"

"Seems like we're trying to cheat death and it doesn't feel right. Besides, once I fill this new journal you gave me, I'm done with my mission."

"Your mission?"

"Yes, to remind the world that an ordinary life can be quite wonderful. That's the legacy I want to leave behind. I want you and my grandchildren to know what an incredible ride it's been."

His grandchildren lived all over the world. If something happened to him, they might not have time to get here. The idea of him dying choked me up so I did what I do best—I changed the subject.

"That wasn't you who pinched old lady Albright on the butt the other night? I heard she screamed for two hours that she'd been manhandled. Margie said it took three sedatives to settle her down."

He chortled. "Old bag. No one pinched her. She's nothing but skin and bone. There isn't anything to grab onto even if you tried. She's one of those high drama types. Needs lots of attention."

Sometimes I thought Mrs. Albright and myself had a lot in common. Drama seemed to be a big part of my life the last few months.

The night ended with me finally convincing Sam that he needed to stay over. I was exhausted and he was genuinely worried about my health.

"Bron, we've got time, you need to rest."

He tried to give me a chaste kiss and send me to bed, but I wanted nothing of it. "Doctor"—I pulled him into the living room with me—"I need some serious healing."

I pointed to my lips. "These hurt really, really bad."

"I thought we had an understanding."

"We do, we do. But you're a doctor, and I need help. I also have pain right here." I slipped off my T-shirt. The sight of my bra made him take a sharp breath. I pulled down my denim skirt to complete my lacy red ensemble.

I smiled. He grabbed the elastic band on the front of my thong and pulled me to him. My breasts tight against his chest, pelvis pressed into his hardness.

"You don't play fair," he said right before he ravaged my mouth with his tongue. His thumb rubbed across my hardened nipple.

I let him take what he wanted, and then pulled back from his mouth. "I never said I'd play fair." Taking his hand, I yanked him upstairs behind me.

"I'm tired of waiting. We want each other and I need to feel you inside of me tonight." I pulled his jacket off and unbuttoned his shirt. "Do you understand that, Sam? Do you have any idea how difficult it is for me to say I *need* someone?"

I hate button-fly jeans. Zippers are so much faster.

He didn't say a word, but he slipped off his jeans and gently pushed me to the bed. The down comforter cushioned the fall as he bent down to slip off the thong, running his hands down my thighs. Not long after that he moved up my body, trailing kisses, and gently removed the bra. He looked down on me, his gaze traveling from my head to my toes. "Never have I seen such beauty."

"Sam."

"I love you." He lay down beside me, his hand resting on my stomach. "Before I make love to you, you have to know how I feel.

"It's scary putting my heart on the line like this, and I don't expect you to do the same. But I've never felt like this about anyone. Ever. It's fast, and scary, and I don't know what will happen."

He started to say something else, but stopped. His lips moved over the circles he'd been making with his hands on my stomach. He slid down my body. Hands pushing my legs apart, his tongue plunged into me. I thought I might die from pleasure. How could anything compare to how this man made me feel? Cherished. Loved. Adored. He gently nibbled and used his masterful tongue to send me into waves of passion. Over and over, until my body ached for him.

"Oh, my," I whispered. I couldn't take much more. But he wouldn't stop and the sweet torture continued as he used his fingers where his tongue had been and slid up my body. Kissing my neck, and suckling my breasts like a man starved.

I couldn't take any more. I pushed him back. He smiled.

"Now." No more begging, I demanded it. I straddled him and slid down his shaft, taking every inch of him. Moving his hands to my hips he met my frantic motion, and made me come again. I leaned forward, hands on his shoulders, and kissed him.

He rolled me onto my back and wrapped my legs around his waist. Faster he pumped me, harder and harder, until I could think of nothing but the joy of his touch.

"Yes, yes!" I screamed, my voice hoarse with passion.

As he poured into me he whispered into my ear, "Forever. I'll love you forever."

I couldn't say the words but I wrapped my arms around him and tried to show him how much I cared. What had started as an extreme hornfest needing to be quenched had turned into something so much more sensual and giving.

In that moment I realized my heart had become very much attached to this man.

He has an early call at work in a few hours, but I think I may have to wake him with a little surprise. Time to return the delicious favor he served me. I think it will involve some lovely whipped cream and my own creative version of a banana split, a la Sam.

I still have a strange feeling, but I've decided it must be jet lag. Too much work and not enough play. Bronwyn's about to change that.

Wakey, wakey, Sammy baby.

Twenty-eight

Saturday, 8 A.M.
New moon
Sweet, Texas
Paranoid witches: 1

Something bad has happened. I feel it. Woke me with a start and it's crushingly horrible. I know it, I know it, I know it.

Sent my mind out to my mom, dad, and annoying brother; everyone was fine. The sheik and PM checked out, and so did Simone. Kira and Caleb slept with their arms around one another.

I can't get into Sam's head. That doesn't mean anything, though, because he's been blocking me since the night we invaded each other's dreams.

He left me with a sweet kiss early this morning and a promise to stop by later this afternoon. After last night, I have no doubts how I feel about him. I just wish I could actually say the words.

Man, I could throw up. It's bad. I hate when this happens. It always means someone I care about is in trouble.

Oh, crap. The phone. Here it comes.

Sunday, 5:30 A.M.
This day has great possibilities. Actually every day does, but this one is special because I woke up next to the man I love. Oh, it took me a while to realize it, but he's the one.

For months he told me we belonged together, but I refused to believe him. What he didn't seem to realize is witches don't have boyfriends. It never works out.

The intimidation factor alone usually stands as the biggest turnoff. A lot of men can't handle a woman with power. The whole reading-minds thing and the ability to turn them into toads sort of makes them insecure.

Even my clients are afraid of me, but they want to use my talents just the same.

Don't get me wrong. I love being a witch. My world's filled to the brim with exciting adventures and people.

But this love thing is all new. My heart's full of an emotion I've rarely experienced. I've cared for people in the past, but loving is something I hardly ever allowed myself to do.

This man changed all of that. I must love him because there are no other possibilities. It's much like being a witch. It is what I am and what I must be.

Look at him, lying there so peaceful. That jet black hair waving around his face and those bulging biceps. Ooh, baby! He's a human cupcake and I could just eat him up.

Now if only I can get him to come back to life it will be a great day. Because lonely as I get sometimes—I don't fuck dead guys.

Stupid, I'm so fucking stupid.

And devastated. There's no other word. The world is a horrible, horrible place. Sam has died twice in the last twenty-four hours and there doesn't seem to be anything I can do to help him.

I love him so much and I can't stand to see him lying there like a vegetable. He could die again at any moment, and this time it might be for good.

The phone was Margie from the nursing home. They'd brought Sam into the emergency room next door and she thought I should know.

"His truck flipped over in the drainage ditch. They didn't see any other cars around, but he was pinned underneath," Margie told me, her voice choked with tears. "You need to hurry, Bronwyn. He died once on the way here and they brought him back. It's not good."

After twelve hours of surgery they mended his two broken legs, wrist, and hip. His beautiful face doesn't have a scratch.

He's so perfect. It isn't fair. When I woke him up yesterday morning we had such a beautiful time together.

My precious man. Why didn't I tell him I loved him? Now he may die, and never have what he deserved from me. What I selfishly held back.

He just died again and there was nothing I could do to help. The doctors and nurses brought him back, but I'm useless and afraid.

His parents are on their way back from some photo safari in Africa and want him moved to a hospital in Dallas. But the doctors here say it would be murder to do so.

Kira and Caleb went to get me some coffee. Talking to them helps, but nothing gets rid of this terrible ache inside. Shortly after they arrived, he went into cardiac arrest again. They jumpstarted the flat line and brought him back.

"You can't die. I'm in love with you," I whispered in his ear. After everyone had left.

"I couldn't tell you before, you big oaf, so don't you go anywhere. You have to stay here with me."

Maybe I wished it, but I could have sworn he pushed into my mind. *He's here.*

"Who's here, baby? Tell me." I pushed back and tried to read him, but saw nothing but blackness.

Kira and Caleb pulled me out of the room when the doctors came in, and back into the ICU waiting area. The cold blue walls did nothing to help the sick feeling in my gut. Did he speak? Or was it my imagination?

"He's so broken and I don't think my magic can heal him." I wanted to collapse into the floor.

Kira held my hand in the waiting room while the doctors examined Sam. She tried to comfort me. "Right now, all he needs is your love. Let the doctors work their own magic."

"But I should be able to heal him. I can help others with potions and spells, why not him?"

Caleb put a hand on my shoulder. "You could ease his pain, but you can't re-create bone and mend it, Bron. He'll be okay. It's tough, but he's a strong man."

"I hope you're right, Caleb." Then I let the tears flow. I crossed my arms across my middle and sobbed. They both hugged me and cried with me. It's good to have friends.

Noon

After only a short time in the waiting room I noticed shadows on the floor in front of me. Peggy and the rest of the coven stood before me.

"Peggy?"

"We're here to offer our assistance. We have powerful healers in our midst and they can help your Sam." She took both of my hands in hers. "His father called me and gave us permission to see him. But we'll only do it if you want us to."

"Of course I do. Thank you all." I squeezed her hands and looked around at the group of men and women.

"He's also going to need our protection."

"Yes, yes."

"No, Bronwyn, you don't understand." Peggy touched my cheek to get my attention. "He was attacked by black magic. We found a dark sludge surrounding the area. He didn't run into anything. Someone picked up his truck and crushed it to the ground."

"I don't— No." The black sludge meant only one thing. The warlock had come for me, here in Sweet.

"We're here to give you strength too, so that you can fight this malevolent evil. My son and two from our coven will take you to your home. You'll be more powerful there."

"I can't leave Sam. He needs me."

"Bronwyn, we all need you right now. As forceful as our coven is, we cannot fight this black magic alone. We'll take care of Sam and protect him, but you must fight for us all.

"Whoever it is came under the guise of another, so beware." She turned and waved her hand to the coven and motioned them into the ICU ward. "This is a powerful warlock; our wards against evil did not bind him as they should have. We'll protect your young man, but you must do what you do best."

I knew what she said was right, and I wanted nothing more than to kill the person who had done this to my beautiful, broken Sam. He'd suffered so much.

But I wouldn't blame myself this time.

I'd make the warlock pay.

I walked to the sheriff. "Take me home, please."

So now we wait. I've made the preparations and covered every angle I can imagine. The sheriff and the two witches are down in the kitchen and, from the clinking of the cups against the saucers, I can tell they're nervous. Can't say I blame them. I might be just a little scared if I wasn't so fucking angry.

The presence is closer. I feel him. He wants me to probe his mind, but I refuse. I'm not falling for any of his tricks. This time we play my game, my rules.

Twenty-nine

Tuesday, 8 A.M.
Sweet, Texas
Spells: 4
Dead guys: I

So tired. Everything happened so fast that I'm having a hard time remembering how it all went down.

My first memory of the fight was the sight of Cole in the conservatory. Relieved and grateful, I sighed. With him here, I might have a better chance of taking down the evil. I might not like him very much, but he had power. And I could use all the help I could get.

He had his back to me but I'd know that curly blond hair anywhere.

"Cole?"

He turned. I couldn't see his face. The sun played tricks that time of the morning. "Bronwyn?"

Pushed my hair behind my ears and squinted to see him better.

"Did you hear about my friend Sam? They found black sludge at the accident site. It's our guy, I know it."

"Yes, yes. Definitely *our* guy." He sounded strange. Like his voice was coming through a bad speaker.

Before I could even raise a hand he threw that nasty black crap at me. I deflected most of it with my wrist but it seeped in.

I'd spent the last few hours recharging so my body could self-heal during an attack without much encouragement. Now I hoped my protection spells worked.

Cole? The cop? I didn't have time to think about the ramifications.

Tried to throw my power at him, but it sizzled at the ends of my fingertips. Nothing.

"I've bound your powers, witch. You can't touch me with your magic." His eyes blazed a fiery red.

Great, just great.

Never, ever underestimate the cute guys. You'd think I'd know better by now.

"Who hired you?" I had to give myself some time. The sludge would wear off in a minute or so, but he didn't need to know that.

"I work for no one." His blond hair flew around his face. Something wasn't right. The voice wasn't the only thing off. It hadn't been the sun playing tricks. Another warlock possessed the cop.

The shape of the man shifted slightly and I knew for certain.

"You aren't Cole, are you?"

No answer.

"If you're going to kill me, the least you could do is tell me who you are. What's the good of being a big, powerful warlock if no one knows it's you?" If I threw magic at him, I chanced killing Cole too. I couldn't do that. I needed the other warlock to step out of Cole's form.

"You have no right to ask anything, young witch. So much trouble you've caused. Upsetting my plans." He pointed an angry finger at me.

"What plans? How am I supposed to know what I've done if you don't tell me?"

The sheriff and the two witches were on both sides of the door behind me. I could hear their quiet chant and feel their power. They were smart not to interfere. If the worst happened they could summon the others.

Cole, or whoever he was, hadn't realized they were there. He must have come in from the side door to the conservatory.

"Come on, Cole. I thought you were one of the good guys."

"This is the body of one who is true of heart. I only borrowed it to get into your small town. Seems you have a strong ward against evil slipping in."

As Cole's body fell to the ground another warlock came forth. Dark hair, with the silver streak. Damn, if it wasn't Wally the Warlock. Cole's body lay in a puddle of muddy earth.

"Wallace? How could you? You're sworn to protect the innocent."

"I've made no such pledge, witch. And perhaps it's time you called me by my true name. Sir William Blackstock."

In the time I'd spent with Wally, or whoever he was, he had to have been the last guy I would imagine as the all-powerful evil dude trying to kill me. Oh, I suspected he worked with someone else, but not that he was *the guy*. The warlock emanated power when we were in Brussels, but nothing like this.

Wait. Blackstock. I'd heard that name, but the sludge had worked its way through my body and my mind didn't click along at its usual pace. "Perhaps I'm dense. But I don't understand why you are doing this. Who are you?"

Then it dawned on me: this was the nasty warlock who had

cursed Darby and her lover. He had to be more than two hundred years old, which would explain the power—and the ability to hide it.

"Why go after me and my charges? I've done nothing to you."

"I don't care for witches, and you are that witch Darby's descendant. That idiot blackened my name with her sorcery. Made me the laughingstock of the town.

"I showed her, in the end—and that lover of hers. You know he stole her from me. They met at our engagement party."

So, all of this was some centuries-old vendetta?

"Why go after my charges, why not just kill me and get it over with?"

"I wanted to discredit you, in much the same way Darby had me. When your sheik's cousin hired me to kill him, it worked out perfectly. Once I'm done with you, I'll kill all the witches of the world. Your kind is a plague upon the magical community."

I felt the binding on my powers loosen and I threw a fireball at him. He deflected but it blinded him for a moment and I called a spell to bind his powers.

He shoved an enormous mound of black sludge at me and I weakened. A wind whipped around us in the conservatory and I realized all the windows had been blown open. His power surrounded me. Drained me. The only thing that kept me from falling to my knees was the image of Sam's face.

This asshole had hurt my Sam and for that I had to destroy Blackstock. I didn't care what he called himself. Yes, the warlock had to die.

I couldn't raise my arms to protect myself and he threw another ball of blackness at me. Pain radiated throughout my body, and my head banged like a sledgehammer had hit it.

I fell against the potting bench. In desperation I used the pruning shears to cut the palms of my hands and slowly turned in a circle as I dripped the red liquid to the ground around me. The one way I knew to beat dark magic was with a combination of blood and earth magic.

I happen to be really good at both.

Raising my bleeding arms as high as I could I screamed:

Mother Earth, take this evil from my sight;
Blind him so no other he harms.
Goddess of Blood, I give this offering;
His soul is yours.
So mote it be.

He threw a bolt of heat to my chest and I couldn't breathe. I fell to the ground, knowing I would die within minutes. My self-healing spells hadn't been meant for magic like this.

A flock of mockingbirds swooped in through the open windows and surrounded Blackstock, pecking him on his head, arms, and legs. One large bird pecked at his black beady eyes and then lifted them from his head.

Well, I would die today, but not before stupid Blackstock got his.

Even as the breath left my body, I felt triumphant. At least the asshole would be blind.

A hand fell across my chest and I turned my head. Cole was kneeling beside me, sending his power into me. The heat from his healing soared through me.

"Thanks."

He collapsed beside me, and I didn't know if he was alive or dead. I had no way of helping him. I couldn't move.

I watched Blackstock through the commotion. He screamed; horrible screeching sounds blasted around us.

The birds could have been hired by Alfred Hitchcock the way

they went about their work. Wally was a bleeding mass of pecked flesh. No eyes, and little nose left. His mouth had been ripped apart, revealing nothing but gums and teeth.

I might have been grossed out but then the snakes rose from the ground. That Blood Goddess is one creative chick. Rattlesnakes encircled his body, biting him and chewing the flesh from his hide.

He only had time to let out one more blood-curdling scream before a great hawk came in and ripped out his tongue.

I thought about firing up just to put him out of his misery, but decided to let the Earth and Blood Goddesses have their fun. Honestly, I had nothing left.

I watched the carnage. Every bit of Wally had been chewed or pecked away; his wicked soul lay there shimmering in a black aura.

Blood Goddess, I commend this soul to thee.
As I will so mote it be.

The light shone brighter and then dissipated into thin air. The Blood Goddess had taken him to her place and he would spend eternity doing her bidding. Wally the Warlock, Sir Blackstock, or whatever he called himself was now the slave of the Blood Goddess.

Cole's chest heaved and he took in a deep breath. He was alive.

The sheriff and the other witches stepped out to gather Cole and me up and move us into the house. At least they'd have some good gossip for the next coven gathering.

Before I could thank them, the blackness swallowed me.

Next thing I knew, I woke in my bedroom to find Garnout shoving some kind of potion down my throat. I coughed and spat.

"Swallow, my dear. You'll heal faster."

I did what he asked. And tried to think.

"Sam?"

"He's doing as well as can be expected." Garnout's kind face smiled as he pulled the covers up to my neck and wiped the spit off of my chin. "The coven and his parents are looking after him. The doctors are pleased with his progress."

"The sheik and PM?"

"Cole called them. The sheik, who is on his way here, sent ten of the best doctors in the country to look after your Dr. Sam. The sheik must be a very good friend."

I couldn't even wrap my mind around that, except I knew that Sam and the sheik had liked each other. If they hadn't both been in love with me they might have been the best of friends. "Yes, Azir's a good man."

"He loves you."

"What?"

"Darby told me. She said the sheik was in love with you. She also gave me the warning about Sir Blackstock but I arrived too late to help you. Looks like you handled everything on your own, as usual."

"It hurt."

"Yes, it did take a great deal from you, but you are even more powerful than before. Once you heal you'll see."

My brain hurt almost as much as my body. "I love Sam," I whispered.

"Well, that complicates things." Garnout knew and heard everything. "It seems your heart has made an important choice for you. I'm sure this Sam loves you, too."

"He does. He told me. But I couldn't say the words to him. I love him so much and now he may never know."

"If he saw what I see in your eyes, he knew. Now, you need to rest."

He raised his hand above my head and I fell into a deep sleep.

I remember the dreams from last night. Sam's hands running over my body. Making me beg with every touch. Our auras mixed into a purple light. He slid into me, his eyes brilliant blues staring into my soul. *I love you. I'm here, and I love you.*

Then he was suddenly yanked away, and my heart ripped into pieces.

He shouted, "Bronwyn! I'm here!"

I sat up, startled. Looked around the room. No Sam. But I could smell him. Called to check on him at the hospital, but his mother says nothing has changed.

Was it just a dream? My body tingles where he touched me. I must still be delusional.

I hear voices downstairs. Have no idea how long I've been out. But I'm afraid to go down. I can't face anyone right now, but I need to see Sam.

Thirty

Heartbroken witches: I

Sam's doing well. The doctors expect a full recovery and thanks to the coven's powers, the need for more surgery is minimal. Most of the wounds have healed, except the one in his head.

I spent all morning in his room with him, hiding. Azir, Sam's parents, some of the coven, Kira and Caleb, and even Simone were all outside in the waiting room. But I was in the room with Sam, willing him to wake up. For all of the healing his body has experienced, he's still in a coma.

"Please, please, wake up, baby. I need to see those beautiful blue eyes again." I squeezed his hand but he didn't respond. Didn't think it possible but my heart is splitting in two. It actually hurts I ache for him so bad.

I joked with Simone about dating dead guys, but she knows I love him.

And I care about Azir. Not in the same way exactly. His kindness and generosity, the way he's taken care of everyone. From me to Sam's parents to the doctors caring for Sam, he's made sure everyone is comfortable and as happy as possible. How could I not appreciate him?

Garnout told me that it would all work out as it should.

"Sam, baby? You have to wake up. We have our whole lives to live together. And I'm not a patient woman."

"Are you trying to will him awake?" Garnout came in and put his hands on my shoulders.

"Yes, but it doesn't seem to be working." I patted his hand.

"You need to rest."

"I'm okay."

"No, you're not. Your skin is pale and you need to eat. How about we stop by the wonderful Lulu's on the way home for some of those artery-clogging chicken-fried steaks?"

"I can't leave him."

"You must. There's a chance your weakened powers may be draining his."

"I'll look after him, dear," Sam's mother said as she walked in. A beautiful woman with dark hair much like her son's, only hers fell to her shoulders in soft waves. She was dressed in an elegant suit. The worry lines around her mouth and eyes were the only things that gave hint to the turmoil she must have been experiencing. "You'll be no good to him if you're too tired."

She made me uncomfortable in my own skin, as if she knew the thoughts rolling around in my head. Impossible. But I got the feeling she didn't like me very much.

Probably just guilt on my part.

She leaned down and whispered to me, "He knows you've

been here, and he'd want you to be healthy. Go and take care of yourself."

I kissed Sam's forehead and walked out.

Before we could leave, Margie ran up and grabbed my hand. "I'm so sorry, girl. But I've got really bad news."

"Oh, Margie, I can't take any more. Really."

"But you told me to let you know. It's Mr. G. He's—bad. Real bad."

I couldn't stop the tears from falling.

"No." My voice croaked. "Is he . . . ?" Azir grabbed my shoulders and held me up.

"It won't be long. I've got to get back. His family doesn't have time to get here. And I don't want him to go alone." Margie blew her nose into a tissue and then handed me a clean one.

"I'll come with you. He feels like my family and I want to be there for him."

Azir and Garnout both started to say something, but stopped. In unison they said, "We'll all go."

So my friends and family gathered around my lovely Mr. G's bed. His breath was raspy and rattling. His gray skin was taut against his cheeks.

I grabbed his hand.

"Witch," he whispered.

"Yes. I'm here. We're all here."

At that he cranked open one eye and then closed it again. A small smile fell across his face.

"Family?"

"Yes."

"Thanks. You're a good girl." He tried to squeeze my hand, but his grip was so weak.

I couldn't hold back the sob.

"Please don't go."

"It's time. She's waiting. And I love her so. . . ."

I knew his lovely wife was on the other side, beckoning to him. I couldn't let my selfishness get in the way of true love.

"Save a dance for me." I cried.

He let out one deep shuddering breath and was gone. I sobbed for half an hour and didn't care who saw or heard.

In a strange way, Mr. G's death helped me realize something important.

But it was hours later before I discovered it. More than anything, I knew he wanted me to celebrate his life and eventually I found my smile again. I kissed his forehead and pulled the sheet up.

I didn't feel like going anywhere, but Azir had arranged for us all to lunch at Lulu's. Ms. Helen and Ms. Johnnie fussed over us like we were children at a birthday party.

We ate chicken-fried steak and chocolate pie. I even wolfed down a piece of apple cobbler. "Now, that's my girl." Ms. Johnnie patted my head like a child as I swallowed the last bite.

"Your food is the closest thing to heaven on earth." I stood up and hugged her. If I didn't know better, I swear I saw a tear in her eye. She sniffled and hugged me back.

"You just take care of yourself, young lady. Helen and I have taken quite a likin' to you, and you need to get back to one hundred percent.

"Oh, and if this sheik friend of yours has any older buddies, send 'em my way. That man's one good-looking fella."

I laughed. She was right about that.

Thirty-one

Wednesday, 10 P.M.
Waxing moon
Sweet, Texas
Content witches: 1

𝐵ack at the house, I watched as Azir organized and told everyone what he or she needed to do. Weird part was not one of them seemed to mind.

Caleb supervised the workers replacing the glass panels in the conservatory. Kira cleaned up the kitchen. Even Garnout, who was in charge of keeping up my garden and seeing to my well-being, followed the orders. Wizards don't take orders, especially from lowly humans.

But Azir had such a way about him. I fell asleep, my mind cluttered with questions. Strange dreams followed. Darby stopped by for a visit. I knew within the dream that what she said was real.

"My darling girl, thank you for bringing back my beloved

Lance." She floated through the white space in my dream and her blonde hair fell in curls around her face. "Because of your bravery all of those cursed by that wicked warlock have been set free."

"Except for Sam." I sighed. "I swear he's under some kind of spell. Why else wouldn't he open his eyes?"

"I don't know. Once Blackstock went into the underworld, which was quite a wonderful feat on your part, all of his power should have been lost." She touched my hair. Even though it was a dream, I could feel the pressure of her fingers.

"Your young man may be trapped in his own dreams. It happens sometimes when one warlock fights another. He may not know he isn't conscious."

Garnout had mentioned the same thing yesterday.

Darby faded a bit, and waved good-bye. "Just love him. He'll find you again. My Lance did." Her lover walked into the picture and took her hands. They disappeared into the whiteness.

Watching them gave me a tremendous sense of peace. At least I'd done one good thing.

The scene shifted in my dream. The sheik's cousin (who, it seems, was killed in a gun battle with the prime minister's security force) waved his hand at me and said I wasn't good enough. Of course it didn't seem to matter to him that he'd tried to murder his own flesh and blood.

Blackstock had used the cousin's hate to destroy the rest of us. I'm not sorry either one of them are gone.

Azir's brother had been possessed and had no idea that he had contributed to the assassination attempts.

I woke up wanting the only two people in my life who weren't here. My mom and dad.

As if by magic they stood in the doorway. "How's my girl?" my dad asked.

I started to cry. Big, strong, brave Bronwyn sobbed like a two-year-old who had lost her way.

"We're here, darling. We know, we know," my mother said. They sat, one on each side of me, and hugged me. No one spoke for a few minutes. As the tears subsided my dad handed me a tissue from the side table.

"The sludge is making my emotions run high. I can't seem to keep it together for very long." I blew my nose and wadded the flimsy paper in my hand.

"You've worn yourself out, honey. There's no need to apologize. Garnout and Sheik Azir filled us in." My mom patted my hand. "We stopped by the hospital and talked to Sam's mother and father. They're very nice. He must be a wonderful young man to have so many people who care about him."

"He is. He's really great, Mom, and I love him."

"Oh?"

"Yes. So much that it hurts." There. I'd said it out loud in front of my parents. It made it more real.

"You're in love with the young man in the coma." My father's puzzled look made me laugh.

"Yes, Daddy."

"I don't—" My poor dad didn't know what to say.

My mom reached across and squeezed his hand.

"Darling Bronwyn. Loving a man isn't the end of the world." My mother looked at my father. "The women on our side of the family have a very difficult time finding mates. Why do you think your grandmother married seven times? You are lucky that you found your true love so young."

"But what about you and Daddy?"

"Well, I wasn't exactly your mother's first choice." My dad blew out a breath.

"What your father's trying to say is that I was engaged to

another young man when we met. A man I loved quite dearly, but he went off to war and didn't come back. But before all of that happened, your father and I had been friends for many years.

"One day I woke up and realized he was the man of my dreams. And we've been together since."

I'd never heard about my mom's past loves, which in hindsight is a good thing.

"So you just woke up one day and that was it?"

"Yes." My mom brushed a hair out of my face and smiled. "You're young yet, and instead of worrying yourself sick, be grateful you love such a wonderful man. Concentrate on helping that young Sam to heal."

"Your mother's right. You just have to take each day as it comes."

"Dad, that's so AA. But you have a point. I love Sam so much more than I thought possible. And now he might die and never know. Oh, I can't think about it anymore. It makes my head hurt.

"Do you know if Mr. G's family showed up?" I circled my neck to release the tension.

"Who?" My dad always had a hard time keeping up with my sometimes-disparate trains of thought.

"The older gentleman, who passed away this morning," my mother reminded him.

"Oh, yes. Your friend—what was her name?" Dad scratched his forehead.

"Margie, dear." Mom took over. "She said to tell you that they were so grateful you were there for him. They're making copies of his journals for you, per his request."

My throat caught. It might be a while before I could read those without crying, but I'd do it. I would remember the man and his life.

I hugged them both, feeling lighter. Funny how parents can always put things in perspective. They seemed so stupid when I was younger; now they're positively brilliant.

"Do you feel up to going downstairs? Your friends Kira and Simone have put together a little surprise for you." Mom stood and grabbed my robe from the bedpost.

After the last few weeks I wasn't much for surprises but it'd be rude to disappoint the girls. They'd been such troopers the last few days. Everyone had.

We made our way down the stairs and I heard the mumble of voices over soft music. The twinkle lights had been hung across the living room and enchiladas permeated the air. Azir, Kira, Caleb, Garnout, and Simone sat talking on the cushy sofa and chairs.

"Welcome, witch." Simone jumped up and handed me a strawberry margarita. "We were worried that we'd have to drink all these wonderful treasures by ourselves."

"Not a chance, girlfriend. Not a chance. And not to look a gift horse in the mouth, but why are you here? Don't you have some demons to slay in L.A.?"

"Haven't you heard?" She put her hand around my waist and squeezed. "The demons have decided to take a holiday."

Everyone laughed.

She whispered, "I had to see for myself that you were okay." The tremble in her voice almost made me cry again. We might not always agree when it comes to men, but I couldn't find a truer friend.

Later that evening, the sheik sat by me on the sofa. Everyone had wandered into the kitchen to check out my dad's homemade peach ice cream.

"He's a good man." Azir took my hand in his.

"My dad? Yes, he makes a mean bowl of ice cream." I smiled as I heard the laughter in the kitchen.

"No, I meant Sam." Azir's fingers moved across mine.

"Um, yes, he is." Okay. Now what? "I should say thank you for all you've done for him. And for me. You've been so generous." I squeezed his hand.

"I would have done the same for any friend."

Confused, I wondered if the black sludge had taken all of my available brain cells hostage.

He stood up abruptly. "When Garnout called the prime minister—I was so afraid you might die before we could get here. I couldn't stand it.

"If something had happened to you, my heart would have died with you."

"Oh." God, I'm so good with the words.

He waved a hand before I could say anything else.

"As much as I want to take you home, lock you in, and keep you safe forever, I know that isn't possible. It doesn't keep me from wanting you, though. I know it's not right." He paced in front of the couch.

"Sam loves you, and I know you love him. He's fighting for his life and he needs you."

"Azir, please." I reached up to him.

He sat down and took me by the shoulders and kissed me. Not a friendly kiss, but the I'm-after-your-tonsils, don't-forget-me kind.

"I'm going home tomorrow. Anything you need is at your disposal, but I can't stay here."

"You're a busy man, I know that."

"That's not the reason. I love you. I know it's not right, and the timing couldn't be worse, but I do." He ran a hand through that thick black hair. His eyes so dark and unreadable.

This had to be hell for him.

He took my hands again. "This is selfish of me, I know, but I had to tell you. If you need me—"

"Hey, Bron," Kira called from the kitchen, "one scoop or two?"

Azir snorted and shook his head.

"Kira, need you ask?" he finally bellowed through hearty chuckles. "It's Bronwyn! She always wants two scoops of everything!"

I smiled and hugged him.

"I'll go get your ice cream." He moved to stand up and I grabbed his hand. "Thank you for everything. For understanding about Sam. Just everything."

He pulled away and almost ran to the kitchen. I'm sure he was feeling as awkward as I was.

Two amazing men cared about me. Okay, one was in a coma and the other lived on the other side of the world, but, hey, a girl could do worse.

Then it hit me hard. I needed to be with Sam. In fact, right then there was nothing more important.

I ran upstairs and threw on jeans and a pink T-shirt. Grabbed my keys from the mantel and ran for the car without ever even thinking to tell anyone where I was going.

On the drive I could hear Sam calling for me.

Sam's parents flanked his bed, and they both smiled when I walked in.

"He hasn't opened his eyes, but he just asked for you." His mother reached for my hand. "Talk to him, Bronwyn. Let him know that you are here." She and her husband moved toward the door. "Please come and get us if anything changes."

"I will." I sat on his bed and leaned in close to his ear.

"I love you, Sam." I kissed his cheek. "And you are so missing out on the good stuff here. Tonight there was a party with strawberry margaritas and homemade ice cream. Ms. Johnnie and Ms. Helen promise that if you wake up you can have a free piece of pie every day for the rest of your life. And Margie's promised free massages. Although I'm not so sure how I feel about her running her hands all over your naked body."

He smiled.

"Sam?"

"Bron." A whisper came through his lips.

"Oh, my God. Open your eyes and look at me." I held my breath.

His lashes moved against his cheeks and he squinted.

I grabbed his face and kissed him hard on the lips.

"Hey." He laughed. "Ouch."

"Oh, sorry."

"No. Good ouch. Water . . ."

I handed him the cup and put the straw to his mouth. He sipped.

Never have I been so happy to see those baby blues.

"What happened?" He tried to sit up, but grimaced with pain. He fell back on the pillow.

"You've been through hell, and probably shouldn't try to move."

"The truck, was it a tornado?"

"No. An evil warlock picked it up and smashed it into the ground. You probably never even saw him. But no worries—he's dead meat."

His lips twitched. "You?"

"Yes, I took care of the bastard."

"Are you okay?" He touched my hand and squeezed.

I couldn't stop the tears from rolling down my cheeks and I bit my bottom lip. I'd cried more in the last few days than I had in the last five years.

"I'm okay. Better now that you are awake. I love you."

He pulled me closer. I kissed him again, this time softer but with no less passion.

"I love you, too. So much," he whispered against my lips. He moved his arms around me.

Yes. Wrapped in Sam's arms, the insecurities melted away. My heart knew the truth.

My Sam. My love. At this moment in life, there was nowhere else I wanted to be.

Is it the forever kind of love Mr. G talked about? I don't know. And it doesn't matter. I'm taking Dad's one-day-at-a-time advice, and loving Sam with everything I have.

A seventeen-year veteran of the entertainment industry, **Candace Havens** has written thousands of syndicated articles and conducted interviews with television and film celebrities, writers, producers, and directors. In addition to writing columns on everything Hollywood, she published a biography of Joss Whedon, creator of *Buffy the Vampire Slayer*, and can be heard weekdays as the entertainment critic on 96.3 KSCS Dallas/Fort Worth. This is her first novel. Visit her on the web at www.candancehavens.com.